PRAISE FOR ADRENALINE:

"If you like **gripping drama, starkly effective description and almost unbearable suspense**, then this book is for you.

The characters and places are engagingly real. It has been suggested by readers that this book would lend itself to an engrossing film.

Throughout intertwining subplots, significant hints are provided to the reader—including one startling revelation. The ending is breathless. I found myself totally unprepared for the plot twists, even though they had been amply prefigured. The rhapsodic tone of lovely inner reflection of love and its beauty when juxtaposed with the ugliness of killing is particularly welcome.

I hope that many will read *Adrenaline*. Without question, it will jolt you to some interesting insights."

— Leslie S. March
Harrisburg Magazine Review

"**This guy can flat out write.** Benedict has a great grasp of the many ways language can be used in telling a story, paired with the skill to do it, which is the thing that makes him stand out… Add in a good feel for the basics of pacing the story and sentence structures, a superb eye for the role of detail, and the priceless ability to draw a reader in until they forget that they're actually reading the story they're in the middle of."

— Poisonedpenpress.com

"**Properly entitled, *Adrenaline* is a thrill ride from the opening chapter.** Dr. John Benedict has written a novel encompassing the intrigue of Michael Crichton's E.R. combined with the thrill of Crime Scene Investigations. This is a top-notch medical thriller and I hope it is the first of many from Benedict. **He could easily become the next Dean Koontz with a medical degree**."

— **Robert Denson III**
Managing Editor of Sunpiper Press
www.sunpiperpress.com

"**Benedict has done an outstanding job** at creating scenes, as well as characters, using every detail no matter how miniscule to evoke clear images and emotional response from readers, thus allowing us to really care about what happens to these characters."

— **Betsie's Literary Page**
betsie.tripod.com/literary

"**Filled with accelerating suspense**, author Benedict builds the plot that moves *Adrenaline* forward with methodical and deliberate subplots and characters, each of which succeed to broaden the mystery and draw the reader deep into the workings of the operating rooms and administrative offices of Mercy Hospital. Characters are pleasantly humanized, his plotting is meticulous, offering a thrilling journey.

Adrenaline offers a new take on the term 'Medical Thriller' that offers a breath of fresh air to the meaning of the term."

— **Denise M. Clark**
Denise's Pieces Author Site & Book Reviews
www.denisemclark.com

"**A series of mishaps and an accidental death at a Pennsylvania hospital raise suspicions of sabotage in the author's debut medical thriller.** Doctors in the anesthesia department at Our Lady of Mercy Hospital are worried about losing their jobs in an impending merger, so it doesn't bode well when a patient dies soon after anesthesia is administered. Dr. Doug Landry and others are unaware that someone in their department is intentionally setting up the anesthesiologists for failure in a series of desperate acts that will ultimately lead to outright murder. **Benedict's novel is a mystery story rife with suspense:** A killer, whose identity is concealed, creeps into dark operating rooms; med student Rusty, searching for his elusive past, finds his way to Mercy; and a patient awakens in the midst of surgery, unable to move but feeling every agonizing cut. There's a hefty number of subplots: Doug's temptation to stray from his marriage vows with a flirtatious hospital employee; sympathetic Dr. Mike Carlucci recalling patients he's lost and trying not to succumb to the pressures of the job; plus Rusty's training and the threat of a suit against the hospital. But through shifting perspectives and a focus on the darker side of medical care--Doug tells Rusty how easily anesthesia, inadvertently or not, can become lethal--ensure that the various plots are less sentimental and more in tune with the murderous saboteur. **Twists and turns abound as the story progresses, and they hit a crescendo in a scene of utter ferocity that's violent and intense.**"

—**Kirkus Reviews**

PRAISE FOR THE EDGE OF DEATH:

"**A deftly written masterwork** in the medical thriller genre, author John Benedict's *The Edge of Death* is the riveting sequel to his earlier novel *Adrenaline* and very highly recommended reading."

— **Midwest Book Review,**
James A. Cox, Editor-in-Chief

"**Soul Satisfying!!!** Another inspired book by Dr. Benedict! The book surpassed all my anticipations and took me to the realm of an incredible combination of scientific learning and mysticism.

I adore the way the book ends with that veiled promise of there being more to follow!!! **All in all, a MUST NEVER MISS magnificent book!** I would recommend everyone to read it.

Thank you, Dr. Benedict. I look forward to your next book, *Fatal Complications* with a tremendous amount of eagerness."

—**Uma I. Van Roosenbeek**

Breathtaking! Once started, there is no way you can put this book down! Suspenseful to the max, this medical thriller is tightly paced and takes your breath away. With a supernatural twist, it keeps you thinking. This book made it all the way to Germany and you can tell that this author knows what he is talking about when he takes the reader to the OR or ICU - since he is an anesthesiologist himself. So be sure not to miss this exciting medical thriller and Dr. Benedict's debut work: *Adrenaline*! These books can definitely be placed in a row with Tess Gerritsen or Patricia Cornwell. **Five Stars!**

—**U. John**

By John Benedict

Adrenaline

The Edge of Death (sequel to *Adrenaline*)

Fatal Complications (coming: December 2014)

ADRENALINE

New 2013 edition

by

JOHN BENEDICT

1st printing by SterlingHouse Publisher: July, 2005
ISBN# 1-56315-355-6
Library of Congress # 2004109498

2nd printing by Createspace: October, 2013
ISBN# 1484897528

EAN# 9781484897522

Cover Design: Jonah Lloyd
Cover Art: Jonah Lloyd

To my dearest wife,
Lou Ann,
whose constant love and support
continually transform my dreams into reality.

CHAPTER ONE

"Shit! Don't give me any bullshit!" said Dr. Mike Carlucci under his breath, as his gaze locked on the unusual rhythm displayed on the EKG monitor. His warning was meant mostly for his patient, Mr. Rakovic, who was scheduled to undergo an arthroscopy of his right knee. Mike's plea was also directed at God, just in case he was listening, and at the monitor itself to cover all bases. Mike didn't expect a reply from any of them. Mr. Rakovic was deeply unconscious with an endotracheal tube sprouting from his mouth. Mike had just induced general anesthesia and was preparing to fill out his chart when the trouble began.

Mike stared grimly at the potentially lethal dysrhythmia known as ventricular tachycardia, or V-tach, and felt the first raw edge of fear scrape lightly across his nerves. It occurred to him that he had never actually seen V-tach during a routine induction in his six years at Mercy Hospital, or during any induction for that matter. It was something that happened in the case reports, not in real life. He wondered if Doug Landry, his best friend and colleague, had ever seen it.

His first instinct was to doubt the EKG. Frequently movement of the patient or electrical interference caused the EKG to register falsely. He rapidly scanned his array of other monitors. Modern anesthetic workstations had upwards of ten sophisticated computer-driven monitors. Substantial redundancy of these instruments allowed him to check one machine's errors against another. The pulse oximeter, a small finger-clip sensor, beeped at a heart rate exactly the same as the EKG. This unfortunately ruled out the possibility of EKG artifact; there was no false reading this time.

Mike absently fingered the gold crucifix dangling from his neck. Grandma Carlucci had brought it back from Lourdes, and had given it to him when he had graduated from med school. The medallion always comforted him. He punched his Dinamap, the automatic blood pressure machine, for a stat reading. The mass spectrometer system, which continually monitored the gasses going in and out of Mr. Rakovic's lungs via the endotracheal tube, registered normal carbon dioxide levels. Mike breathed a sigh of relief; it meant the breathing tube was properly positioned in his patient's trachea and not in the esophagus. He quickly checked breath sounds with his stethoscope to ensure both lungs were being ventilated normally. They were. The pulse oximeter showed a ninety-eight percent oxygen saturation level, confirming beyond doubt that his patient was being adequately oxygenated. Again good. However, nothing to explain the sudden appearance of V-tach.

The blood pressure reading would be key for a number of reasons. First and foremost, Mike knew he must treat the offending rhythm; its cause was of secondary importance at the moment. A normal blood pressure reading would mean Mr. Rakovic would still have adequate blood flow to his vital organs—brain most importantly—in spite of the rhythm disturbance. Mike knew that as V-tach accelerates, the heart can beat so fast it doesn't have time to fill and fails as a reliable pump. The blood pressure can fall drastically or disappear altogether.

"C'mon you piece of shit! Read, damn it!" Mike hissed under his breath to his Dinamap. Fifteen seconds never seemed so long. While waiting for the blood pressure, he opened the top drawer of his anesthesia cart and pulled out two boxes of pre-mixed Lidocaine, a first-line emergency antidysrhythmic drug. He ripped open the boxes and assembled the syringes. He glanced up at Diane, the circulating nurse. She was busily filling out her paperwork, oblivious to any problem.

"Diane," Mike called out, "I got trouble here. Get the crash cart!"

"Jesus, Mike! Are you kidding?" asked Diane, eyes bugging wide, pen frozen in mid-task.

"Serious badness," Mike said, trying to keep the dread he felt out of his voice. "Looks like V-tach." His voice sounded a little higher than he had intended.

"Oh shit!" she said as she hurried out of the room, almost tripping over the trash bucket. Mike was thankful that Dr. Sanders, the orthopedic surgeon, was still out of the room scrubbing his hands. No time to tell him just yet; he wouldn't take it well. If the blood pressure were unacceptably low, Mike would need to shock the patient back into a normal rhythm. He injected one of the syringes of Lidocaine into the intravenous line and simultaneously felt Mr. Rakovic's carotid pulse. It was bounding, arguing against a low blood pressure.

250/120! "Holy shit! Where'd that come from?" Mike asked the leering LED face of the Dinamap. Accusatory alarms screeched from the Dinamap in response. Mike truly had not expected such a high blood pressure and was momentarily confused. The temperature in the OR seemed to have jumped twenty degrees, and he felt rivulets of sweat coursing down his arms. The fear was back and not so easily dismissed this time. *Think, damn it, think! What would Doug do?*

He quickly reviewed what he knew of Mr. Rakovic's medical history and his own induction sequence. Mr. Rakovic was a sixty-two-year-old hypertensive with a history of coronary disease and a prior heart attack. But, his hypertension was well controlled on his current regimen of beta and calcium-channel blockers. Mike knew his patient had a bad heart, and had taken care to do a smooth induction along with all the usual precautions to avoid stressing the heart. A blood pressure of 250/120 and V-tach at 160 beats-per-minute were about the worst stresses any heart could undergo. Mike knew this, but was still baffled. *Be cool, Mike. Be cool.*

He had been stumped before; medicine was by no means an exact science, and anesthesia was one of the frontiers. Mike also knew better than to waste precious time pondering this. As long as he had reviewed it sufficiently to make sure he hadn't overlooked something, it was time to move on to the immediate treatment. He could replay the case to search for subtle clues when Mr. Rakovic was safely tucked in the recovery room.

What lurked in the back of Mike's mind during these first few minutes, prodding him along, was the specter of ventricular fibrillation or V-fib. V-tach was reversible with rapid proper treatment. V-fib, on the other hand, was often refractory to treatment, leading to death. The problem was that V-tach had a nasty habit of degenerating into the dreaded V-fib without warning. The longer V-tach hung around, the more likely V-fib would appear. So Mike knew time was of the essence.

"Gotta bring that pressure down," Mike mumbled to himself. He reached back into his drawer for Esmolol, a rapidly acting, short duration beta-blocker designed to lower blood pressure. He drew up 30 mg and pumped it into the IV port. He also punched in the second syringe of Lidocaine. Mike tried hard not to take his eyes off the EKG monitor for long as he drew up and administered the drugs. He wanted to see if the V-tach broke into a normal rhythm or converted into V-fib. Irrationally, he felt that if he continued to watch the rhythm it wouldn't convert to V-fib; if he took his eyes off it for too long, the demon might appear.

His Dinamap on STAT mode continued to pour forth BP readings every 45 seconds. 290/140.

"What the hell!" Mike said. Alarms were now singing wildly in the background, adding to the confusion.

Just then, Dr. Sanders charged into the room demanding answers. "What's going on here, Carlucci?" roared Sanders.

Mike didn't have time to deal with the irate surgeon. A wave of nausea swept over him as he felt events slipping out of control. Things were moving so goddamned fast. Fear threatened to engulf him. "Hypertensive crisis!" he managed to blurt out while he grabbed for some Nipride, his strongest antihypertensive. Unfortunately, it had to be mixed and given as an intravenous infusion rather than straight from the ampule. This would take a minute Mike and his patient could ill-afford. Diane returned with the crash cart and several other nurses. She looked at Mike and said, "Do you need help?" It certainly sounded like she thought he did.

"Get Landry in here stat!" Mike yelled in response. He took his eyes off the monitor as he worked on the Nipride drip. Just as he got the Nipride plugged into the IV port, he heard an ominous silence.

The pulse oximeter had become quiet. Usually the pulse ox signaled trouble, such as a falling oxygen saturation, by a gradual lowering of the pitch, not an abrupt silence. Mike could think of only three possible causes, and two of them were disasters—V-fib or cardiac standstill. The third reason could be as simple as the probe slipping off the finger. Although this third possibility was enormously more likely, Mike doubted it. As he turned his head toward the EKG monitor, he knew with eerie prescience what awaited him.

V-fib greeted him from the monitor. He had failed to get the blood pressure down fast enough. The V-tach had degenerated into

V-fib as the strain on the heart had become too much. His Nipride was now useless; in fact, it was harmful. He immediately shut it off. Mike knew that in V-fib, the heart muscle doesn't contract at all; it just sits there and quivers like a bowl full of jello. No blood was being pumped. High blood pressure had ceased to become a problem; now there was no blood pressure. Brain damage would ensue in two minutes, death in four to five minutes.

Doug Landry, the anesthesiologist on call that day, burst through the OR door. "What d'ya got Mike?" he asked, slightly out of breath. Doug glanced at the EKG monitor and said, "Oh shit! Fib!"

"Paddles!" shouted Mike, comforted by Doug's presence. "He went into V-tach, then shortly into fib," said Mike, nodding at the monitor.

"Yeah, I see," Doug said. His large sinewy frame looked like it was coiled for action. Diane handed Mike the defibrillator paddles.

"400 joules, asynchronous!" Mike barked.

Diane stabbed some buttons on the defib unit and it emitted some hi-pitched electronic whines. "Set," Diane said shrilly.

"Clear!" Mike shouted.

Mike fired the paddles, and a burst of high-energy electricity pulsed through Mr. Rakovic's heart and body. The EKG monitor first showed electrical interference from the high dose of electricity, then quickly coalesced into more V-fib.

"Shit!" Mike said. "No good." He had never appreciated how ugly those little spiky waves of V-fib were.

"Hit em again, Mike," Doug said.

"OK. Recharge paddles." The paddles took several seconds for the high amperage capacitors to charge between countershocks. "Better start CPR," Mike said as he began pumping on Mr. Rakovic's chest. His hands soon became slimed from the electrolyte gel left by the paddles on Mr. Rakovic's chest. God, he hated chest compressions.

"Paddles are ready, Doctor!" said Diane. Her eyes were wider than before, and her mask ballooned in and out, as she gulped air.

'Boom' went the paddles again, and Mr. Rakovic's body convulsed a second time. Mike stared at Mr. Rakovic's face as it contorted, reminding him of a medieval exorcism. Mike held his breath and waited for the monitor to clear, pleading with it to show him some good news.

"Still fib!" Mike growled. He resumed chest compressions as he nodded to the circulator to recharge the paddles yet again.

"Epinephrine? Bicarb?" asked Doug.

"Doug, I don't think he needs epi," Mike replied quickly. Mike wondered if Doug was also feeling the pressure. His voice was too damn even, though. "His pressure went through the roof on induction. I don't know why, but I just can't believe he needs epi."

"Okay," Doug said. "The paddles are ready." Doug's forehead creased momentarily, then he added, "V-fib in an elective case. Unusual. Any history, Mike?"

Mike stopped compressions long enough to fire the paddles a third time. He smelled the ozone coming off the arcing paddles. The V-fib continued. *Gimme a break, Mr. Rakovic!*

"Shit! Charge the paddles again," Mike said to Diane. He turned to Doug. "Yeah, prior MI, stable angina, hypertension. Doug, I think we better try Breytillium. I already gave him two doses of Lidocaine." Sweat was now soaking through his scrub top, pants and surgical cap, and running down his face.

"Yeah, sounds like a good idea," said Doug. "I'll take care of it."

Mike glanced over at Doug and cursed his calm efficiency. He knew 'the Iceman' was a veteran of the OR wars. Doug had worked at Mercy for twelve years. He had been on the front lines before and had always performed well. Doug reminded Mike of his mentor in residency days, Dr. Hawkins. Mike thought he could hear Dr. Hawkins now: "Retaining control and being cool are critical in these situations. Split second decisions need to be made. Panic is a luxury you can't afford." The advice sounded hollow.

"Any allergies, Mike?" Doug asked. "Malignant hyperthermia? Breytillium's ready."

"No allergies." Mike was breathing hard now and had to space his words with short gasps. "Doesn't look like MH—no temp. Hurry Doug. Run that shit. He's been in fib for a while. We're running out of time. He may never come out."

"I'm bolusing now," Doug said as he injected a large quantity, "and here goes the drip."

Mike clung to Doug's steady voice like a lifeline. Mike realized that he was in danger of losing control. He could see it in the trembling of his own hands and hear it in the huskiness of his own voice. He wondered if Doug noticed. *Deal with it, Mike. Deal with it.*

Hawkin's words floated back to him again. "It's just like being in combat. Soldiers can train and drill all they want, but they never really knew how they'll react until the bullets are real and start to shriek by their heads. Will they turn tail and run, or fight back?" *Leave me alone, Hawkins!*

Mike looked around the room. He felt they were all staring at him; he could read the expressions in their eyes: "It's your fault! You screwed up!"

"Try it now, Mike," Doug said, jolting him back to reality.

Mike grasped the paddles tightly to prevent them from slipping from his slick hands and applied them to Mr. Rakovic's hairy chest for the fourth time. He pushed the red trigger buttons on each paddle simultaneously to release the pent-up electricity. All 280 pounds of Mr. Rakovic's body heaved off the OR table again and crashed down, sending ripples through the fat of his protuberant abdomen. Mike now smelled an acrid, ammoniacal odor and realized it was coming from the singed hairs on Mr. Rakovic's chest. He frantically wiped the burning sweat out of his eyes so he could see the monitor. The V-fib continued stubbornly and had begun to degrade into fine fibrillations. "Damn you!" Mike yelled at the monitor.

"I'll give you some bicarb," Doug said. Out of the corner of his eye, Mike thought he could see Doug shaking his head slightly.

The next fifteen minutes were a blur to Mike. More chest compressions, more emergency last line drugs, many more countershocks were tried. Nothing worked. Mr. Rakovic continued to deteriorate, his pupils widening until at last they became fixed and dilated. His skin was a gruesome, dusky purple-gray. He was dead. Doug finally called the code after fifty-three minutes and gently persuaded Mike to stop chest compressions. Dr. Sanders walked out of the room without saying a word.

Mike was numb as he stared at the corpse in front of him. One portion of his brain, however, continued to function all too well. It kept replaying his initial encounter with Mr. Rakovic in the holding area. He could see Mr. Rakovic in vivid color and hear him plainly, as the rest of the OR faded to silent gray. They had joked about the Phillies' pitching staff. They wondered whether Barry Bonds would break Big Mac's homerun record. God, he wanted this to stop, to get his laughing, living face out of his mind. But he couldn't. His mind was a demonic film projector playing it over and over. He felt very sick to his stomach and had an overwhelming need to get out of the room and get out of the hospital with all its stinking smells. Just go, anywhere but here.

God, this was what he hated about anesthesia. One minute you're having a casual conversation with a living, breathing, laughing, for God's sakes, human being and the next you're pumping on his chest. He becomes subhuman before your eyes as his face turns all purple and mottled. He cursed his decision to ever become an anesthesiologist. What in God's name was I thinking? Frail human beings were not meant to hold someone's life in their hands. The responsibility was just too awesome.

"Mike. Hey, Mike. You OK?" Doug put his hand on Mike's slumped shoulders. Mike came out of his trance enough to nod his head. Several tears rolled down his cheeks. "Mike, there's nothing else you could've done," Doug continued. "We were all here too. He must've had a massive MI on induction. Not your fault. Some of those guys just don't turn around no matter what you do. Don't blame yourself. We tried everything."

"Yeah, I know Doug. But I just can't get his face out of my mind. We were talking, joking just an hour ago. Now he's dead."

"C'mon, let's get out of here." Doug led Mike out of OR#2. "I know you might not be up to this, but Mike, you've got to talk to the family. Did he have any relatives here with him?"

Mike didn't answer immediately. As the adrenaline haze faded, he struggled to regain control. He felt completely drained with an enormous sense of loss, but coaxed sanity back into place. "Yeah, he came in with his wife. Nice lady." Mike paused, feeling his vision blur again, this time with tears. "What do you say, Doug?"

"Listen, I'll go with you. Just tell her what happened. Everything was going fine. He went to sleep and then bam, out of the blue, he had a massive heart attack. Nothing in the world was going to save him. We worked on him for almost an hour and tried everything. Tell her we're really sorry."

"OK. Help me, Doug." He would've rather stuck nails in his eyes than face Mrs. Rakovic at that moment.

The two men walked through the electronic entrance doors toward the OR waiting room. Mike swallowed hard and entered the small windowless room. Doug was right beside him. Mike searched the faces until he found Mrs. Rakovic. It wasn't hard. As soon as she saw him, she immediately leapt out of the chair with a quickness that belied her bulk. Her frantic gestures revealed the depth of her hysteria. Mike walked over and she collapsed into his arms. "Tell me is not so!" she wailed in her thick, Slavic accent. "Tell me Doctor Sanders made mistake. Not my Joey!" She cried convulsively.

"I'm so sorry, Mrs. Rakovic," Mike said, blinking fast. "He had a massive heart attack. We tried everything." He felt her tears burn into his shoulder and then felt his own tears stream down his face. "I'm sorry." Her wracking sobs shook them both.

CHAPTER TWO

Doug Landry juggled his cup of coffee and his heavy notebook as he fished out his keys. The sign posted on the Radiology classroom door read, "Keystone Anesthesia Corporate Meeting, Tuesday, December 10th - 7:00 p.m." Doug walked in, flipped on the lights, and surveyed the small room. He resented for a minute that the anesthesia department didn't even rate their own meeting room anymore. The hospital was always looking to cut costs these days. Where would it end? he wondered.

The classroom was windowless and had a long table in the center with about ten chairs gathered round. A beat-up lectern sat in front of a huge chalkboard, which all but covered one wall. Two other walls were devoted to the radiology library with countless textbooks and journals interspersed with life-sized anatomic models. On either side of the door could be seen framed photos of the graduating classes of X-ray tech classes all the way back to 1969 when Mercy opened its doors.

Doug sat down in his usual seat and chuckled; they always sat in the same seats in these meetings. Pecking order didn't just apply to birds. Bryan Marshall, the chief of the department, occupied the head of the table. Doug and the younger members of the group sat on Marshall's left, while Joe Raskin and the old guard sat on Marshall's right. Mike Carlucci generally sat to Doug's immediate left. Doug sipped his coffee and wondered how Mike was holding up after his hellish case yesterday. He knew Mike was high-strung; hopefully, he could shake it off.

The door opened and Mike walked in balancing a box of pizza in one hand and a six-pack of Coke in the other. "Hi, Doug," Mike said as he laid his cargo down on the table. "Shit, it's cold out there! I brought some pizza. I'm tired of starving at these damn meetings and eating when I get home at ten o'clock."

"Great idea," Doug said, the smell of fresh pizza already filling the room. "What kind—no, wait, let me guess. Pepperoni, right?"

"Yup."

"You Italians. So predictable," Doug said, smiling.

"Hey, you don't like it—more for me." Mike removed his ski cap, took his coat off, and slung it over the chair to Doug's left. He helped himself to his own slice and popped the top on a Coke. "So, what do you think this emergency meeting is all about? Have you seen the agenda?"

"No, I haven't," Doug replied. "I'm not sure what it's about, Mike. I know Marshall's been agitated all day. He and Raskin have had lots of hush-hush conferences in the hallway today."

"Not just today, Doug. All last week. I swear something's up." Mike ran his fingers through his prematurely graying black hair in a futile attempt to straighten out the mess left by the cap.

"Probably just some B-S about our contract with the hospital," Doug continued. "I think it's coming up for renewal."

"Do you think it's about my, uh, case?" Mike asked, his thin face darkened by a heavy five o'clock shadow, turning very serious.

"I don't think so, Mike. You just said this has been brewing for a week. Marshall likes to call these emergency meetings to rile everyone up." Although Doug *was* worried that Marshall might bring up Mike's case. It would be just his style to rub Mike's nose in it.

"Yeah, I guess so, and to demonstrate his power over your life. Colleen and I were going to take the kids to Chuck-E-Cheese tonight. She wasn't too happy about me bagging out at the last minute."

Doug could picture Colleen taking that call. She was such a sweetie, but Doug knew she hounded Mike relentlessly about spending time with their two little girls. "Sounds like you're in the doghouse now, buddy," Doug said, and proceeded to make howling noises. Mike smiled tiredly but said nothing. Normally, Doug knew, Mike would've joined the dog team, but not tonight.

"Let's just hope Kim gets here on time," Mike said.

"Yeah, remember last time?" Doug asked, matching Mike's serious tone as he busied himself with the pizza.

"Marshall ripped her a new one," Mike said. "She was only ten minutes late." Mike paused to sip his Coke, a thoughtful look coming over his face. "Why does he have it in for Kim so bad?" Mike glanced at his watch and eyed the door nervously, then added, "Marshall usually has a soft spot for attractive women."

Doug lowered his voice a notch and said, "Mike, it's like this. Marshall hates Kim and everything she represents."

"What do you mean?" Mike's bony hands tapped out some rhythm on the table.

"Marshall's from the old school when it comes to doctors, nurses, and women in medicine. It killed him to take Kim in as a partner last year. He believes only men have the necessary devotion to make reliable partners. Haven't you ever heard him rattle off one of his favorite sayings? 'Men don't get pregnant' or 'Women are ruled by their emotions.'"

"Yeah, I guess I have."

"There's two other things that really stick in his craw. You know that Kim will call off when one of her kids is sick. Marshall can't stand that. As far as he's concerned, dedication to Keystone is Job One; kids and family take a backseat—way back." Doug finished his slice and washed it down with more coffee. The cold coffee almost made him gag, but he forced it down, figuring he needed the caffeine to make it through the meeting.

"What else?" Mike asked. "You said two things."

"Well—and this is probably the main reason he hates her— her husband's a fricking doctor. He's an internist with Lombard Associates, the busiest practice in Central Pennsylvania."

"I know that. Why is that such a problem?" Mike made little popping sounds with his empty Coke can as he repeatedly dented it.

"Marshall likes his docs to be sole breadwinners with families. The reason is simple. These suckers are much more likely to be loyal to him because they're dependent on him for their livelihood."

"Oh, you mean like me?" Mike asked and smiled ruefully. His hands became still for a moment.

"Yeah, just like you. And me. You're not going to gripe about working seventy hours a week. You need the money. So do I. Kim *does* gripe about the hours."

"OK, I get it," Mike said quickly. "Maybe we should change the subject before he gets here."

"Fine, but you asked me." Doug didn't add that Marshall also liked his doctors in debt and encouraged this with low interest corporate loans. Doug knew Mike had recently made use of this and bought a huge new house and was in big-time debt.

Bryan Marshall moved to the lectern, glanced at his watch, and gruffly called the meeting to order at precisely 7:00 p.m. Even though he had been in the states for thirty years, he still retained traces of his South African acquired British accent. Doug could see he was in a foul mood. Where was Kim? he thought anxiously. He glanced around the table at the other members of their group.

Marshall cleared his throat, and Doug refocused on him. He was a large man, just shy of sixty, with a generous potbelly somehow supported by thin spindly legs. He had a thick mane of white hair that was disheveled at the moment thanks to the surgical cap he had worn all day. His massive head rested uncomfortably on his shoulders with only a hint of neck showing, as if the weight of his head compressed his neck. His coarse facial features appeared slightly swollen and inflamed due to the deep ruddiness of his complexion. Tortuous blood vessels snaked across his temples and neck adding to the impression that his head contained too much pressure.

Doug watched him scan the room and saw his scowl deepen. He was clearly annoyed, and this amused Doug. After spending twenty-eight years as chief of the department, Doug knew that Bryan Marshall was unaccustomed to being delayed by anyone.

"Well, it seems Dr. Burrows hasn't seen fit to arrive yet," Marshall said. He practically spat out the word "doctor." Doug knew Marshall was capable of thickening his accent at will, a technique he often employed to telegraph his authority and command respect. Tonight, it sounded like he had just stepped off the boat from Johannesburg. "No matter. We have a lot to cover and I'd like to commence."

Doug turned to Mike and rolled his eyes in anticipation of yet another long meeting. There had been too many in the past month.

"As you know," said Marshall, "Mercy is engaged in merger negotiations with Osteo and General." Doug knew Lancaster Osteopathic Hospital and Lancaster General Hospital were Mercy's chief competitors in the area. "The nuns are running scared. Sister believes that with the increasing market penetration of managed care in Central Pennsylvania, she needs to align or merge with someone to obtain sufficient bargaining clout."

Doug was always irritated by the flip manner Marshall and his sidekick, Joe Raskin, would refer to the nuns. By Sister, Marshall meant the head administrator of Our Lady of Mercy Hospital where Keystone Anesthesia was based. She ran the Catholic hospital with the help of a cadre of nuns from the special order, the Sisters of Christian Benevolence.

Marshall continued. "She's afraid that as a single entity, the large HMO's and managed care corporations will dictate her fees and low ball her right out of business. She might be right." He paused to clear his throat.

"Those fuckers!" exclaimed Raskin, who smacked his flattened palm on the wooden table. Doug turned and gave Raskin a hard stare. He had never cared much for Raskin. From the day they had met twelve years ago, Doug had quickly put Raskin in the major pain-in-the-butt category. Raskin was a contemporary of Marshall; the two of them had founded the anesthesia department at Mercy back in 1969. Doug knew Raskin could always be counted on to support Marshall's point of view. However, Raskin rarely added anything of substance. Raskin caught Doug's stare and returned it, eyes glowering. He then added sourly without dropping his eyes from Doug, "Pardon my French."

"General's better than Osteo," said Omar Ayash in his Middle-Eastern accent. Ayash was also a member of the old guard. He had emigrated from Lebanon in the late sixties, and after bouncing around New York and Pennsylvania, wound up at Mercy in 1972. Doug was surprised to hear from Ayash; he was usually silent during these meetings.

"Not nearly so many AIDS cases or Lancaster knife and gun club members," Ayash continued, referring to Osteo's inner city location and the patient population this entailed. "Besides, half of Osteo's patients are medical assistance. No money there."

"Bryan," said Doug, "a lot of the surgeons seem to think we're going with General."

"That's what I heard as well," added Mike. Doug turned to look at Mike. Something about him, his tone or expression wasn't quite right, but he couldn't put a finger on it. To the rest of the group, Mike probably appeared to be fully engaged in the discussion, but Doug sensed a preoccupation or a faraway look in his friend.

Bryan Marshall cleared his throat loudly in an effort to silence further interruptions. "Sister called me up to her office for a meeting this afternoon. That's why this emergency session was necessary. I can shed some light on the merger talks but there's been some, uh, new developments." Marshall enunciated the word "developments" peculiarly, imparting an ominous tone. He paused for further emphasis, and a hushed silence fell over the room.

I can't wait to hear this, thought Doug. These merger talks were unsettling enough. What now? Everyone leaned forward slightly in their seats.

"You're right, Doug," Marshall said. "Sister *is* favoring General. She likes the administrator over there. He's willing to make concessions so she can preserve her autonomy at Mercy and keep her precious Catholic mission intact. And you all know bloody well what that means—no abortions or tubals." Marshall hammered his fist down on the table as he said the word abortions.

"She'd flush this place down the fucking toilet," said Raskin angrily, "and us with it before she'd back down on abortions!" His face turned red and Doug couldn't help but wonder what his blood pressure was.

Doug fired another look of disgust at Raskin, but Raskin had his eyes on Marshall. Doug realized this was not the main point. He knew Sister's feelings on abortion were non-negotiable, but it really didn't matter. Assuming a merger did take place, all the abortions could easily be performed at the original institution. What else did Marshall have on his mind?

"Apparently," Marshall continued, "Thompson's been engaged in talks with Pinnacle." He delivered the word "Pinnacle" as if he had lobbed a grenade into their midst. He stopped abruptly, as if he had no more to say—as if what he said was enough.

The silence was broken by a loud snort as Ken Danowski sneezed. Ken was one of the younger members of the group, seated to Mike's left. "Sorry," he said, although it came out muffled through his handkerchief.

"Oh shit! Pinnacle—that's just great," said Mike.

"The turd's in the punch bowl now," added Raskin profoundly, eyes sparkling.

Doug grimaced and figured this was what the emergency meeting was really all about—Pinnacle. The door opened, and Kim Burrows entered the room. She quickly headed for the empty chair next to Ken Danowski. Doug saw Kim and Ken exchanged meaningful glances. Doug knew they were the neophytes of the group and looked to each other for support.

"Nice of you to join us, Doctor Burrows," Marshall growled sarcastically as he took a lingering look at his watch. "Even *you* might find this meeting important. We were just talking about Pinnacle Anesthesia."

Kim took off her parka and slid into her seat. Her cheeks were bright red from the cold and almost matched the color of her lipstick. Doug thought she was an attractive woman, small and slim with fine features and short blond hair. She'd recently celebrated her thirty-second birthday and had been with Keystone for two years. "What's Pinnacle Anesthesia?" she asked in a weak voice.

"You've never heard of Pinnacle?" Raskin asked, as if he couldn't comprehend the fact that there was actually one person on the planet in the dark on this matter.

"No, should I have?" Kim answered defensively, her voice taking on a strident tone. She was unable to hold Raskin's stare; she dropped her gaze and busied herself with her pen.

"They're the bastards that come into a hospital and take over the anesthesia department," Raskin explained with rancor. "They clean house and bring in their own people to run the fuckin' place. Right,

Bryan?" Raskin paused momentarily to get a confirmatory nod from his superior, and continued with renewed vigor. "They contract directly with the hospital to run the department for a fixed fee, and turn the billing over to the hospital. Administration goes ape-shit over that. They get the docs on salary, where they've always wanted 'em, and have a chance to make a profit from the billing, too."

"Joe's right, Kim," Doug said. "This is serious bad news for us."

"But," Kim said, "Joe mentioned profit. What does—how can they run this place any more efficiently than we do? We work sixty-plus hours per week!" Doug knew Kim despised their present work schedule. This time she gave Raskin a burning glare, which she didn't drop.

"They bring in newly trained docs or docs with questionable histories who are willing to work for half of what we do," Doug responded. "Remember Kim, the job situation out there is tight."

"That's the catch, Kim," Mike went on. "The people they bring in are usually inferior or downright dangerous."

"None of them are board-certified," noted Raskin with pride. All of the Keystone group were board-certified except for Omar Ayash—three failed attempts at the written exam, and Kim Burrows—who had passed her writtens and would sit for her first oral exam in July.

"Don't you think the surgeons would be outraged and rally behind us?" Kim asked.

Marshall's head swiveled with surprising speed to lock his gaze on Kim. He cocked his head slightly, like a hawk evaluating his prey. A cruel smile materialized on his face. "Unlikely my dear girl. Do you really think so?" He wielded his vast experience like a mace and bludgeoned people for their naiveté. Of course, Doug knew, naiveté was defined as any opinion contrary to Marshall's own. "The surgeons wouldn't care if chimpanzees were providing the anesthesia, so long as their cases didn't get held up!" Marshall didn't bother to add "You stupid bitch", as it was clearly implied by his tone.

Doug hated when Marshall did this, and sadly it wasn't all that rare. Doug occupied a strange place in the group. He knew he was sort of the middleman between the junior and senior partners. People on both sides came to him with their various gripes, and he took it on himself to be a kind of peacemaker—the glue that bound the group together. He didn't particularly care for the role, especially when Marshall or Raskin started to run roughshod over the younger members.

Doug knew Kim was stung by Marshall's response; he could see it in her face. He wanted to help her, but it was no fun sticking his head on the chopping block either. What *was* she thinking!? She knew the surgeons weren't known for their loyalty to the anesthesiologists. Doug sighed and said, "However Bryan, the hospital does have a credentials committee that might make it tough to bring in poorly qualified people."

"You're missing the point, Landry!" Marshall boomed with exasperation, his head swiveling once again. "For Godsakes man, the credentials committee is made up mostly of surgeons. Plus, if the nuns smell money, they can bloody well railroad anyone through that blasted committee. You know that!"

Doug groaned inwardly. *Nice job, Doug.* He had succeeded in deflecting Marshall's anger away from Kim all right, right onto himself. "Yeah, I guess so," he said weakly. Doug decided to retreat a bit, lick his wounds, and consider the situation. Now was not the time to challenge Marshall directly. He needed to gather more information, plan his course of action.

Although Doug was not thrilled with the prospect of Pinnacle Anesthesia, he realized panicking was premature. Many factors would need to be decided before this was a done deal. The merger could collapse at any point. Pinnacle might well not be able to come to a suitable fee agreement with Mercy. Kim was right when she said that Keystone ran the place efficiently.

Second, even if Pinnacle did come in, they usually didn't clean house as Raskin had suggested. Doug knew from several of his friends in other parts of the state that Pinnacle usually retained about half of the existing department, expelling the less desirables. However, the chief frequently got the axe, as they liked to bring in their own man to head the new group.

One reason Pinnacle kept on several former partners was specifically to address Kim's concern. They didn't want to stir up surgeon outrage; this was bad for business. They needed these people to provide continuity and smooth over the transition period. With passing time, however, the old members often found themselves becoming excess baggage as their usefulness faded and newer, cheaper labor became available.

The meeting droned on for another hour with the typical bickering, back-biting, and ass-kissing that Doug figured exemplified corporate meetings across the country; from the small town school board meetings held in cafeterias, to the elegant polished teak enclaves of General Motors, human nature remains remarkably constant, he thought. Nothing was really agreed upon or resolved, as was usually the case in these emergency sessions.

Doug believed this latest development could easily have been discussed next week at their regularly scheduled corporate meeting. But he knew Marshall liked to call these emergency meetings to demonstrate the central importance of work in one's life. Besides, Doug thought, Marshall had little else to do. His children were all grown up, and his wife was frequently out of town on extended vacations. Marshall didn't have any soccer teams to coach, baths to give, or homework to help with. He wouldn't have the faintest concern for these anyway.

By the time the meeting broke up at 9:15, Doug was tired and anxious to go home. It had been a long day, and he knew he'd have to be in here bright and early the next day. He walked out of the building together with Mike Carlucci. The two men stopped at Mike's Suburban.

"Well, what'd you think?" Doug asked. He spoke in a hushed tone as they both noticed Bryan Marshall and Joe Raskin engaged in a similar post-meeting chat at the far end of the parking lot.

"I dunno Doug—I wish we coulda waited 'til next week to discuss it. I mean he really doesn't know anything yet."

"Yeah, you're right," Doug said, shivering in the December wind. "Hey, wanna grab some coffee or dessert? It's too cold to stand out here and talk." Frequently, the two of them would stop somewhere after corporate meetings to conduct the post-mortem analysis.

"Not tonight, Doug. I gotta go home."

Doug, for the second time in the evening, sensed a slight distance in Mike. "You OK Mike? You know, with your case and all?"

"Yeah, sure. I'm dealing with it." Mike paused as a gust of wind roared by, rendering speech impossible. "Wonder how long it'll take 'em to sue?"

"Not sure, Mike—you don't know they will," Doug offered limply. The two men stared past each other. There was an awkward silence as Doug struggled to find other words of comfort. He couldn't.

"I'll see you tomorrow, Doug," Mike finally said with a pained expression. "Take care."

"Yeah, you too." They each headed for their vehicle. Doug realized that a lawsuit was virtually guaranteed and that they both knew it.

Doug paused at his truck, turned, and gazed up at the hospital. The wind bit into him, urging him to seek cover inside his truck, but he stood his ground. The hospital loomed dark and massive in front of him, blotting out half the night sky. The building, cloaked partly in shadows, was a Frankenstein patchwork of ill-fitting additions, and clashing architecture. Its jagged roofline was littered with microwave antennae, ductwork, and chimneys. A monstrous concrete parking garage, newly constructed, attached to the body proper via two enclosed aboveground walkways.

Doug wondered about the future of Mercy's anesthesia department. Was it about to undergo radical surgery? Was the answer somehow linked to the department's murky past? He realized he knew precious little about the department's early years, and for the first time, it bothered him. Discussions of the past were conspicuously absent. Details about it were glossed over; direct questions rebuffed.

What were Marshall and Raskin talking about?

CHAPTER THREE

Bryan Marshall walked back into the building from the cold parking lot and headed to his office. He thought the meeting had gone about as well as could be expected, although he noted Carlucci wasn't holding up well with the strain of his case.

He unlocked his office and stepped in. He knew it was late and he should be getting home but figured he had time for a quick look. He sat down at his desk and unlocked the bottom drawer. Toward the back, behind some files, was a metal box with another lock. Using the small key hung on the chain around his neck, he unlocked the box. Marshall pulled out a stack of photographs and riffled through them until he found the one he was looking for. The chosen photo was faded somewhat and looking a little worn, but he didn't care.

"Karen, Karen," he muttered to himself. He closed his eyes and leaned back in his chair, coaxing the old memory to life; it wasn't the first time. He could see and hear her as plainly as if she were in the room.

"Stop that! What are you doing?" Karen McCarthy squirmed out of his embrace.

Marshall nodded slightly at her shrill tone; it definitely pleased him. "I'm just trying to gauge your interest in your current position, Miss McCarthy," he said.

"What do you mean?" she asked flustered, as she backed toward the wall of the cramped office. Her elbow collided with one of the many framed diplomas covering the wall and sent it seesawing crazily on its mounting. Her face registered mostly surprise, but he believed he could detect a delicious hint of fear.

She eyed the door, as if calculating the distance, and then edged a few steps to her left toward it. Marshall didn't pursue her, but was content to study her, aware vaguely of the heaviness of his breathing. She was such a small thing, and so young. Not much older than his daughter. He knew he could easily overpower her. He debated his course of action for a moment, but something about her eyes got to him. She had the look of a cornered animal; he thought she might scream at any moment. He realized he was going about this all wrong—this was virgin territory after all. Time for a new tack, he thought.

With effort, Marshall manufactured a gentle smile and slowed his breathing. "Look, Miss McCarthy. I'm sorry about the—ah, hug. It's just my Old World upbringing." He searched her delicate face and dazzling, light-green eyes. He thought he could see the panic recede a notch. He retreated behind the oak desk that consumed half the room and settled down in the leather chair, its wooden frame groaning beneath the load. The casters on his chair squealed as he rolled closer to the desk. He shuffled some papers, cleared his throat, and said, "Have a seat." He gestured to the only other chair in the room.

"I'd prefer to stand," she said, her face trying to manage defiance, but her voice wavering and barely audible.

"As you wish," he said. "The reason I called you in early for this meeting is so we could discuss several things. You've been a student here six months now and it's come to my attention that you've had some problems." He looked up at her. She remained standing, staring at the newly carpeted floor. He cleared his throat again and continued. "The Department of Anesthesia is like a big family. The school of Nurse Anesthesia is part of that family. Your problems are our problems and vice versa." He maintained his smile, trying hard to add warmth to it.

After slipping on his reading glasses, Marshall opened a folder on his desk and began leafing through papers slowly as if performing a distasteful task. "Hmmm, let's see here," he said sadly. "Failure to intubate the trachea, unrecognized esophageal intubation." He paused and looked over his glasses at her. She didn't meet his gaze. He continued, "Poor manual dexterity, technical skills below average, D on the pharmacology final." He leaned back in his chair, shook his head wearily and sighed. "Karen, Karen—your evaluations say it all. What *am* I going to do with you?"

"B-but sir, I'm improving, sir." She clasped her hands and began to wring them. "M-most of those were early on. It's been a rough year, sir." She looked up and made her first direct eye contact with him. Her eyes were pleading.

"Ah, yes. A rough year, indeed." Marshall sat forward in his chair suddenly, elbows landing on the desk, and fixed her with a hard stare. His tone changed abruptly from concerned professor to Gestapo interrogator. "You neglected to mention on your application that you had a baby!" He slammed his fists on the desk and the phone handset rattled in its cradle. A hint of a smile surfaced on his face, but he quickly suppressed it.

She let out a muffled cry of surprise and tears began to roll down her flushed cheeks. "How did . . . ? Who told . . . ?" Her lithe body trembled, and she swayed back and forth slightly.

Much better, he thought. Now we're getting somewhere. His plan was paying off. Marshall reflected back to his first meeting with Karen. He had known early on that she had lied on her application about the out-of-wedlock baby. He was well con-nected and had his sources. Normally, this would have doomed any chance of admission to the rigidly Catholic Mercy Hospital. But he had intervened on her behalf; he had chosen not to reveal her secret to the committee. He said he saw real promise in her, and in this, he had been quite honest. "It would be such a shame if the hospital found out about the baby. Why, they'd have no choice but to expel you." Marshall turned both palms upward in a help-less gesture as he let this sink in.

"I need this job," she said meekly. "My baby—"

"I know you do, Karen. I know you do." His soothing voice continued, "I understand perfectly. I want to help you." Hope flick-ered across her face. Marshall felt a stab of remorse as she gazed at him imploringly with her doe eyes. He broke eye contact, but like a moth to light, his gaze soon returned to her breasts. His hands had taken a preliminary measure of them moments earlier and had dis-covered they were much larger than her baggy scrub suit had let on. This excited him immensely and served to obliterate his hesitation. Nothing would deny him now. "Remember what I said about the department being family? Well, family members help each other, don't they? But help is a two-way street, isn't it Karen?"

"W-what do you want?" she asked, although he could see from her anguished expression she understood.

"Nothing you haven't done before, I assure you," he said and stood up from his chair. The panicked look returned to her face.

"I can't," she said, and then bolted for the door. She grabbed the knob with both hands, yanking it hard. When she realized it was locked, she froze, still facing the door. Her shoulders col-lapsed and soon began to bob up and down as fresh tears came.

Marshall closed the gap between them. Being so close to her again, seeing her tightly curled, strawberry hair peek out from the surgical cap, breathing in her clean, young woman smell, he found it hard to concentrate. He reached out and took off her surgical cap. Her hair seemed to expand as if spring-loaded and tumbled down to just below her shoulders. He was amazed that it had all fit into her cap. He turned her gently to face him. Her limbs moved waxily as she released the doorknob; she wore a blank, resigned expression. She looked past him toward the shelves of books and journals, but appeared to focus on nothing. Marshall put his arms around her, drew her close to him and ran his fingers through her coppery mane. He towered over her, his chin resting on the top of her head.

"There, there now, Karen. No need for tears." He selected a kindly, fatherly tone as he continued to stroke her hair. "I'm not the uncaring ogre that you imagine me to be. I don't want to have to throw you and your baby out on the street all because of some bad grades and a little lie."

All she could manage in response were muted sobs.

Marshall caressed her body and nuzzled her. "Don't make me do that, Karen," he said in a husky voice. "I want to help you. I need you to help me." He slid his hand under her scrub top. He felt her shudder, but she offered no resistance. "And call me Daddy."

The twenty-five-year-old memory, one of his favorites, still held considerable power and never failed to excite him. His heart was thumping rapidly and his breathing was uneven as he put the photographs back and locked up. Poor Karen, he thought. Such a pity.

CHAPTER FOUR

At 5:30 a.m. Wednesday morning, Doug's clock radio alarm did its best electronic impression of a screech owl. God, he hated that noise. Doug had already been awake for ten minutes and was resting comfortably waiting for the alarm. He had the uncanny ability to know what time it was anytime at night. After twelve years of getting called at all hours, he could gauge the time by how fatigued he felt. He liked to get seven hours of sleep, but his brain had carefully cataloged the different feelings of one hour of sleep, two hours, three hours, and so on up to seven. He actually enjoyed waking shortly before his alarm, so he could savor the relaxation of his bed, rather than be oblivious to it in sleep.

He got up, shut off the alarm, and headed for the shower. He rarely utilized the snooze button, regarding this as a moral weakness. His morning routine was timed down to the minute. Surgeons did not tolerate late starts.

Doug's mind wandered back to last night's meeting as the hot water pulsed across his body. He had set the adjustable shower massage head to hard pulse; his seven-year-old son, Steven, called this setting "bombs." It helped him wake up and relieved some of his morning stiffness.

Would the hospital really get rid of us? He would've thought it impossible a couple years ago, but now in the era of health care reform and managed care all bets were off. Surely, even if Pinnacle came in, they would offer positions to some of them. He began to mentally dissect his own group, Keystone Anesthesia.

He smiled when he thought of the large differences between the members of his group. Just as in every walk of life, some people are particularly well suited to their jobs and some are not. Doug was often amazed by how much effort some patients would expend to select a surgeon, only to leave the choice of the anesthesiologist to potluck. He knew that in many operations the two are equally important in determining the outcome of the procedure.

Doug cringed when he thought of two members of his own group. Omar Ayash was in his late fifties and had a bad habit of falling asleep in the OR while administering anesthesia. Sometimes he would nod off for a few seconds, and the circulating nurse would have to shake him to rouse him. He had been written up numerous times, and his personnel file was replete with incriminating reports, but somehow they couldn't get rid of him. The hospital didn't want to get entangled with disciplining a physician and felt the responsibility lay with the anesthesia group. Keystone was loath to fire him, as he had already threatened lawsuits for age and nationality discrimination. Doug couldn't wait for him to retire.

Then there was Joe Raskin, a strange mix of a man. He was in his mid-fifties and aging poorly. He was barely 5' 7" and unable to convince anyone that the 260 pounds packed on his frame belonged there. He was dark complected and sported a thick, unkempt black beard generously streaked with gray. His beard was so heavy that Doug figured Raskin needed to trim the upper portion if he wanted to see. He had intense, dark brown eyes and a broad nose smeared over the center of his face.

Doug reflected that Raskin was one of those guys that every place is obliged to have: a great talker. He could sure talk the talk, but stumbled when walking the walk. Raskin's story was actually tragic; he had fallen into one of the common pitfalls of anesthesia practice. Doug recalled bits of one of their earliest conversations twelve years ago, when they had first met.

"Where did you train?" Doug asked.

"Mass General," replied Raskin, his voice caressing the name in reverence.

Doug couldn't help but be impressed. It was one of the premier anesthesia training centers. "When did you finish?"

"Sixty-nine."

"Was Mercy even open then?" Doug asked.

"Yeah, sure. It opened in sixty-eight. Bryan Marshall started the department. I came six months later."

"But why Mercy? It couldn't have been much more than a clinic back then. You probably could've gone anywhere."

"You got that right, Doug." Raskin paused and seemed to recall memories, possibly of his forgotten youth. "I was hot shit back then. They didn't come any better trained. I coulda written my own ticket."

"Yeah, but why Mercy?" Doug persisted. "Why not Penn or Columbia or Cornell?"

"I was hot shit."

Raskin never did answer the question, but Doug finally figured it out over the years: laziness. Raskin had opted for the easy life when he took the job at the shiny new Our Lady of Mercy hospital. It was a nice posh job in a sleepy community hospital, complete with nurse anesthetists (CRNAs) to do the work. He couldn't pass it up.

Therein lay the trap. Raskin's job consisted of supervising the CRNAs. This was supposed to mean an intimate involvement in the cases, helping with the critical induction and emergence phases, and troubleshooting any problems. Probably Raskin started out that way, but eventually the money and his laziness must've gotten in the way.

Raskin worked during the heydays of anesthesia. He and his early partners (Omar Ayash joined in 1972) made a fortune supervising thousands of cases. They ran three or four rooms with low-paid CRNAs, and billed the fledgling insurance companies full freight decades before the days of cost-containment and the powerful HMOs.

Somehow, Raskin's supervision evolved until it looked like what it did now. Raskin no longer bothered to set foot in any of the ORs. He spent most of the day on the phone to his various brokers keeping tabs on his several million dollars in pension, profit-sharing, and personal accounts. He walked up and down the corridors of the OR complex rubbing his hands together, and signaled the "girls," as he referred to the CRNAs, to proceed. He gave them a peculiar hand sign, a cross between a military salute and a traffic cop gesture, through the window in the OR doors.

The essential drawback to this technique, Doug figured, besides having the CRNAs make fun of Raskin behind his back, was that his skills, his actual hands on procedures, deteriorated badly.

This might have been okay; Raskin might have been able to slide by until his retirement except for several gigantic unforeseen changes that swept over the anesthesia field in the late 1980's. First, CRNA salaries skyrocketed, doubling or even tripling in a five-year period. Second, the supply of well-trained anesthesiology residents was at an all-time high. Third, because of the advances in surgery and anesthesia, many more complicated procedures were being done on older and sicker patients. What this all translated into was that many anesthesia groups were leaning toward more physicians and fewer CRNAs to run their departments. This meant less supervision and more personally administered anesthetics by the physicians themselves.

Doug remembered very well when this change had come to Keystone Anesthesia Associates. Early in his employment, the group had voted on more physician anesthesia and less supervision. He had been thrilled. After just two years of supervising CRNAs at Mercy, he could easily make the transition back to administering his own cases. To someone like Raskin, however, this must have been his worst nightmare.

Raskin was a very intelligent man and surely realized what was happening. But again, Raskin's innate laziness prevailed and prevented him from taking any meaningful steps to remedy his situation. It must've been just easier to let someone else do all the work, and deceive himself into thinking that he could've done it himself.

Doug often wondered how much Raskin actually realized. Did he understand the depth of his fears and incompetence? Or had he, after lying to himself for so many years, come to believe his own lies?

Doug felt uncomfortable with his own skills when he took a two-week vacation. When he came back, the first day he was a bit rusty and might blow an IV or something before getting back into the swing of things. He couldn't imagine a twenty-year vacation.

The real irony of the situation was that Joe set foot in the ORs only when he was summoned to help out in an emergency. Doug thought this was especially ridiculous. How is the guy who hasn't intubated anyone in a year going to waltz in and do the one the experienced CRNA cannot? Invariably, the answer was he could not. So another anesthesiologist, frequently Raskin's friend, Bryan Marshall, came in and bailed him out.

In addition to losing skills he'd once possessed, Raskin also became deficient in techniques that hadn't even existed when he'd trained. All branches of medicine progressed rapidly, and the highly technical field of anesthesia was no exception. New procedures, techniques, and monitors were constantly coming on the scene with the rapid growth of microchip technology. New drugs were also constantly appearing. Doug knew that the anesthetic of 1999 bore little resemblance to an anesthetic of the 1970s.

Raskin's knowledge didn't actually become obsolete. Raskin prided himself on keeping up with all the latest, through reading extensively in journals and attending numerous meetings. Raskin could carry on a wonderful discussion of any of the cutting-edge techniques or pharmacodynamics of modern day anesthesia. This was where the talk the talk part came in and served as a highly effective smokescreen.

What Raskin really lacked was the technical expertise, gained only from hands-on experience, to apply the new technology. But more than that, Doug surmised, what he really suffered from was fear, a deep-seated fear, approaching phobic proportions. He avoided any hi-tech, complicated case like the plague.

Doug often speculated on the enormous effort Raskin expended manipulating the schedule. Wouldn't it just have been easier to learn the newer techniques and do the cases, then to constantly avoid them and live in perpetual fear that he would be assigned to one that he couldn't weasel out of? The constant fear surely took its toll. He became meaner and nastier, prone to temper tantrums and displays of rage. His interaction with the patients and the nursing staff suffered. Whereas Omar Ayash's file was thick with reports of incompetence, Raskin's file was filled with patient and staff complaints.

As hard as Raskin's predicament was to understand, what was even more difficult to comprehend was why Bryan Marshall put up with Raskin. Marshall didn't suffer *anyone* lightly. Did having a yes-man for all occasions justify his forbearance? Doug had gnawed on this one for years but had never come up with a truly satisfactory explanation.

Doug turned off the water and stepped out of the shower. He toweled off his six-foot-two-inch frame, wrapped the towel around his waist, and got ready to shave. He studied his image in the steamy mirror for a moment. He was comfortable with what he saw, but he chuckled when he thought it had not always been so. Throughout his teens and early twenties, Doug had believed his nose was too big and chin too small. But over the years he had come to accept that maybe his initial assessment, perhaps skewed by his shyness, had been harsh. It seemed that women were indeed attracted to his features. His wife, Laura, insisted he was handsome. He still didn't quite get it, but had moved beyond the questioning state.

The steam did a good job hiding the gray sneaking in at his temples and the bags developing under his eyes. He knew his looks and youth were following the well-worn trail to middle age. He couldn't quite figure out how much it bothered him.

He walked into the bedroom where Laura was still sound asleep. She looked especially pretty; her face was so peaceful, framed by her long black hair. Snuggled up next to her was Anthony, their three-year-old little boy, vigorously sucking his thumb. He was the youngest of their three sons. Anthony had a habit of climbing into their bed early in the morning. Doug smiled as he remembered twelve years ago, when their first son, Teddy, was a baby. They had discouraged him from sleeping in their bed, believing that their marriage bed was no place for little children. It might foster hard-to-break habits of dependency likely to warp a child's development. Being first time parents was not easy. Now, he looked forward to Anthony snuggling with them and believed this sense of comfort and protection would only help the child in later life.

Doug loved to take Anthony out to breakfast after being on call. The older boys were in school, and Laura appreciated the opportunity to get some housework done unimpeded. The two generally gravitated to the Country Oven, a little coffee shop just down the road off the interstate. Anthony especially liked to retrieve the *USA Today* from the "slamming door," and to sit on the stools at the counter rather than at the booths or tables. He also enjoyed taking his toy-du-jour to show the waitress and paying the bill with Dad's help.

At times like these, when the house was so quiet and everyone was still asleep, Doug was overwhelmed with love, thankfulness, and serenity. Sadly, guilt also surfaced. Just this past weekend, Laura and he had had another monster fight, this time over something really critical, like did he have time to go the gym. Strange how minor issues could explode into nasty fights so easily. This worried Doug almost as much as the fact their fights had become more frequent. *What was happening?*

Doug shook off this worry only to have uglier thoughts replace it. Would someone die today at his hands? Would this be the day the sleeping serpent reared its ugly head and sank its fangs into him? Strange thoughts for the Iceman. Doug smiled briefly. He didn't believe he was as cool as they thought he was. He wasn't sure anyone really could be. He was thankful for his experience and knew he was stronger for it, but he could never be absolutely sure of himself. How's that expression go? Past performance is no guarantee of future results.

Over the years he had dealt well with these fears, banishing them quickly whenever they appeared. They barely grazed his consciousness, as he kept them imprisoned in the subterranean depths of his subconscious. However, because of Mike's unfortunate case Monday, his fears were launching a bolder assault.

Doug arrived at the hospital at 7:05 a.m., the same time he always did. He slid his plastic card into the slot to activate the security gate into the doctor's parking lot. To this day, he was slightly embarrassed to park in this special lot. One of the OR nurses said that as long as they had Doctors' parking lots, it would be hard to have much sympathy for all the doctors' whining about dwindling reimbursement. She was referring of course to all the shiny new Mercedes, BMWs, and Lexus's that inhabited this particular lot. She had a good point.

Doug maneuvered his eight-year-old, 120,000 mile Toyota 4X4, which he was secretly proud of, next to Ken Danowski's

Explorer. He knew everyone's vehicle. One could glean a surprising amount of information from a quick glance around the lot. He saw Dr. Marshall's car and realized he must've been called in last night. Undoubtedly he was still working on an emergency case. He also saw Dr. Johnson's Lexus and because he was an OB-GYN specialist, the case was most likely a cesarean section or less likely a ruptured ectopic pregnancy.

Doug grabbed his gym bag, hopped out of the truck, and strode briskly to the back entrance to the hospital. Cold still gripped the air and Doug breathed out large plumes of vapor. He glanced at the eastern sky and wondered if the sun was frozen somewhere below the horizon and might never rise. He knew as late man today, he didn't have a prayer of seeing it on the way home.

Doug looked forward to seeing some of his co-workers in the locker room where they changed into scrubs. The locker room was one of the few places where everyone showed up at once and had several minutes to talk. First on the agenda was the previous call-person's tale of woe. This was particularly interesting because your turn in the barrel was never far off. Doug entered the locker room wondering again how Mike was holding up.

"Hey Doug, good morning," Ken Danowski offered cheerfully. "How are you?"

"Not bad," responded Doug. "Sounds like you're getting a cold, though." Doug peeled off his bulky jacket and stuffed it in his locker.

"Yeah, the baby's picked up some crud, and I always seem to get it," Ken said, punctuating his remark with a loud snort into his handkerchief.

Doug picked out some scrubs and proceeded to change. "Feels like we just left."

"Yeah, I know. Nothing like an emergency evening meeting to screw up a week. Looks like Marshall's here doing a case." Ken glanced around quickly and added at half volume, "Too bad."

"Yep, it's a damned shame," Doug echoed.

"What did you think of the meeting last night?" Ken asked.

"I wouldn't worry too much about Pinnacle. We don't have all the facts yet."

"That's easy for you to say. You're not low man on the totem pole," Ken said, grinning.

"Yeah, you're right. Better worry." Doug paused to smile, then asked, "What're you doing today?"

"I'm a regular guy," Ken said as he pulled a scrub shirt over his head, "but I got the frigging vascular room with Shindler. I'll be here till the cows come home and then some."

"You're breaking my heart." Doug liked Ken and thought he was much more animated and personable when Marshall or Raskin weren't around. He was a good addition to the group, just what they needed—some new blood.

The locker room door opened and an unfamiliar face entered. The face belonged to a young, clean-cut kid in his early twenties with short, cropped red hair and med student written all over him.

"Uh, hi, I'm Rusty Cramer. I'm here to see, uh, Dr. Bryan Marshall, the chief of anesthesia."

"Hi Rusty." Doug held out his hand to shake. "I'm Doug Landry, the real chief of anesthesia around here," Doug said, as he broke out into laughter. Rusty gave him a firm hand and smiled clumsily.

"You must be our med student for this rotation," continued Doug.

"Yes, that's right Dr. Landry."

"Call me Doug. I believe the good Dr. Marshall is involved in a case right now. We'll meet him shortly. And that's Ken Danowski over there." Doug grinned and lowered his voice slightly for effect. "He's kinda low man. You want to avoid him at all costs."

"Pleased to meet you, Rusty," said Ken. "Just ignore that turkey," he said motioning at Doug. "He's been sniffing the gas for so long it's rotted his brain. Why don't you suit up and join us for a fun-filled exciting day. The scrubs are over there. You can use this locker over here." Ken paused to sneeze. "Stick with me and I'll show you some *modern* anesthesia."

"OK, thanks." Rusty laughed nervously again and appeared slightly confused. Doug realized that coming from the Penn State University Medical Center, Rusty was no doubt accustomed to a more formal interaction with his staff men.

"So, you've come from the mecca to mingle with the peasants," Ken said.

"The mecca?" Rusty stripped down to his T-shirt—the front of which was emblazoned with a large picture of the Amazing Spiderman. Doug had to work hard to suppress a grin.

"That's how we peasants refer to the big university teaching hospital—to show proper homage," Ken said.

"Oh, I see," Rusty said, smiling. He hesitated for a moment, then added, "You may kiss my hand now." Doug and Ken both snorted in laughter.

The locker room door opened again and Mike Carlucci stalked in.

"Hi Doug, Ken," Mike said. He ignored Rusty.

"How's it going, Mike?" Doug asked, grimacing slightly. He could tell immediately from Mike's agitated tone, haggard appearance, and tense body movements that things were far from all right.

"Bad, Doug. They filed suit already!" Mike spit the words out as he flung his locker door open with a clang. "I just got the notice last night. Ten fucking million dollars!"

The playful mood in the locker room evaporated, being replaced by a cold gloom. Doug suddenly found the pattern of cracks in the linoleum floor mesmerizing.

When the long day finally ended, Doug walked out wearily to his truck. The sun had set several hours earlier and darkness was descending in earnest. It had been a typically busy Wednesday with lots of scheduled cases and a slew of emergency add-on cases. He hadn't seen much of anybody all day and felt like he had been chained in his room. They were short nurses and breaks had been scarce.

Doug glanced around the virtually empty parking lot. Ken's truck was gone; so was Mike's. They had been lucky and escaped earlier. Doug unlocked his door and hopped up onto the vinyl seat. It felt like he was sitting on a block of ice. He vowed his next vehicle would have heated seats. Doug wondered what the day must've been like for Mike. It had to have been hellish. Doug had never been sued, but knew it could happen at any time. Mike was an extremely conscientious individual and seemed to be taking his patient's death quite hard. Although, he thought, maybe that was unfair. Who could say how they would react to playing such an intimate role in another's death? Doug shook his head. He hoped never to have to answer that one. At least there were no emergencies today, thank God. No patients arresting in the OR, no difficult intubations, no bloodbaths. Maybe with Christmas just around the corner, things would settle down for a bit. They could all use a break.

CHAPTER FIVE

He checked the hallway for people, and slipped as silently as a shadow into OR#5. He knew his chances of being observed were slim because the entire complex was deserted this early in the morning. The OR nurses wouldn't start setting up the cases for another thirty minutes, and Ken Danowski, the anesthesiologist scheduled to be in here today, never showed up before seven o'clock.

Once inside, he adjusted the switch so the operating room was bathed in dim light, barely enough to push back the shadows. He paused to take in his surroundings, sensing vaguely that he needed to rekindle his anger. He surveyed the walls first, walls he had seen a thousand times, covered with their dingy, green tiles. Puke-green was how he always referred to them. Abruptly, he had the sensation someone was watching him. Turning quickly, he shot a glance above the heavy wooden door he had just come through. There it was, just as he had known it would be—a small wooden crucifix staring down at him.

"Leave me alone," he muttered. He turned and walked past all the laparoscopic equipment, the electrocautery generator, and the OR table toward the anesthesia machine at the far end of the room. That was it in a nutshell, he thought. Catholic hospitals were just too damn cheap. Austerity was a virtue. He remembered Sister Catherine drilling that and other such nonsense into his head in school. What a load of crap!

He stood before the Drager Narkomed 3B, one of the most advanced anesthesia machines on the market. It was a behemoth, standing seven feet tall and four feet wide, bristling with hoses, cables, and metal support struts like so many alien appendages. Thoughts of the impending hospital merger swirled through his head. Would he really lose his job? Is this how his institution, Our Lady of Mercy, would repay his years of service? Would his career be sacrificed on the altar of managed care in the name of the almighty dollar?

His gaze swept to the three vaporizers mounted on the machine at eye-level: Halothane, Forane, and Suprane, the anesthetic gases currently in vogue. His hand reached out involuntarily and caressed the cold, smooth metal cylinder of the Forane vaporizer. Sliding his hand to the top of the vaporizer, he gripped the large, finely knurled knob like he had done countless times before when anesthetizing his patients. Could they actually take away his hospital privileges and bar him from these ORs? The answer was all too clear. He reminded himself how Mercy Hospital had dealt with Good Friday.

Mercy had always closed its ORs on Good Friday out of respect. This was the decent thing to do, he thought. Since his earliest memories, he had always gone to mass on Good Friday; it was one of the holiest days of the year, for Chrissakes. Now, thanks to the gun-to-your-head, bottom-line accounting demanded by those managed care pricks, Good Friday was just another day of the week. The OR doors were wide open. Crank those little doggies through. Yee-hah! Business decision, they had called it. Well, if the nuns could make a business decision, then so could he.

He stared beyond the vaporizers, and his thoughts returned to the haunting theme that had stuck in his brain like a catchy tune. Would those smug-faced, know-it-all bastards he called partners, walk away with his job? Especially galling were the young punks, so confident with their recent training. They didn't have a clue what work, loyalty, and sacrifice were all about. His hands clenched tightly into fists, and he felt his heart begin to pound away in his chest. But the anger felt good.

Trembling slightly, he fetched a fresh bottle of Forane and a bottle of Suprane from the anesthesia cart. Any hesitation he had earlier was gone. He produced an empty bottle from his pocket and unscrewed the caps on all three bottles. He chuckled to himself as he thought of the ingenious fill spouts that had been engineered to prevent accidental cross-filling of the vaporizers. Too bad they wouldn't work this time. He poured the contents of one bottle into another and played mix and match with the bottles and fill spouts. He was thus able to defeat the fail-safe mechanism and fill the Forane vaporizer with the wrong agent, Suprane. The volatile liquid gurgled quietly as it transferred. The room smelled of Forane and Suprane, but he knew the pungent odor would quickly dissipate. He cleaned up his handiwork and made a rapid exit from the room, not bothering to give the crucifix a second look. Again he took note that no one was in the OR complex to notice him.

CHAPTER SIX

Ken Danowski hadn't gotten much sleep last night. He dragged himself wearily from his Ford Explorer out into the biting December wind. God, it's cold, he thought as he trudged the hundred yards or so from the parking lot to the hospital. The raw air burned his sore throat and his head throbbed miserably.

He keyed in the combination to the Doctor's locker room. Encumbered by his heavy winter parka, gloves and briefcase, he struggled with the door that seemed heavier than usual. Once inside, he walked over to his locker and set his briefcase down with a grunt. Doug Landry was standing close by with his nose buried in his own locker, rooting around for something. Ken smiled. How Doug ever found anything in there was beyond Ken. Doug was the butt of many jokes about his sloppy locker habits. But Ken knew better then to be fooled by this. Doug Landry was a sharp anesthesiologist, as sharp as they came. "Lose something in there, Doug?" asked Ken as he pried off his gloves.

"Oh, hi Ken," said Doug, pulling his head out of his locker and revealing a big grin. "Naw, not a chance. A place for everything and everything in its place. See, right here where I left them." He held up his narcotic keys like a trophy fish.

Ken smiled back at Doug. Even though Doug was ten years his senior, he related well to him.

"You're kind of late," Doug said, eyeing his watch longer than necessary. He frowned and shook his head slowly. "You probably can kiss that partnership thing goodbye."

Ken chuckled as he slipped his parka off and stuffed it into his locker. "Whoever said anything about wanting to be partners with you turkeys?"

Doug smiled again, but soon his face became serious. "You look a little rough, Ken."

"Yeah, the baby was up last night with croup, and I don't feel so hot either." Ken cringed as he recalled the scary night he had spent with his ten-month-old son. "God, I can't stand bad airway stuff with kids in the OR. But, at home with your own kid . . ." His voice trailed off and he shook his head.

"Yeah, nothing worse than a sick kid," said Doug. "You're right. One night when Teddy was a baby—oh, ten years ago or so—they had to admit him to the hospital and put him in a croup tent."

"Thank God, Ryan didn't get that bad." Ken peeled his turtleneck and sweater over his head and felt his hair crackle with static electricity. He instinctively sucked in his bare midsection and then smiled inwardly when he realized he was succumbing to petty machismo. All the same, he maintained his beach pose. Somehow, he thought, Doug always managed to look fit—muscular, actually—and he didn't want to be shown up by the older man.

The hospital intercom crackled to life, interrupting the men. Ken knew it must be 7:15 as the obviously taped voice of the president of Mercy Hospital, complete with annoying background hiss, blared from the speaker. "This is Sister Emmanuel with the morning prayer. Dear God, please help us remember that we are not alone in our suffering. We are not the only ones . . ."

Ken tuned Sister Emmanuel out; he had heard the same prayer or something similar every morning for three years now. Soothing, she was not. Fingernails across a chalkboard would be an improvement, he mused. He finished suiting up and clanged his locker door shut.

"Hey, you better say your prayers," said Doug, also finishing with his locker. "You gotta long day ahead, pal. I saw the schedule. You're in OR#5. Better get some coffee in you so you can stay awake."

"Thanks for the advice," Ken said sarcastically. "Where'd you get your degree from again—mail order, right?"

Doug laughed in response.

"That caffeine shit will kill you," continued Ken, knowing full well that Doug was a notorious coffee fiend. He'd seen him put away three or four cups a day, twice that on a call day. "Didn't they teach you anything in med school?"

"Med school?" Doug asked. "Whoever said anything about med school?"

Laughing, the two men headed out of the locker room. But, kidding aside, Ken knew he'd be right up there with Doug in the java department.

"Speaking of med school," Doug said, "Have you seen Rusty this morning?"

"No, but his beat-up Jeep was in the parking lot when I came in."

"Hmmm, I wonder where he is?" Doug paused to tie on his surgical mask. "Well, if you see him, send him over to me in outpatient surgery. The schedule's light and it should be an easy day."

"Okay, will do," Ken said, also reaching for a cap and mask. "Have a good one."

"Thanks, you too." Ken certainly hoped he would feel better as the day went on.

Ken started to page through the medical chart of Dorothy Lubriani, his first patient of the day scheduled for a laparoscopic gall bladder removal. Her name seemed vaguely familiar to him, but he couldn't place it. He sipped his coffee and turned to the patient information sheet to check for clues as to who she might be. She was a forty-five-year-old, married RN on disability he discovered. No other personal information was available, and this didn't ring any bells for him. He groaned audibly when he saw a three-page, typewritten summary of his patient's medical history produced by the patient herself and clipped to the inside of the chart. This was never a good sign, he thought. Probably has a list of allergies a mile long, too.

Ken absently rubbed his hand over his chin as he read further. The coarse stubble was rough on his hand and surprised him. He realized he had forgotten to shave this morning, one of the early casualties of a sleepless night. He forced some more coffee down. He saw Dorothy had made no fewer than nine visits to the OR in the last five years. Nothing serious—an assortment of lumps and bumps excised and a few hernias repaired. Ken let out a resigned sigh, chugged the remainder of his coffee, screwed on his best happy face, and walked across the hall to the holding area to meet his patient.

"Good morning, Mrs. Lubriani," Ken said. He knew immediately he had seen her before, but still couldn't say where. She was medium height, overweight, with dark hair and makeup appropriate for a night out, not the operating room. "I'm Dr. Danowski. I'll be your anesthesiologist this morning." Ken spoke quietly because the holding room was crowded with several other patients awaiting surgery.

"Hi, Dr. Danowski," Dorothy said loudly in a high-pitched nasal voice. "You took care of me two years ago for my hernia. I'm so glad to get you again."

"Ah, the hernia, of course," Ken said, feeling himself blush slightly. He still didn't remember her; his sluggish brain refused to cooperate. "So, how are you doing today?"

"Well, not so good, Doctor. I have the beginning of a migraine right behind this eye." She tapped on her right temple emphatically.

"And my irritable bowel is acting up. Or do you think that's gall-bladder? No, too low. And wouldn't you know, my fibromyalgia is singing this morning."

Oh shit, thought Ken. He remembered her now and realized his blunder. He had violated a cardinal rule of medicine: Never, under any circumstances, ask a patient such as Dorothy Lubriani how they are feeling.

"But my asthma's doing pretty well—only a touch of wheezing. Dr. Jefferies says the new regimen he has me on—you know, alternating the three inhalers—has been shown in recent clinical studies to be most effective."

Ken looked around the holding area for moral support. Mike was several litters away but was too engrossed starting an IV on his patient. He didn't look to be in a joking mood anyway. Ken returned his attention to Dorothy who had paused to take a breath. "That's great," he said and fought hard to keep a straight face.

"Thank God she's asleep!" Ken said to himself as the Diprivan finally hit. He noted that Dorothy had taken a relatively large dose, probably owing to her frequent reliance on painkillers.

"Cripes, Ken. What took you so long?" asked Babs Honeywell, the circulating nurse. "I thought you'd never get her to sleep."

"Me either," said Ken.

"Thank God, it's a general," said Sandy McCoombs, the scrub nurse as she noisily made last-minute rearrangements of her instruments.

"Yeah, she's some piece of work," muttered Ken as he proceeded with the anesthetic. He knew the intravenous Diprivan would wear off in about five minutes, and in order to keep Dorothy anesthetized, he would need to quickly administer a gaseous anesthetic agent. He dialed in the Forane vaporizer to two percent. To provide muscle relaxation, he also administered Atracurium intravenously, which would temporarily paralyze his patient.

"What's wrong with you today, Ken?" asked Babs, good-naturedly. "Cat got your tongue?"

"I'm out of it today, Babs. Ryan was up half the night with croup. After we finally got him settled, I was too keyed up to sleep."

"How old is he now?"

"Ten months." Ken scanned his monitors—everything looked good—sat down, and started to fill out his anesthetic record.

"They're so cute, then," Babs said. "Well, if I see you nodding off, I'll bonk you one."

Ken looked up. "Yeah, you do that," he said. He broke off eye contact again and busied himself with his record, hopefully signaling an end to the conversation.

The surgeon, Dr. Bruce Watkins, came through the door, his hands dripping wet and held high. "Hi, Babs, Sandy." They proceeded to gown and glove him. "Morning, Ken."

"Hi, Dr. Watkins." Ken still didn't feel comfortable calling the older surgeons by their first names, even though he had worked with them for three years now.

"What do you think of my patient, Mrs. Lubriani?" Watkins asked.

"She sure can talk a blue streak," Ken said. Looks like everyone's in a talkative mood this morning, he thought glumly.

"Ah, you noticed. Any trouble putting her to sleep? She's got a slew of medical problems."

"No, not really. Once you take her brain out of the picture, she's really quite healthy."

"You're probably right, Ken. I'm not sure how diseased her gallbag's gonna be, but she's been hounding me for six months now to take it out."

"I can imagine." Ken didn't want to be rude, but he hoped Watkins would pick up on his disinterested tone soon.

"She's got the symptoms down pat—she was a nurse you know—but her papida scan doesn't show much."

"Well, we'll see," Ken said. "She's awful big, though."

"You know what they say: female, fat, and forty—think gall-bladder," Watkins said and cracked up at his own wit.

Ken yawned under his mask.

* * *

Dorothy regained consciousness slowly. She felt very peaceful and relaxed. She wasn't quite sure where she was but didn't let that concern her. She was probably home in bed making a late morning of it. She *could* open her eyes if she wanted. Naw, just savor the floating sensation. Bits of a faraway conversation drifted by her ears. She chose to ignore them. Then one word, a name, penetrated her stupor—Dr. Watkins—her surgeon. That's right! This was the special day she had waited so many months for. She was supposed to have her gallbladder out today. She also heard her name and the beeping of some monitor.

Oh, of course, silly. You've already had your surgery and you're in the recovery room. I remember seeing that nice Dr. Danowski and drifting off to sleep. Wow! That was fast. And no pain. Isn't modern medicine wonderful? I knew laparoscopic procedures were less painful, but this is fantastic!

Dorothy Lubriani figured it was time to wake up and perhaps see about some additional pain medicine, just in case. She tried to open her eyes and found she couldn't.

That's strange. She noticed that she wasn't breathing normally. In fact, the air was being pushed into her lungs instead of her sucking it in. Very strange.

Fear began to creep into her sodden brain. What was going on? Was something wrong? Since she couldn't see anything, she focused on listening.

"—female, fat, and forty—think gallbladder."

That's Dr. Watkins, she thought. Hey, who's fat!?

Dorothy had had enough of this little game. It was time to stop playing possum—time to get up and go. Only when she tried, she found she couldn't move a muscle.

* * *

That's weird, Ken wondered to himself. His patient's heart rate had just shot up from the 70's to over 120, and her blood pressure had increased to 190/110. Normally, heart rate and BP jumped on incision, but they hadn't touched the patient yet. Watkins was still BS-ing with the nurses, and they were in slow gear hooking up all the video equipment necessary for laparoscopic surgery.

She seems light. Ken quickly dialed the Forane to three percent, a very high setting he rarely used, while he reviewed his anesthetic. He knew he had given her plenty of Fentanyl and already had the Forane on a hefty amount. She can't be light on three percent Forane on top of the Fentanyl and Diprivan. Maybe she really does have a bona fide medical problem after all—untreated hypertension. If so, the only way to bring down the pressure and pulse was with an antihypertensive. Ken drew up some Labetalol and gave it, hoping to control the pressure before incision.

"Okay to go, Ken?" Watkins asked as he grasped the scalpel in his gloved hand.

"Uh, yeah, sure," Ken replied, feeling uneasy. He knew Watkins wouldn't really wait for an answer. The question was more of a formality designed to denote incision time, rather than actually ask permission. Ken drew up more Labetalol and watched his monitors closely.

* * *

"Okay to go, Ken?"

Whoa—wait just a minute here! What's going on? Why can't I move?

Dorothy's questions were all answered when she felt the searing pain just below her umbilicus as the scalpel blade bit in.

She screamed, but no noise came forth. Her mouth didn't even twitch.

Stop! Stop! You can't do this! I'm awake, damn it! She thrashed as hard as she could, but she might as well have been a statue. The pain intensified. Tears came to her eyes.

* * *

C'mon, Dorothy. Fly right. Ken wanted to stabilize his case and veg out a little. He wasn't in the mood to tackle any big diagnostic dilemmas or emergencies this morning. He gave several more large doses of Labetalol before he got the pressure under control.

He sat down and started to draw up his drugs for the next case, but uneasiness still tugged at the edges of his mind. Ken had been doing anesthesia long enough to know that many patients didn't follow the textbooks. However, he also knew it was generally not a good idea to ignore his sixth sense. More often than not, there was something he had overlooked. He reviewed his anesthetic once again. Nothing amiss. *She just runs high, that's all.*

* * *

Oh, sweet Jesus! Don't let them do this! The pain was becoming unbearable. *Please, dear God, just let me die. Help me! Help me!* Dorothy continued to sob.

* * *

God, it's only 8:30, thought Ken. *I'm wasted already. Gonna be a long day.* Ken yawned for the hundredth time. His mind drifted and he imagined himself sitting in his easy chair at home watching TV with his wife, Lynn. The baby was asleep upstairs and all was so peaceful.

In his daydream, his black Labrador came over to him and pawed at his arm. "Leave me alone, Trooper," he mumbled. Ken snapped awake at the sound of his own voice. Something was wrong!

He sat bolt upright and shook his head to clear it. He scanned his monitors once again and went through a mental checklist, forcing himself to look carefully at each one.

Was she getting enough oxygen?

> O2 Sat - 99%
> FiO2 - 0.52

Yes. Oxygen saturation was excellent and inspired oxygen concentration was a normal 52%.

Was the tube in?

> EtCO2 - 35 mmHg
> FiCO2 - 0 mmHg

Again, yes. He had normal readouts showing the presence of carbon dioxide in the exhaled gases and no rebreathing of CO2.

> BP-170/95
> P-76

All still OK, except for a mildly elevated BP. He couldn't find anything wrong with any of the other monitors. Ken was baffled.

He turned to examine his patient. One of the casualties of the hi-tech explosion in anesthesia, he knew, was that recent grads focused almost wholly on their computer screens instead of their patients. For the most part, this worked out well. After all, modern advances in monitoring had largely accounted for the increases in anesthetic safety. But Ken also understood there was a danger to this approach.

He looked at Dorothy's face. Her color was good, the tube looked fine—no kinks, disconnects, or secretions. Then he saw something about her eyes, which he had taped shut at the beginning of the case. Wait—she's tearing. That's odd.

Tearing could be a sign of lightness, but he thought he had ruled that out early on when he had turned the Forane to the max.

He quickly pulled the tape off one eye and opened the lid. What he saw froze him and a sickly fear gripped him.

Holy shit! Her right pupil was hugely dilated. Ken's adrenals squeezed hard, and he felt the rush of adrenaline slam his tired brain into overdrive. He ripped the tape off the left eye. It's blown, too! Damn it, she's stroked!

Ken suddenly felt ill with crushing guilt; the gut-wrenching sensation spread like wildfire through his body before the analytical part of his mind had a chance to respond. His breathing became labored. No reason to stroke, though, he finally reasoned. He grabbed the flashlight out of his drawer and clicked it on. He opened Dorothy's right eyelid and held the light about two inches from her eye. He moved it off to the side and quickly brought it back to shine in her eye.

* * *

The flood of light came crashing through Dorothy's right eye and then left eye. She stopped sobbing for a minute. *That was Dr. Danowski I saw—why, he looked like he had just seen a ghost.* Darkness again. *Help me, Dr. Danowski! Help me, Dr. Danowski!*

A bright light shone directly into her right eye. It was so intense, it hurt. *This must be the light they talk about. I'm dying. I'm heading for the light.*

* * *

"Oh, thank God," Ken sighed with relief. Dorothy's pupils had contracted briskly to the light, indicating her brain was still functioning. There was no stroke. The conclusion was inescapable. *She's light! How did I miss it? She's light, possibly even awake!*

"Everything OK up there, Ken?" Watkins asked.

"Yeah, fine," Ken lied, his voice a bit shaky. He didn't want to upset Watkins, who had a nasty reputation for turning ugly if all didn't suit him.

"Makes me nervous when I hear my gas-man praying," Watkins said, breaking up again.

Ken injected large doses of Fentanyl, Versed and Diprivan into Dorothy's intravenous line while he tried to figure out what had gone wrong. He whispered in Dorothy's ear, "Everything's OK, Dorothy. You're all right."

* * *

Dorothy sensed herself being carried away again into oblivion. The awful pain was finally going away. *God's answering my prayers and taking me.* As she lost consciousness for the second time that morning, Dorothy thought she could hear the Almighty telling her: "Everything's OK, Dorothy."

* * *

Ken checked his infrared agent monitor again. It was reading -

	Insp	exp
Forane	2.9%	2.9%

Just what he had dialed in. That should have been plenty to keep her asleep. What went wrong? Computer glitch? Monitor malfunction? Broken vaporizer? Sudden instinct propelled him to action before he fully comprehended what he was doing.

Ken tore the rubber breathing bag from the circuit and sniffed the contents. Almost three percent Forane should be easy to smell.

What the—that's not Forane! It's Suprane!

In a flash, it all made sense. Two-point-nine percent Suprane isn't enough to keep anyone asleep. Eight to ten percent Suprane were the typical concentrations used. Poor Dorothy had been light all along, probably even awake.

But, how could it've happened? he wondered sickly. And, how much would she remember?

CHAPTER SEVEN

Maybe now, I'll get some answers, Rusty thought as he waited in the hallway for Dr. Landry to come out of the locker room. The two had hooked up this morning and done several cases in the outpatient surgery wing, a stand-alone unit separate from the main hospital OR. Rusty's investigation of his past had amazingly led him to Mercy Hospital, but here the trail went cold. Ever since his days at the orphanage, he had wondered about his parents. Who were they? Why did they put him there? What had really happened to them?

The locker room door opened and Dr. Landry stepped out, interrupting further thoughts. "C'mon, Rusty," Dr. Landry said. "I'll buy you lunch."

"Sure, you're on!" Rusty replied. He was always eager to humor his attendings—they were, of course, responsible for his all-important evaluations. Rusty knew he was quite adept at adapting himself to please people. In fact, he had dubbed himself, "Plasticman," not really having a shape of his own but able to take any form the other person wanted to see. A true shape-shifter, just like on <u>Star Trek</u>. He had gotten along very well with Dr. Danowski yesterday and figured it would be even easier with Dr. Landry. This skill had served him well through college and the rigors of medical school. He viewed life as an endless series of cranky attendings to be hoodwinked in order to achieve his goals.

But he had to admit that Mercy felt very different from the Med Center. There was a feeling of freedom here to be away from the Med Center's stiff professors, endless rounds, boring case presentations and countless students. He was getting a taste of medicine on the front lines with real-life doctors. Plus, he was getting one-on-one training, something that just didn't happen at the Med Center.

"OK, follow me," Dr. Landry said. "We'll head down to the coffee shop. The cafeteria will be too crowded this time of day." He led Rusty back down the OR hallway and out through the imposing automatic doors guarding the entrance. Outside of the OR, they went to the elevator and Dr. Landry pushed the down button. He turned to Rusty and said, "You did a nice job with that intubation."

Rusty was puzzled because he knew he had struggled to put the breathing tube in. He glanced at Dr. Landry's face to see if he was putting him on, but saw only sincerity. One of the benefits of being Plastic-man ironically enough, was that Rusty was a rather good judge of honesty. "Thanks for being patient with me, Doctor Landry. That's the first one I ever got in."

"Good for you," Dr. Landry said, smiling broadly. He patted Rusty on the back and said, "We'll make an anesthesiologist out of you yet."

Rusty laughed and returned the smile, although he was still locked in his kiss-ass med student/attending mode. The bell sounded and the door slid open revealing a crowded elevator. Dr. Landry and Rusty squeezed on and conversation halted while the elevator descended one floor to the lobby level. Rusty stole several glances at Dr. Landry and reflected that he held the key to an extremely valuable learning experience; a good mentor was hard to find. There was no telling how many procedures Dr. Landry might let him try.

Rusty exited the elevator and came face-to-face with a huge wooden crucifix, handcarved and beautifully painted, mounted on the marble wall facing the elevators. Dr. Landry steered them through the busy hospital lobby toward the little coffee shop. Rusty hadn't been on the first floor much and took in his surroundings, trying to get his bearings.

The lobby was an interesting cross between a Roman Catholic chapel and a greenhouse. Numerous large potted plants, hanging ferns, and tasteful flower arrangements were crammed into every nook and cranny, competing for space with religious statues. Large portraits of the Virgin Mary, Baby Jesus, and the Pope adorned the walls. There was also a dignified looking nun Rusty didn't recognize. He paused to look at her picture.

"That's the hospital administrator. The coffee shop's right down here," Dr. Landry said gesturing forward.

"I'm not used to working in a hospital that seems like it's half church. Doesn't it, uh, bother you?" Rusty instantly regretted his choice of words.

"No, Rusty," Dr. Landry said and chuckled. "I've been here so long, I barely notice it."

Rusty felt relieved; he certainly didn't want to offend Dr. Landry.

"Actually," Dr. Landry continued, "come to think of it, I like working here. The sisters do a nice job running the hospital. They have a reputation for being, uh, thrifty, but in today's competitive market this works well. Also, I think the patients appreciate the religious atmosphere."

"It just seems funny to have a nun for a CEO," Rusty observed, fixated on the business end of things. "Can she really hold her own with the HMO corporate sharks?"

"Yes, I believe she can." Dr. Landry turned and opened the heavy glass door to the coffeeshop. The sound of conversation and laughter flowed out mixed with the aromas of frying bacon and coffee. Rusty realized he was very hungry.

They both ordered chicken salad sandwiches, the specialty of the coffee shop, at Dr. Landry's suggestion. After their orders were filled, the two men took seats at a small table in the back of the noisy, crowded room.

"So Rusty, which specialty are you thinking of?"

"I'm not really sure yet, but I guess I'm leaning toward cardiology or internal medicine," Rusty said as he proceeded to wolf down his chicken salad sandwich. "Mmm, this is good," he managed to get out between considerable bites.

"Medicine? Yuck, kinda boring," Dr. Landry replied, also munching away.

"What made you choose anesthesia?" asked Rusty. "Do you like it?" Normally, Rusty would never have asked an attending such a personal question, but with Dr. Landry it seemed okay to push it.

"Yeah, I do like it. Not many people have a good feel for what it's really all about, though. Even after my rotation through it my third year—two weeks, just like you—I didn't have much of a clue. Seemed dull just watching these people sleep, but I liked all the computer and chemistry stuff. So I took a month of it early fourth year and loved it. I've always liked doing procedures and always disliked having long discussions with patients about their aches and pains."

"Yeah, I know what you mean. How long have you been here?"

"About twelve years."

"Wow," Rusty said and meant it. "I hear Doctor Marshall and Doctor Raskin have been here since the place opened."

"Pretty much."

"Do you think I'll get the chance to work with Doctor Marshall?"

Dr. Landry smiled wryly and said, "I'm sure you will."

Rusty decided to switch gears. "How's the job situation in anesthesia?"

"Not so good, Rusty. With all the mergers, managed care pressures, and Medicare cuts, the job situation is tight. Some people are desperate just to keep their jobs." Dr. Landry said it in a funny way, like he knew more than he was saying. "But for good people, opportunities always exist."

"But still, don't you find it boring?" Rusty asked. "You know in *The House of God*, he says anesthesia is ninety-nine percent boredom and one percent sheer terror."

"That guy was obviously never an anesthesiologist. It may look easy watching someone skilled do it, but let me tell you something, Rusty. When they walk out of the room the first time and you're alone with the patient—it ceases to become boring real quick. When you realize it's just you, your hands and brain, between a deadly arsenal of drugs and a patient's life, it's very sobering."

Rusty raised his eyebrows and murmured, "Hmmm." His mouth was too full to speak. Out of the corner of his eye, Rusty noticed several nursing students who had just come in and were standing in line. One in particular, a tall brunette with shiny white stockings, seemed to be looking right at him and smiling. Rusty returned the smile, but then quickly forced himself back to the conversation. Can't appear rude to Dr. Landry. Medicine required sacrifices, and this was one of them.

Rusty looked at Dr. Landry, expecting him to be in mid-sentence or frowning at him. But, he noticed that Dr. Landry was also staring off in the direction of the stockings, and hadn't said anything. Amazing, thought Rusty. He knew from talking to Dr. Danowski that Landry was married with several children. He seemed good-looking enough, although Rusty felt he was a poor judge of these things. But, the thought of him checking out the nurses amused Rusty. Why, he must be over forty! "Very sobering," Rusty said.

Dr. Landry shook his head, smiled quickly, and resumed eye contact with Rusty. "I'll never forget the day I soloed. My attending was just ten feet outside the OR door looking in and I was still scared shitless. What if the patient goes brady, loses pressure, or bleeds too much? What if I can't ventilate, or intubate, or get laryngospasm? A million what-ifs go through your head, and you try to figure if you know how to treat each one fast enough. Don't let the boredom part fool you." He shook his head.

"Hmmm, you make it sound kinda scary or dangerous. But Dr. Landry—"

"It's Doug, Rusty."

"OK, don't you think surgery is a lot scarier? After all, they're doing the real cutting." Rusty couldn't help but notice the brunette and her friends had occupied a nearby table. He smiled in their direction.

"No way. It's a very popular misconception, though. Now I'll grant you that some branches of surgery, like CT or major vascular, are very demanding . . ."

"CT?"

"Cardiothoracic. And I don't mean to make their job sound easy. It's not. I'm not sure I'd ever want to do it. But, consider the bread-and-butter surgeries—the hernia repairs, the knee arthroscopies, the gallbladder removals, and so on, that make up ninety percent of all operations. The likelihood of the surgeon inflicting a mortal wound during one of these procedures is extremely remote."

"Why do you say that?" Rusty asked.

"Well, because the area being operated on is far from any vital organ or large blood vessel," Dr. Landry continued. "And that's not to say all surgeons are perfect and don't botch things up. On the contrary, mistakes do happen."

"You mean like amputating the wrong leg or something." Rusty thought Dr. Landry seemed a bit touchy in this area; perhaps he was jealous of the surgeons.

"Exactly," Dr. Landry went on, "although that represents an extreme case. Sometimes hernias need refixing in several months or ear tubes fall out. The point is that the mistakes almost never cause immediate loss of life or brain damage."

"OK, I get it. But what makes anesthesia so different?"

"Glad you asked." Dr. Landry paused to take a bite of his sandwich. "Putting someone under a general anesthetic is completely different. Now, *every* case carries with it a small, but real risk of death or brain damage. You can die from anesthetic complications just as easily going to sleep for a five-minute D&C as you can for a five-hour spine fusion."

"Jeez, that's comforting. Good thing no one knows that."

"Rusty, it doesn't mean that being anesthetized is incredibly dangerous. It's not. In the hands of a competent anesthesiologist, it's very safe, carrying a risk similar to driving to the hospital. The point is that a general anesthetic involves the perfusion of all the vital organs; it's not a peripheral procedure. Didn't they teach you anything about perfusion in med school?"

"S-sure," Rusty stammered, suddenly trying to buy time. "It's, uh, means getting blood flow to the tissues." Typical attending— they're all alike. Just when he thought he was away from the Med Center.

"Right," Dr. Landry said and smiled. Rusty relaxed a bit and took another bite of his rapidly disappearing sandwich. "Now what's the purpose of having tissue blood flow?" Dr. Landry asked.

"Well, the tissues need oxygen."

"Exactly. You *have* been paying attention in school. Oh, that reminds me of the old joke. What's the deadliest substance known?"

"Uh, I'm not sure."

"Oxygen, of course. It kills in levels as low as one part-per-billion."

"Hmmm . . ." Rusty didn't get it, but vowed to work on it later.

"Anyway, here's the important part. What can disrupt tissue oxygen delivery or perfusion?"

"Well let's see." Rusty put on his best studious look as he thoughtfully sipped his Coke. "If there's a cardiac or BP problem, not enough blood will be pumped. That'd mess up perfusion." Rusty suddenly realized where Landry was going with this. "Or if the patient's not breathing, his O-two intake will stop."

"Precisely!" Dr. Landry beamed. "And this is what we deal with in anesthesia. Any airway or blood pressure problem can deprive the heart or brain of oxygen with disastrous results in minutes."

"When we put someone to sleep, what's the first drug we give them?"

"The white stuff, uh, Diprivan?"

"Right. Diprivan, otherwise known as propofol. They lose consciousness quickly and then they don't breathe, so we start ventilation by mask."

"What's the problem?" asked Rusty.

"What if you can't ventilate them with the mask?" Dr. Landry countered.

"Why wouldn't you be able to? Anyway, then you could just intubate them with the endotracheal tube, right?" Rusty asked.

"Right, but you're getting ahead of yourself. Which drug did we give next to facilitate the intubation?"

"The muscle relaxant, succinylcholine," Rusty said.

"Very good. You're with me. But there's a major trap lurking here that I don't think you're even aware of."

Rusty hated when he missed major traps; there were so many in medicine. He concentrated very hard trying to come up with an answer. Dr. Landry appeared to wait patiently. Finally, with some disappointment Rusty said, "OK, you're right. I don't see it."

"Take it from me, there are some people you can't mask ventilate. Usually, it's the big ones, the three-hundred-pounders, but you never know for sure until you try, until they're asleep."

"So you intubate them," Rusty replied quickly, irritated that he was still missing the point.

"You mean push the succinylcholine, paralyze them and then intubate?"

"Yeah, right." Rusty knew he had made a mistake but wasn't sure how yet.

"Herein lies one of the most dreaded situations in all anesthesia, my friend." Dr. Landry paused to crunch on some chips, and took a quick look at the brunette's table. "There are also people you can't intubate. If you've just paralyzed this patient who you can't ventilate with the mask, and now you discover you can't intubate him, you're screwed big time. Up the creek. Shit out of luck. You can't breathe for him, and you just paralyzed him, so he can't breathe for himself either." Dr. Landry sat straight back in his chair, fiddled with his surgical cap, and looked straight at Rusty. "Get the picture?"

"Yeah, I do," Rusty said softly as the meaning sank in. "So, like, he dies?"

"Well, hopefully not, although that's possible. It's emergency trach time."

"Yeah, right. I've seen that on *ER*."

"It's not as easy as it looks, Rusty," Dr. Landry said grimly. "By the time the shit hits the fan, and you've finished mucking around with your unsuccessful intubation attempts, your patient's blue as hell and headed south fast. You probably have about one minute left to get the trach tray in the room, use it, and hook it up before he dies. Not a lot of leeway for error." Dr. Landry wasn't smiling anymore and looked more intense than Rusty would've thought possible.

"Man, this airway stuff is pretty serious," Rusty said in a subdued tone. He quickly switched his facial expression to match that of Landry's. "Have you ever had a patient, uh, like that. You know, you couldn't ventilate or intubate?"

"'Fraid so and even worse." A troubled look clouded Dr. Landry's features.

"Did they, uh, it turn out okay?" Rusty asked tentatively.

"You be the judge. Back when I was a second-year resident, I once gave the wrong drug to a patient."

Rusty was shocked. He couldn't imagine Dr. Landry making a mistake; he exuded such an air of capability. And he really couldn't imagine an attending telling him about it.

"Her name was Stephanie," Dr. Landry said, "and she was having her first baby." His eyes drifted as he focused inward on the memory. "She was my age at the time, and we hit it off nicely. I had just finished putting her epidural in. It worked great. She was so relieved that she couldn't feel her contractions anymore. She gave me the sweetest smile, took my hand and shook it, and thanked me profusely. Then her BP dipped, which isn't that uncommon. I was a little nervous and reached for the ephedrine syringe to give her BP a boost. I gave her Atracurium by mistake." Dr. Landry's face twisted in pain as he said this. "Do you know what Atracurium is, Rusty?"

"Yes, it's a muscle relaxant." Rusty felt sick as the implications of paralyzing an awake patient sank in. But, he was also fascinated. "What happened?"

"When she started gasping for air and whispering 'I can't breathe,' I realized quickly enough what must've happened and began to try to ventilate her with a mask. I can still remember her eyes, her beautiful blue eyes wide with panic, staring up at me. I told her everything would be all right to calm her down, but I didn't believe it. I don't think she did either. To this day, I can't think of anything worse than being paralyzed awake and not being able to breathe."

"Jeez, that's horrible."

"Unfortunately, pregnant women don't have the best airways and I wasn't able to ventilate her well enough."

"Oh, shit," said Rusty. He felt his own heart begin to pound as he imagined himself dealing with such a situation.

"So, I tried to intubate her and guess what." Dr. Landry wore a sad expression.

"She was a difficult intubation?"

"You got it. I realized I was in deep shit. She was turning dusky and time was running out." Dr. Landry paused, and a frightened look gripped his face. He was obviously reliving the memory.

"Did she make it?" Rusty asked, on the edge of his seat. He had forgotten all about the brunette.

"She did, no thanks to me. The OB nurses had called the senior anesthesia resident. He came up stat and trached her while I stood by helpless and shaking." Dr. Landry was staring at his plate, his hands playing with his napkin. Rusty wasn't sure, but thought he could detect a slight trembling of Dr. Landry's hands.

"Wow, that's some story," Rusty said and took some deep breaths. He was genuinely touched that Dr. Landry had shared this experience with him. He had never had such a discussion with an attending before.

"You don't ever forget a case like that," Dr. Landry said. "It goes through my mind every time I put someone to sleep. I learned a lesson that day. You can care too much for people." He shook his head slightly and a weak smile spread across his face. Rusty thought he looked a bit embarrassed, probably he figured from baring more emotion than he liked. Dr. Landry seemed like one of those people who like to keep a tight rein on their emotions. Rusty knew the type. They projected a happy-go-lucky, go-with-the-flow attitude, but shied away from any real positive or negative swings of emotion.

The two sat there not saying anything. Dr. Landry wiped his hands on his napkin for the third time and Rusty played with the little plastic swords that had held his sandwich together. The silence quickly became uncomfortable, so Rusty said the first thing that came to his mind. "Dr. Carlucci seemed pretty upset yesterday in the locker room. Is he gonna be OK? What happened?"

"Well," Dr. Landry answered slowly. "He got sued, big time."

"Yeah, but why? Did he have a bad complication?"

"You could say that," Dr. Landry replied. "You shouldn't get me started on this, Rusty. Lawsuits are always a sore subject with physicians, and I've got more opinions on the matter than you'd probably care to hear."

"I doubt it." Rusty wondered if he had picked such a hot topic to switch to. "Remember, I'm gonna be out there too one day."

"Yeah, you're right. But we don't have a lot of time," Dr. Landry said as he glanced at his watch, "so I'll give you the short version."

"OK."

"Now this is probably one part philosophy, one part psychology, and one part cynicism, so bear with me."

"OK, sure."

"First of all, what you have to realize is that *any* bad outcome, and an intraoperative death is about as bad as you can get, is promptly rewarded with a suit. I believe the evolving societal psychology on this is twofold." Dr. Landry mimicked a scholarly tone. "I call these Landry's laws of litigation."

"You *have* given this some thought," Rusty said.

"Law Number One: Any badness happening to one human being must ultimately be due to the fault of another human being, or its short form corollary: one cannot harm oneself."

"I like that," said Rusty, who was relieved at the lighter tone the conversation was taking.

"To illustrate," Dr. Landry went on, "if someone drinks too much at a bar and wraps his car around a tree or injures another driver, it's clearly not his fault. Rather, the bartender may be at fault for serving him too many Coors Lites, or perhaps the car manufacturer is at fault because the brakes should've worked better, or maybe the bottles themselves failed to warn the individual clearly enough that drinking them might cause drunkenness, or maybe a combination." Dr. Landry paused to finish his sandwich.

"Impeccable logic, counselor," Rusty deadpanned. Again, Rusty noticed how easy it was to talk to Dr. Landry. For stretches of time, he'd even forgotten Dr. Landry was his attending. He'd have to watch himself.

"The second law is that there are no such things as natural causes. Acts of God no longer occur. For instance, if the roof caves in on you in a hurricane, your injury is not the result of an Act of God. Someone, perhaps the local news or the police or fire departments, should've warned you better of the approaching hurricane, or—"

"Or, sue the builder 'cause he didn't build the roof strong enough!" Rusty cut in excitedly.

"Exactly. Now, two inescapable conclusions flow directly from these laws. One, compensation is due anyone who gets hurt because it's already been determined that someone *else* is at fault—"

"Uh-huh," Rusty said nodding his head in agreement.

"and two, since it doesn't cost me anything, it's a nice thing to handsomely reward the injured person."

"Makes sense. What about malpractice, though?" Rusty asked.

"No-o-o problem. The laws are universal." Dr. Landry's smile reappeared. "If someone has a heart attack and dies in the hospital, clearly it didn't just happen. This violates Law Number One: people can't harm themselves. It can't have anything to do with smoking two packs a day for thirty years, a lifetime of eating fats, or the strict avoidance of any type of exercise. And surely, he didn't die of natural causes. This violates Law Number Two: there are no naturally caused deaths. So that leaves us with the inescapable conclusion that something in the hospital killed him."

"Amazing!"

"It becomes easy then, with this presupposition, to find the smoking gun. Was it the aspirin he got for a headache? Or perhaps the stress of his dinner being ten minutes late? God forbid his nasal prongs slipped for a minute. You see, the inept doctors and nurses did him in."

"Those villains!"

"Something sure as heck caused that heart attack, and any lawyer with half a brain can comb through the medical chart looking for one hair out of place, one 'i' not dotted, to hang his case on. You see, with the two laws already firmly established in the American consciousness, he's won the case before he starts. The only thing up in the air is the amount of the award."

The two again consulted their watches and stood up together. "So, what do you think?" Dr. Landry asked as he gathered up his trash.

Rusty smirked and replied, "We shoulda been lawyers."

"You're right," Dr. Landry said. "C'mon, let's go. We have two more cases to go, and I believe one of them could use a spinal."

"A spinal. You don't say." Rusty felt himself get excited and tried to put a lid on it. This was more than he could hope for.

"Ever done one?" Dr. Landry asked casually.

"No, but I'd sure like to try!" Rusty felt he had died and gone to procedure heaven.

CHAPTER EIGHT

Doug left the hospital in good spirits and headed for his truck. Still pretty darn cold, he noted. It was one of those winter days where the sun put in a good appearance, but did little actual work and looked to be in a hurry to leave, even though it was only four o'clock. Doug was glad to be heading out because he had a rough weekend ahead. He was on call Saturday which also meant being late-man on Friday, and back-up call on Sunday. Call was a gut-wrenching, twenty-four hour shift in the hospital, starting and ending at seven o'clock in the morning. On-call weekends were never something he looked forward to.

He climbed in and turned the key. The engine was slow to turn over and took several tries but finally caught. However, he thought, it was better than it had been in the morning when the night's deep freeze had turned his motor oil to sludge. He'd have to remember to get the battery checked.

Doug decided he had time to stop at the gym on his way home. He tried hard to squeeze in several visits to the gym a week; he needed it to help deal with the stress of his job. As he sped down the interstate, radio tuned to The River, a classic seventies and eighties soft rock station, he thought about Rusty. Doug had forgotten what a pleasure it was to work with bright young students. Teaching the medical students used to be one of the high points of his residency at Pitt. Seeing Rusty get his first intubation was a treat. His enthusiasm was refreshing, something foreign to the usual life-in-the-trenches at Mercy. Walking him through the spinal was also special. Rusty's smile reminded him of watching his son, Teddy, get his first hit in Little League. Doug remembered running out to first base to give Teddy a congratulatory high-five. He would never forget the look of sheer joy on his son's face.

But Doug sensed there was a calculating side of Rusty as well, one that wasn't all that visible from the surface. He had asked a lot of questions about Marshall and Raskin, and the early days of the Mercy anesthesia department. Why would he care? Was Rusty for real or was he just playing the med-student game for grades? Maybe, Doug reflected, it hadn't been such a good idea to tell him the Stephanie story. He hadn't even told Mike, whom he considered one of his best friends.

Doug stamped hard on the brake pedal when he saw the traffic in front was almost at a standstill; the construction zone had snuck up on him. God, he couldn't stand this mess. This particular stretch of I-283 had been torn up for what seemed like ten years. Doug especially loathed the concrete barriers, which herded the traffic single file for several miles. He always thought they were dangerous. Too damned narrow.

As he crawled forward, Doug's mind drifted back to his final days as an anesthesia resident at the University of Pittsburgh. Whenever he thought of teaching medical students, he wondered if he had made the right decision when he left academics and had opted for private practice twelve years ago. He knew that a rather large gulf separated the academic world from the world of private practice, or "real world" as he now chose to call it. The academicians, holed up in their ivory towers, believed they were the sole masters of hi-tech, rigorous medicine and medical theory, and looked down their collective noses at the lowly grunt on the front lines. Here, they preached, was to be found only incompetent losers practicing outdated medicine poorly.

Of course, across the divide, the private practice docs viewed the academicians with similar contempt. Their credo was: If you can't do it, teach it. They viewed their university counterparts as arrogant stuffed shirts with abysmal bedside manner coupled with poor skills, who would quickly starve in the real world of patients, referrals, and word-of-mouth advertising.

As is frequently the case, Doug figured the truth was lost somewhere in the middle. Some academicians would have performed brilliantly in private practice, but chose rather to focus their talents on didactics or research. Similarly, many physicians in community hospitals practiced state-of-the-art medicine, honed to an unequaled level of perfection through sheer volume of cases.

Doug pulled into the local Gold's, which was not far from his home. In the locker room, he encountered two of his 'favorite' individuals, "Chowder" and "Mule." The two had given themselves the nicknames for unfathomable reasons. Doug decided he could easily detect them with his eyes closed; they gave off an unpleasant odor of testosterone sweat mixed with body oil. He had reason to believe they lived at the gym, for he couldn't recall a time he had come in when they weren't there.

Both men were posing their formidable, jock-strap-clad physiques in front of the full-length mirrors. They were flexing various muscle groups hitherto unknown to Doug, despite his detailed knowledge of human anatomy. Neither was tall. Mule, at about five-foot-six, stood several inches taller than his white counterpart, Chowder. Both exhibited massively muscled bodies plus the thinning hair and acne associated with anabolic steroid use. Their conversation consisted of grunts and guttural noises peppered with several discernible expletives and punctuated with raucous laughter.

At times like these, Doug wondered about the evolution of the human race. Could this possibly be the same species that had produced the transistor, the microchip, airplanes, and space flight? No, scratch that. Was this the same species that came up with the wheel?

Out on the gym floor, Doug made his way to the bank of Stairmasters and climbed onto one of the empty ones. He programmed the Stairmaster to Pike's Peak, entered his 180-pound weight, set the time and level, and began pumping away. This day would have to be an aerobics day; he only had about thirty-five minutes before he had to leave to take his middle son, Steven, to Cub Scouts. He immediately checked out the "scenery," as the guys at Gold's quaintly referred to the female members. When in Rome . . .

Until recently, Doug's scouting sessions had been a harmless activity. Oh sure, there had been several occasions where he had gotten into trouble with his wife, Laura. Doug remembered one particular night when they had gone out for dinner and a drop-dead gorgeous blond sat down at the next table. She had on a very short, very tight, very low-cut dress. Doug tried mightily to look at his wife, but his eyes kept getting pulled off target as if drawn by a strong magnetic field. Laura didn't say anything at first. After about twenty minutes, she glared at him and whispered hotly, "You're making me real dizzy, Doug. Your eyes are bouncing back and forth so much I feel like I'm watching a damned ping-pong game. You better take a good look at those boobs over there, cause you sure aren't gonna see any tonight!"

Doug scanned the gym, but didn't see much of interest. His Stairmaster was squeaking a little as it relentlessly increased the pace, and he was beginning to breathe hard. Doug had learned to control his wandering gaze around Laura. He was genuinely sensitive to her feelings and didn't want to offend her. He knew he had no real interest in these women; he just liked to look.

Over the past six months or so, a subtle change had seeped into their marriage. Communication was somehow more difficult. Laura seemed unhappy and even depressed. He never thought he'd see Laura like this; depressed just wasn't in the equation for her. In fact, Doug remembered that Laura's happy, bubbly personality was what had attracted him in the first place.

They had met while both attending Cornell at an ice hockey game. Hockey at Cornell was huge. It was a Division One sport and permeated every aspect of campus life. Doug had worked as an usher at the home games and had noticed her instantly. She came in with several of her girlfriends, but stood out as if a spotlight shone on her. What impressed him more than the way her silky black hair framed her pretty face, was her smile. Her face was transformed when she smiled, taking on an angelic glow. He couldn't stop staring. What also got his attention was her laughter; it was so clean and genuine. She radiated such an aura of joy, she positively sparkled with the pleasure of life. He just had to get to know her. After several hockey games and some impressive small talk such as, "You can see better from these seats," Doug finally mustered the courage to ask her out. Actually, they agreed to meet at a Friday evening public skating session. He recalled the evening vividly. She showed up wearing a tight blue and white ski sweater and jeans and looked awesome.

Despite her athletic build, Laura couldn't skate that well, but this worked to Doug's advantage. He skated backwards, relying on his intramural hockey skills, and held her hands. Frequently he would have to stop to avoid hitting someone on the crowded ice, and Laura would plow into him, laughing all the way. Several times, she even made Doug lose his balance, and they both went down in a sliding heap. Normally he would've been embarrassed, but that night he didn't even notice.

He drove her home afterwards in his 1968 VW beetle with the broken heater. They both froze, but neither seemed to mind. She invited him up to her apartment for some hot chocolate to warm up. They talked the night away until three in the morning before either of them noticed the time. Embarrassed, Doug got up to leave. She tugged on his shirt and wouldn't let him go unless he promised to come back for breakfast; she said she made killer pancakes. He promised. They shared a long goodnight kiss and finally said goodbye. Doug walked outside into the night oblivious to the cold, his head spinning and lips tingling but feeling happier than he had ever been. The crescent moon smiled and the stars winked at him as he skipped to his car. He went home but couldn't sleep. He couldn't wait to see her again. They saw each other constantly over the next two weeks, and separations longer than several hours were painful. By the end of the school year, they were engaged.

The Stairmaster chimed, proclaiming he had reached his goal, and Doug was yanked back to the present. The emotive part of his brain was still resonating with the memory of Laura, basking in the afterglow of their newfound love, and he was reluctant to relinquish the feeling. He hadn't thought about their first date in a long time. The pleasant memory made their current troubles all the more strange and difficult to understand. What was happening with their marriage now was hard to put a finger on. Doug wondered if the problem was simply due to the hectic nature of their lives with two children in school and a preschooler. But he wasn't sure this was enough to explain it. Other things came to mind.

Laura was a stay-at-home mom who excelled at it, but she had a strong work ethic, possibly the result of a father who had abandoned the family early in Laura's life. She tended to be extremely sensitive to the other women around her who had jobs. She felt they viewed her as a lazy wife who sat at home having coffee with friends, watching soaps, and chatting on the telephone. Being a doctor's wife didn't help because she felt guilty that she *could* stay at home with the kids, and the family could survive on one income.

To assuage her guilt over being a stay-at-home mom, Laura volunteered for everything from homeroom mother for the boys in school to assistant soccer coach to Cub Scout den mother. If there was a job opening for a parent—the more onerous the better, no money please—Laura was always first in line. She managed to squeeze in delivering Meals-on-Wheels to the elderly shut-ins between shuttling the kids back and forth to activities.

In addition to being an avid volunteer, Laura lacked the capacity to say "no" to anyone asking a favor. If her friends asked her if she'd mind feeding their dog while they went away for the week, she'd respond, "No problem. I'm home all day anyway." Unfortunately, she made it sound like she had nothing to do and that she'd be thrilled to help out, so that her friends did wind up taking advantage of her.

Ironically, Laura wound up working twice as hard as any "working" mother. Sadly, no one realized this except Doug. The neighbors and Laura's friends and acquaintances still thought she had it pretty easy. After all, she found time to volunteer for all sorts of things; she *must* be bored. Even Laura herself didn't perceive herself as taxed to the limit; her sense of work ethic/guilt clouded her view.

Doug, however, realized his wife frequently bit off more than she could chew, and sometimes he and the kids got caught in the crossfire. Their lives seemed to be an endless array of activities centered around the three children. There were constant soccer/baseball/swim team practices and games, homework, science fair projects, piano lessons, cub scouts, etc. Laura orchestrated the scheduling of all these activities with a precision the Pentagon would have been proud of. Doug plugged into the scheme of things whenever he was available. Their conversations consisted mostly of planning the logistics of the busy evening or weekend. Minor concerns were often left unaddressed until they became unbearable and blossomed into full-fledged shouting matches.

Doug was startled out of his introspection by a voice and a blur of blond hair coming from the Stairmaster to his right.

"Hey, you come here too!" The voice and blond hair belonged to a surgical intensive care nurse at Mercy.

"Yeah, uh, you work at Mercy, don't you?" Doug managed to get out. He was horrible with names. They both had to talk louder than Doug was comfortable with to be heard above WTPA, the heavy metal station cranked up on the gym's sound system.

"Yep, I'm Jenny Stuart. I work in SICU. I just joined Gold's a couple of weeks ago."

"Hi, I'm Doug Landry. I work in anesthesia."

"I know who you are. I was there the other night when you brought that ruptured triple-A in. That was some case!"

"I remember you now. You look, uh, sort of different," Doug stammered. *God, she's pretty!*

"Different? Hmmm. Now there's a compliment."

"No, no. I mean your hair and all. I just didn't recognize you, that's all. You look great." Doug felt himself blush, and they both laughed.

"How's he doing?" Doug continued quickly, eager to get back on safer ground. "He was pretty sick when they brought him to us—no blood pressure—the typical abdominal aortic aneurysm. Bled like stink when they opened him."

"He's doing really well. In fact, he's being transferred out tomorrow. You do good work, Doctor." She punctuated this with a big smile as she gazed a bit too long into his eyes.

"We got pretty lucky with him. I didn't think he was gonna make it there for awhile. Must've had good nursing care postop." Doug smiled back and returned an equally long stare. He'd never seen her with her hair down or dressed in a tight gym suit before. She was slim, about five-foot-four, with shoulder-length blond hair and a body Demi Moore would have envied. He had trouble keeping his eyes on her face as they talked.

"So, how long have you been coming here?" she asked.

"Oh, a couple of years now. It's a nice gym and right on the way home from the hospital." Funny, he thought, *her lips are so full. He never cared much for full lips, but suddenly found them irresistible.*

"Where do you live?" she asked.

"Just down Route Thirty, three or four miles down the road in Heatherfield."

"Which days do you usually come to the gym?"

"Kinda whenever I can. I try to get in two or three times a week, although I do come in pretty regular Friday nights after work." *Why is she asking so many personal questions and why am I so willing to answer?* He felt sort of guilty talking to her just after he had been reminiscing about Laura, but the twenty-year-old fading memory couldn't compete with the here and now in the flesh. Doug's Stairmaster program was over again. He quickly punched in another ten minutes and adjusted it to Level One so he wouldn't get too out of breath.

"I used to belong to a Gold's in California," she said. "They're all over the place out there."

"Yeah, you look like you're pretty serious about your exercise."

"Whatever do you mean?" She flashed another big smile at Doug, who could feel his heart accelerating even though he had turned down his machine.

"You have a really nice figure."

"Well, thank you. I do believe you're getting better at giving compliments. You look like you're in pretty good shape too." Her eyes slid up and down his torso and legs.

"Naw, not really." Doug felt the blood threatening to return to his face. "I don't exactly belong at Gold's. You know, the image is serious body builder and all that. Look at the guys around here— they're animals." Doug nodded toward Mule and Chowder. As if on cue, Mule let out an inhuman scream as he successfully squat- ted over five hundred pounds, the bar literally bending over his shoulders. "I just come here because it's the only gym on the way home from work. I do some basic weight stuff to keep my back in shape. But, muscle-head I'm not."

"Coulda fooled me." She lit up her smile again. "Can I ask you a personal question?" she asked coyly.

"Sure," Doug answered, feeling a bit sheepish. He figured she would ask if he were married now and spoil all the fun.

"Why did you go into medicine?" she asked, her face turning serious.

"Well, it's kind of a long story. But if you want to hear it—"

"Please," she said quickly and then did something with her face, some sort of adorable pleading look, that made Doug wonder if he'd be able to refuse her anything.

"OK. I started off as a chemical engineering major at Cornell." He didn't feel it necessary to add that Laura was a pharmacology major there also.

"Engineering?"

"Yeah, I got my degree in it. I was always into math and physics. Nice and clean—no emotional stuff to get tangled up in."

"I always knew you were weird," she said and laughed.

"But then in my senior year my dad got sick and was diagnosed with colon cancer." She winced in response. Doug couldn't help but notice that even her pained look was cute. "So I decided I would go to medical school, learn all I could, and rid the world of cancer."

"So did you?"

"No, but thanks for playing along." Doug stopped climbing and focused on her. "My dad died when I was a second year medical student. I wasn't very far in my training and had little extra to offer him." Doug recalled the bitter helplessness of watching his dad wither away, consumed by the cancer.

She stopped climbing and returned his gaze. "I'm sure you were more helpful than you realized." They both stood silent for a moment looking at each other.

Doug shook his head to break the spell. "Anyway I got side-tracked into clinical medicine somewhere along the line and then gravitated to anesthesia. I haven't looked back since."

"Wow," she said and pushed a stubborn lock of hair out of her eyes.

"So, you used to live in California?" The more he looked at her, the prettier she got. He couldn't quite put his finger on it, but he knew she was beautiful. No, exotic-looking. Maybe it was the high cheekbones? Some sort of Slavic background?

"I just moved back East three months ago," she said. "Messy divorce and all that."

"Oh, sorry to hear that," Doug lied. He felt self-conscious; he looked around to see if any of Laura's friends were there. He didn't see any.

"Don't be. I'm not—definitely for the best. That's what I'm doing back in good ol' P–A. I grew up outside of Philly. Figure I'd make a clean break and a fresh start. Mercy had the opening I was looking for."

"Yeah, it's a good hospital. I've been there about twelve years."

"Wow, twelve years! You don't look that old, Dr. Landry." Long stare again.

"Call me Doug." Landry glanced at his feet, suddenly afraid that he was about to stumble off the Stairmaster. He also glanced at the clock on the wall. *Shit! I gotta go soon.*

"Sure, Doug." Her voice lingered a bit over his name. "Or maybe it's *Doogie* Howser?"

"Uh, not hardly. You don't look so old yourself."

"Old enough," she said and started to laugh lightly.

Doug laughed too, and then said, "So, what happened in California, if you don't mind me asking? I don't mean to pry."

"No, not at all, *Doug.* I guess we just got married too young. I was still in nursing school, and Paul was a local musician when we met."

"Oh, what'd he play?"

"Piano, mostly, but some guitar and trumpet, too. He's really quite talented—or was. He's also quite the bullshitter."

"Ah, I know the type."

"Well, I fell hard for him and bought into all the bullshit. You know—the record contract, TV appearances, Grammys. Paul used to dream big. We got married, both thinking success was right around the corner."

"What happened?" Doug asked although he was having trouble concentrating on the story; her rhythmic pumping and perfume were hypnotic.

"Well, the dream was just that—a dream. When his career didn't take off as fast as he thought it should, he started drinking—first just at the clubs, then at home, too."

"Sounds rough."

"Yeah, and he began to spend more time with the college groupies. It was as if he thought I felt ashamed of him, that he failed me. I never thought that—I loved him—I was just happy to be with him." Her cheerful expression gave way to a wistful, pained look.

Doug genuinely felt sorry for her and wished he could comfort her in some way. "Some guys just figure they're not worthy of real love unless they earn it somehow," he said. "Sounds dumb, I know."

"If he couldn't be successful at his music, he tried to demonstrate his success in other areas—with the women. I got jealous, and the marriage started to crumble."

"That's a really sad story."

"Like I said, that's all behind me. We've been apart for two years now. So, how about you, Doug?"

"I, uh, just lead a perfectly boring life." *With my wife and three kids. Now's the time to tell her, Doug.* But he didn't feel like mentioning this. He was enjoying the flirtation too much.

"What do you do for fun?" she asked.

"Fun, well, I like to play tennis. I play over at the racquet club, and I like to hike. There are some nice mountains just south of here."

"I love to hike, too. You'll have to show me those mountains sometime. Tennis, I'm not so good at."

"Anyone can learn." He paused and swallowed hard. "Wow, a fellow outdoors-person. It would be fun to show you those mountains sometime." Doug glanced at his watch. "Oh boy. Listen I gotta run and . . ." He almost said pick up Steven for Cub Scouts. "See you round the hospital, Jenny."

"When are you on call next?" she asked. "I work mostly nights."

"Ah, let me think," he said. "This Saturday."

"Hey, great!" Her face lit up again. "I'm working flex then, too. See you Saturday. Maybe we'll have more time to talk," she said, eyes twinkling.

"Yeah, I hope so. See you." Doug retrieved his stuff from the locker room and practically ran out to his truck with a strange mix of emotions. Yeah, I hope so? Show you the mountains? What the hell was that? However, he couldn't deny the feeling of exhilaration he had. She was coming on to me—big time. Unbelievable!

Doug slammed his truck into reverse and pulled out of the parking space, mad that this turn of fate should befall him. He realized he had crossed a line somewhere. This was more than eye games; this was serious. He had surprised himself with his shameless ability to flirt. But then again he thought, he'd never been tempted by a woman like Jenny Stuart before. The devil had definitely pulled out all the stops this time. Could any man with a pulse resist? He jammed the shift into drive and roared away muttering to himself over and over, "What the hell are you doing?"

CHAPTER NINE

Mike Carlucci screamed. He sat up in bed, T-shirt sweat-soaked and heart pounding.

"Baby, baby, what's wrong?" Colleen asked as she wrapped her arms around him. "You scared me."

Mike searched the darkened bedroom. "It was here, Colleen. I felt it." He climbed out of bed and turned on the light.

"Baby, what are you talking about? You just had a bad dream," Colleen said soothingly. "Come back to bed." She patted his place in bed. "It's three in the morning."

"Yeah, bad dream." Mike took some deep breaths, and the pounding of his heart eased. He sat down on the side of the bed and felt Colleen snuggle up against his back. Her warmth was nice. "It was Kotzmoyer," he said.

"Poor baby," Colleen whispered in his ear and stroked his shoulder.

"I need a dry shirt." Mike got up, opened his bureau drawer, and put on a new T-shirt. After all these years, he thought, shaking his head. *Kotzmoyer's back.*

Mr. Kotzmoyer had been a patient of Mike's as a resident who had had a heart attack. Thanks to the nightmare, Mike recalled the events vividly.

Mike was on call the night Mr. Kotzmoyer's urine output had ceased. At the time, Mike didn't think it was a serious problem. The nurses called incessantly through the night, usually with concerns that weren't important and could easily keep until the morning. Mike couldn't really think of anything to do short of encouraging fluids and ordering a diuretic, but the patient was asleep. He decided to wait until morning rounds, a scant three hours away, when he could confer with his more senior residents and see if they had any better ideas. He figured it wasn't that important to call and wake his R3 at home. In the morning, after getting one hour of interrupted sleep, he discovered he'd made a bad decision.

His senior resident raked him over the coals unmercifully on rounds. Mike knew that medicine residents regarded anesthesia interns rotating through their service as hopelessly dull individuals who could never actually grasp the finer points of internal medicine. They were also eager to humiliate such interns in front of others to perpetuate the prejudice.

"Let me get this straight, Carlucci," demanded Calhoun, the medicine R3, his eyes boring into Mike's. "He had no, zippo, urine output since one a.m. and you did nothing!?"

"Well, I didn't hear about it until three," Mike answered softly. "I ordered some Lasix."

"Lasix! Lasix! Did you have a clue as to this man's volume status? You gas-passers are all alike. You just don't get it." Calhoun shook his head sadly.

Snickers erupted from Mike's fellow interns on the service; all of them were internal medicine interns.

"Does anyone know what Carlucci should've done?" Calhoun asked.

"Of course," chimed in Shapiro, who could always be counted on to have a knife handy for your back. "He should've transferred the patient to the MICU, swanned him, and depending on the results, either fluid bolus, pressors, and/or diuretics."

"Bitch," Mike mouthed, glaring at her.

"Right!" Calhoun said to Shapiro. He turned to Mike. "Carlucci, write the transfer orders and get this man down to the MICU stat. Line him up and page me when you get some numbers. Clear!?"

"Yes, sir!"

"His beans will probably shut down and kill him, thanks to you," Calhoun graciously informed Mike.

Mike was bone-tired after less than an hour of sleep and depressed over the prospect of another long day, but Calhoun's dire prediction energized him. Rather than wait for the transport aide, he pushed Mr. Kotzmoyer's hospital bed by himself down to the MICU. He felt sick all over; his screw-up might seriously endanger another man's life.

Hours later, the situation worsened. Despite the application of hi-tech medicine of the day, Mr. Kotzmoyer's condition deteriorated. His kidneys did indeed shut down, and each drop of urine was considered a treasure. Sitting in the MICU nurses' station poring over Kotzmoyer's chart and the latest lab printouts, Calhoun was calling the shots now and appeared deeply worried. Mike sat next to him, feeling as bad as Kotzmoyer looked.

"Like trying to get pee from a stone," Calhoun said. "Nothing's working. Dopamine's on, wedge is good, got megadose Lasix and Bumex. What else is there?"

"How about Dobutamine?" suggested Mike.

"Are you crazy?" answered Calhoun. However, Mike noticed he couldn't give him any good reason not to try it.

Just then the monitor watcher shrieked out, "V-tach! I got V-tach! It's Kotzmoyer!"

Mike and Calhoun raced into the room ahead of several ICU nurses. They arrived in time to see Kotzmoyer's eyes roll upward into his head as he lost consciousness. Mike glanced at the arterial line trace to check for any blood pressure. There was none.

"Paddles!" screamed Calhoun. He was never very calm at codes, and this one proved no exception. "Call the code, damn it!"

Mike went to the head of the bed, hooked up the Ambu bag, and began ventilating Kotzmoyer with the mask. Thankfully, this was before the days of pulse oximetry, so they didn't know how low their patient's oxygen saturation really was.

The nurse rolled in the crash cart. Calhoun applied the paddles and fired. The V-tach broke into an irregular sinus rhythm. Mike noticed pressure waves reappearing on the art line trace as BP was restored.

Kotzmoyer opened his eyes and let out a groan. Amazingly, he spoke. "Where am I? What's going on?"

"You're in the intensive care unit, Jack. Your heart's giving us some trouble," Mike responded, not really knowing what to say. Calhoun couldn't be bothered.

"Oh, I see—"

The rhythm degenerated into V-tach again and Kotzmoyer went out in mid-sentence.

"Shit! Have to hit him again!" roared Calhoun. "Get that Lido drip running STAT!"

This time it took two shocks. Kotzmoyer regained consciousness again. "Tell Helen, I love her. The boys, too."

"Hang on, Jack," Mike implored him. "You're gonna be OK. Hang on." Mike's eyes began to blur with tears.

This time didn't last long. V-tach again. A third set of electroshocks barely restored proper rhythm. Mike sensed where things were heading. Mr. Kotzmoyer, the Lazarus man, awoke yet again.

"Helen—"

Mike couldn't stand it; he was being driven insane. He felt as if Death itself was in the room and playing games with the mortals, jerking the marionette strings, taunting them with the inevitable. He cursed the monster over and over.

Mr. Kotzmoyer died shortly thereafter, this time succumbing to V-tach, which no longer responded. Mike wept softly, while Calhoun stormed out of the room in disgust.

The memory of Kotzmoyer always affected Mike, but he hadn't thought of it in years. Mike could never shake his feelings of responsibility and grief over Kotzmoyer's death. Even after his attending pulled him aside and told him that nothing they could have done earlier or later would have altered Kotzmoyer's fate, he still didn't feel absolved of his guilt. He could also never forget the look in Kotzmoyer's eyes as he had stared at him from beyond the grave. Mike climbed back into bed.

"Feel better?" Colleen asked.

"Yeah," he lied. "Night."

"Night." She turned over, kissed him on the forehead and rolled back. Soon he could tell from her rhythmic breathing that she was asleep. He stared up at the ceiling, knowing that the odds of himself sleeping were slim.

Mike swerved into the doctor's parking lot, tires spitting gravel, about an hour earlier than he normally arrived. His hands trembled a bit as he fumbled with the plastic card at the gate. What little sleep he'd gotten seemed to have been riddled with more ghastly dreams. Mr. Rakovic continued to haunt him, as he had all week.

Last night his dreams had centered on his early encounters with the Angel of Death. He was replaying the highlights again now, as he trudged toward the hospital, his boots crunching on the frozen ground. The parking lot was a ghost town. It was still dark outside, although troubled clouds could be made out in the pre-dawn eastern sky. The bitter cold and rude wind failed to make significant inroads to his consciousness.

He remembered his first encounter clearly. He had been a third-year med student at the University of Virginia, new to the clinical part of his education. His first rotation was cardiology, which he thought was fascinating, but which also brought home the life-or-death nature of medicine. After all, what signified man's mortal frailty better than the heart. He'd been at lunch when his red code beeper went off.

"Code Blue! Nurses' Station, 4 East, STAT!"

He left his lunch and sprinted to the fourth floor nurses' station. They directed him to room 408; it was familiar to him because it was one of his patient's rooms, Mr. Nagle. He could barely stick his head in the door, because it was jammed with residents, med students, and nurses, all engaged in frenetic activity. No attendings were in sight; they rarely made appearances on the wards.

Mr. Nagle apparently had suffered a cardiac arrest. He was lying on his back on the floor, wedged between his bed and the wall, vomitus smeared all over his face and hospital gown. Mike was shocked at the almost comic nature of the resuscitation effort, or "code," as it was called. It seemed to be nine parts chaos and one part medicine. Residents at the bedside shouted out demands for equipment or meds as they pumped on Mr. Nagle's chest, inserted tubes, and stabbed him repeatedly with needles of frightening size. Their demands were relayed to the nurses in the hallway, who frantically searched their carts for the desired items; drawers were ripped open and slammed shut.

Luckily, as a third-year med student, Mike had very little actual responsibility for his patients other than knowing their histories, medications, and latest lab values for presentation on rounds. He watched with rapt attention as the code unfolded, inwardly cheering his team like a spectator at a football game; craning his neck to get a better view of the big plays. He was overcome with emotion when Mr. Nagle's heart rhythm was restored and it was clear he was going to make it. Touchdown in sudden death overtime. Mike felt noble about his pursuit of medicine that day.

Aside from being his first encounter with actual life-and-death medicine, what Mike remembered most about the resuscitation were two things. One was the nurse giving CPR to Mr. Nagle. Her name was Colleen. He found out later she had discovered the patient unconscious in bed and called the code. By a twist of fate, Mr. Nagle's erratic heartbeat had led to the start of a relationship between Mike and Colleen that eventually blossomed into marriage. They still told the story of how they met at a code and how Mr. Nagle survived in spite of them.

The second thing that Mike recalled was the distinct feeling that Death had been cheated that day, and wasn't particularly happy about it. He had sensed the presence of the creature and could've sworn it whispered to him, "I'll be back." He believed the creature had paid him a visit last night.

Mike walked mechanically through the back entrance of Mercy Hospital up to the second floor and keyed in the combination for the doctors' locker room. It was empty. Good, he thought. Mike changed into scrubs and searched through his locker for several items. He retrieved a single, shiny glass ampule and a syringe. Mike fished around in his locker for a rubber tourniquet. He shut the locker door quietly.

He went into a bathroom stall, closed and latched the door, sat down, and snugged the tourniquet around his left arm. He cracked the ampule and drew up two cc's of Fentanyl, a powerful narcotic, one hundred times more potent than morphine. He hesitated for a moment with the needle poised above one of his distended veins. *Should I?* He paused, clutching at his gold crucifix, hoping for some divine inspiration, something to draw strength from. Instead, one final demon flowed into his brain. Mike remembered Bryan.

Bryan was a five-year-old little boy with an angelic face and unruly blond hair. Mike was doing his pediatric heart rotation as a senior anesthesia resident. Children came in from all over the state for their open-heart surgery. These cases were enormously complex and carried with them mortalities approaching fifty percent for the more seriously deformed hearts. This meant half the children would die.

Bryan had a disorder known as Tetrology of Fallot, a wicked genetic affliction where the heart is horribly malformed. The cardiac surgeon had called it a "frog heart." Bryan was blue at birth and barely able to survive on his own, but he was too small to undergo the extensive repair surgery required. His parents were instructed to do their best to raise the boy, coax him along, get him to grow, so he would have a fifty-fifty shot at surgical cure. Talk about tough jobs. Mike did his pre-op assessment of the child the night before surgery and met the parents. Mike noticed that the five years growing time had indeed accomplished its purpose, but at a fearful price. The parents were hopelessly attached to their little boy and naturally overprotective. They asked question after detailed question about the anesthesia, as Bryan squirmed first in his mother's lap, then his father's. Mike did his best to answer all fully; they deserved it. He assured them the boy looked to be in good shape for anesthesia, and they would all do their best tomorrow. He mentioned that the surgeons would discuss the surgical risk involved; he couldn't bring himself to discuss the high mortality rate with them. As Mike left the room, Bryan smiled and waved goodbye from the safety of his mother's lap.

Initially, everything went smoothly. Bryan went to sleep at 6:30 a.m. without a hitch, and all the complicated monitoring lines were inserted without problem. The child was placed on the heart-lung machine at 8:05 a.m. This allowed the surgeons to stop the heart temporarily so they could operate on it. The surgeons were telling jokes and laughing, a sure sign that the surgery was progressing nicely, but when they attempted to restart the reconstructed heart and come off bypass, no dice. The heart stubbornly refused to pump any blood at all. The operation was a failure. They couldn't go back on bypass either; the heart had been stopped too long and would never tolerate another bypass run. The surgeon ordered the perfusionist to shut down the bypass machine and walked out of the room leaving the anesthesia and surgical team with his words of wisdom: "Well, you win some, you lose some."

"But, he'll die. Bryan'll die," Mike pleaded with his attending. "We've got to do something. I promised his mother."

"You know there's nothing we can do, Mike. I'm sorry. Turn off the ventilator. We're done here."

The grief from that day had never really left him; rather it festered inside and sensitized him. For the first time, sitting in the bathroom stall with his arm throbbing from the tourniquet, Mike saw his life as it really was. He had been running from grief and fear, from the Kotzmoyers and Bryans all his adult life.

He knew this had been largely responsible for his choice of anesthesia as a profession. He didn't like getting to know his patients and their families and then watching them die. He took it all too personally, too hard. Anesthesia was better in this respect. Patient relationships were generally not deep to begin with, and the patients rarely died.

Mike realized that all doctors must face this crossroads at some point in their careers. If they detach too much from their patient's pain, they become heartless bastards with no sense of caring or empathy, no ability to heal the soul, the most important part of their patient. If they don't detach at all, they risk being dashed on the rocks of human suffering.

However, Mike had never before felt the full, crushing weight of responsibility for another man's death. He believed he had killed Rakovic. The lawsuit had been the final straw. He felt like a total failure to himself, his chosen profession, and to his family.

Colleen had tried to reassure them that things would be OK; they'd make it through this together. She was a good wife. In fact, she was too good, and Mike couldn't bear the thought of letting her down.

But he couldn't set foot back in the OR the way he was. He just couldn't face the thought that harm might come to another innocent person through his hands. Just thinking about it made him tremble and his palms sweat. He was in no shape to deliver anesthesia; he was quivering all over. But, he couldn't let his family down. He had only one card left to play.

It took him two sticks to enter the vein, until red swirls of his blood mingled with the Fentanyl in the barrel of the syringe.

He pushed the plunger.

Within seconds the Fentanyl coursed through his entire body and brain, scorching all the fear out of him, like a mighty, fire-breathing dragon, searing his self-doubt. His breathing evened, and his pounding heart slowed. He walked out of the stall and faced the mirror above the sink. Other than pinpoint pupils, he appeared to be the old Mike Carlucci. Steady hands and all, he emerged to take on the day.

CHAPTER TEN

Doug finished his tuna fish sandwich, washing it down with his kiwi-strawberry Snapple. He was sitting at a desk in the center of the anesthesia on-call room, which doubled as the lunch table. The fifteen-foot square room, adjacent to the OR proper, was their home away from home. Doug felt like it was his cell, he had spent so much time imprisoned there over the years. The place could get pretty crowded if all six anesthesiologists on duty for the day ate together, but the busy OR schedule virtually guaranteed that would never happen.

He glanced at his watch—11:45 a.m. Soon time to get back to work. He would just have time to eat some Oreos, hit the head, and proceed to the holding area to meet his noontime patient. He pulled out the OR schedule crammed in his pocket. He still had three cases to go. He hated being the late man, and this day didn't look like any bargain. He'd be lucky to leave by seven o'clock tonight.

Mike Carlucci breezed through the door wearing a big smile and carrying his lunch.

"Hey Mike, have a seat," Doug said as he pushed his briefcase aside, clearing space on the crowded desk.

"Geez Doug, every time I come back here you're loafing," Mike said. He set his lunch down and pulled up a chair.

"Yeah, right. I did two lap choleys this morning. Did you see my first one? Over three hundred pounds. Don't talk to me about loafing. You did local standby feet all morning—a real tough one."

"Them's the breaks," said Mike as he opened his styrofoam container. The smell of fried chicken quickly filled the room.

"I gotta go soon," Doug said sadly. "I have Hartman at noon." One of his favorite workday activities was to spend lunch yakking it up with Mike.

"Is he chomping?" Mike asked as he attacked a greasy drumstick.

"You know Hartman," Doug replied. "When isn't he chomping? He's always in such a goddamned hurry." Doug rolled his chair sideways to the file cabinet that served as a pantry, grabbed a couple of Oreos and rolled back.

"Hey, listen. What are you guys doing next weekend?" asked Mike. "I'm pretty sure Colleen got a sitter."

"No good, Mike. I told you how badly I need CMEs. I lined up a course in Baltimore." Again, Doug was genuinely disappointed. He enjoyed their evenings out with Mike and Colleen. In fact, they didn't really have any other close friends.

"Inner Harbor?" Mike asked as he swiped a napkin across his face.

"Yeah." Doug took a closer look at Mike. Something about his face didn't seem right. It appeared thinner, if that was possible, and his eyes had dark circles around them.

"How many credits?" Mike asked.

"Twenty."

"Wow, decent," Mike said. "Are you taking the kids?"

"No, Laura's not even going."

"What!" Mike set down his drumstick and looked up at Doug. "You guys fighting again?" he asked in a quieter, more serious tone.

"No, of course not," Doug answered quickly. "The kids have rehearsals for the Christmas pageant and surprise, surprise, Laura's involved."

"Hmmm. She let you go by yourself?" Mike asked incredulously.

"Yeah, I need those CMEs." Doug stood up and gathered his trash. "What do you mean, anyway? She trusts me," Doug said and chuckled but felt a slight irritation creep in nonetheless.

"Well, I'm glad she does, 'cause I sure don't," Mike said and laughed easily.

"What the hell are you talking about?" Doug asked, grinning.

"I see the way you can't keep your eyes off them pretty young thangs."

"Cut me a break!" Doug said. "You don't know what you're talking about."

"Must be that midlife crisis they talk about," Mike said. "They say that's what happens when you get older."

"You don't have to worry about getting old eating that stuff." Doug pointed to the drumstick. "Haven't you heard, fat's bad for you?"

"Do I look fat?" Carlucci asked, patting his trim belly proudly. "You wish you were in such good shape."

"You Italians just don't get it." The old give and take felt good. He hadn't seen Mike so cheerful in weeks. But then Doug got an odd sensation that Mike's good humor didn't quite fit with his haggard appearance.

"You're just jealous."

Doug glanced at his watch. "Shit, I really gotta go. Who's relieving you, anyway?"

"No one," Mike answered, awkwardly suppressing a grin.

"When's your next case?" Doug asked in mock alarm, as he stood up. He already knew the answer.

"One o'clock," Mike replied.

"An hour and fifteen minutes for lunch!"

"I deserve it."

"Unbelievable!" Doug managed to get in before the two broke down into laughter. "Well, some of us have work to do," Doug said and headed out the door. Over his shoulder he called back, "I gotta grind out three more cases."

Doug was relieved after his conversation with Mike; he had been very worried about how Mike was holding up. Things seemed back to normal, and Doug was thankful. He dismissed his earlier thought about Mike's tired appearance; maybe he had just had a rough night with the kids. The two men had become very tight in the six years they had worked together. They shared similar philosophies on many things from work to family, and Doug felt he could read Mike pretty well. Mike was just too happy for anything to be seriously wrong.

* * *

"Geez, Doug, it's seven-thirty," said Mike, as he and Doug entered the locker room. "Sorry to keep you here so late." Mike didn't need to change clothes since he was on call and staying the night, but was in the habit of seeing Doug out. Tonight, he wanted to make it quick though. He had other things to attend to.

"No problem, Mike," replied Doug, as he stripped off his scrubs. "When it's busy, it's busy. Nothing you can do." Doug sat down on the wooden bench and rubbed his eyes and forehead. "I just hope tomorrow stays sane. Saturdays really suck."

"Yeah, I hope so for both our sakes," said Mike. "So far, there's only a hip on for Clark. Shouldn't be too bad."

"Right," said Doug as he put on his jeans. "He doesn't fool around too long on anything."

"Laura and you doing anything tonight?" asked Mike. He tried to put his key in the lock but his hand shook so badly it wouldn't go in. Mike quickly checked on Doug to see if he noticed. Doug was busy lacing his boots.

"Naw, are you kidding?" Doug asked. "I'm beat after you slaved me all day. How many more years we gotta do this?"

"Twenty to twenty-five, I reckon," said Mike. He took a step sideways to block Doug's view of his hands.

"Is that all. Sounds like a prison sentence." Doug pulled his turtleneck shirt over his head. "We might try to watch a video after we get the kids to bed, if I can stay awake."

"Yeah, I know what you mean," said Mike. With one hand steadying the other, he managed to get the key in and open his locker. "You should see Colleen. She loves watching movies and all, but I swear she's never made it more than ten minutes into one. I get hooked and watch the whole damn thing."

Doug smiled at him, and Mike tried hard to smile back. Mike felt the closeness between them and was tempted to tell Doug his secret. They could talk about anything. He remembered telling Doug about Colleen's miscarriage last year. Doug had confided in him about how broken up he was over his father's death.

Certainly, it would feel good to unburden himself. But a part of him wondered how Doug would react. Doug was so cool; he might not understand what it meant to be afraid. He knew he couldn't tell him yet. Maybe he'd tell Doug after he got through the trial and stopped using. Doug was good at keeping secrets. Maybe someday, they'd laugh about it together.

"Hey, space cadet," Doug said interrupting his thoughts. "I said, have you heard the weather?"

"No," Mike replied.

Doug zipped up his Woolrich down parka and closed his locker door. "It's supposed to drop down to ten degrees tonight. Big windchill, too."

"Shit, why so cold this early in December?" Mike asked. *Just go, Doug.*

"Some jetstream bullshit, arctic air mass and all that," Doug replied. "Well, I'm outta here, Mike. I'll be at home, but try not to call me, OK?"

Mike forced a grin. "Don't worry, pal. You know me."

Doug headed for the door, but then turned and said, "It's good to see your old cheerful self back, Mike. I was a little worried about you earlier in the week."

"Yeah, yeah, me too. Don't worry, Doug. I got it under control." Mike paused and flashed Doug another fake smile. "See? Happy. Now go on. Get out of here before I put you back to work." Mike motioned toward the door.

"All right, all right. See ya."

As soon as Doug left, Mike dropped all smiles. Mike was irritated with Doug. He was a good friend, but sometimes he was a little too perfect. Well, that wasn't entirely true. Mr. Cool was having his own set of problems at home. He didn't admit to it, but Mike knew. When the couples had gone out recently, he had seen the tension between Doug and Laura. Besides, Doug had never gone to a meeting before without her. What was that all about?

Mike knew Doug had always had a wandering eye, but his affliction seemed to be worsening. Mike didn't get it. Laura was as pretty as they came and nice to boot. She'd do anything for you—not the typical, bitchy Doctor's wife. No, he didn't understand Doug's behavior. Doug even seemed touchy when he brought it up.

The hospital PA system barked to life, startling him. "Doctor Campbell, call the emergency room, two-one-six-four, STAT." Oh shit, Mike thought. They're stat paging the vascular surgeon to the ER. That can't be good news.

His fears were returning with a vengeance. He still had several cases to go that he knew of. And Friday nights, all bets were off. Anything could come screaming up from the ER: ruptured aneurysms, trauma, pediatric emergencies or obstetrical nightmares. He knew it was time for a re-dose if he was going to make it through the next twelve hours of call.

His heart began to pound and the trembling intensified just thinking about it. *How the hell am I going to make it twenty-five years? Don't think about it. One day at a time and all that shit. You know, desperate times call for desperate measures.*

He retrieved the necessary supplies from his locker and proceeded to one of the bathroom stalls.

* * *

Doug made it all the way out to his truck, before he realized he'd forgotten the schedule book.

"Damn it!" he said, as he flung his bag into the truck. He couldn't decide whether to get it or forget about it until tomorrow. "Feels like ten below!" He didn't relish another trek back to the hospital, but he'd promised Laura he would bring the book home tonight, so they could plan the family's summer vacation.

"Damn it! I'll never get out of here," he said, as he began retracing his steps to the hospital. The wind did its best to punish him for his forgetfulness.

* * *

Mike closed the door to the bathroom stall. A small part of his brain noted how quickly he had progressed from moral dilemma stage, to figuring out when it would be time for his next dose. Was it really possible to become drug dependent that fast? Could someone sink so low in a period of hours?

The remainder of his brain quickly overwhelmed these concerns, flooding him with images of panic and naked fear. He felt powerless to resist. A man's gotta do what a man's gotta do. He repeated this mantra over and over while he drew up the Fentanyl and performed the venipuncture on himself. Mike pushed the plunger for the second time that day, this time with considerably less reluctance. He took a deep breath, sat back and waited for the Fentanyl to kick in and deliver him from his fear.

He didn't have to wait long. He was still amazed by the rapidity of it all. He likened it to the crashing surf of a swiftly incoming tide; his fear was a small sandcastle, obliterated in an instant by the rushing torrent. The tourniquet dropped from his arm to the floor as he sat entranced by the pounding waves.

* * *

Doug was walking fast and still shivering as he entered the locker room. He had to go through the locker room to get to the on-call room where the schedule book was kept. He noticed that Mike's locker door was ajar, but didn't think much of it.

He strode past the bathroom stalls and glanced over as he was about to exit the room. What he saw stopped him in his tracks.

There on the floor, visible underneath the first stall, were Mike's Nike Airs. He recognized them immediately. What stopped him, however, weren't the sneakers, but the rubber tourniquet draped over the left one. That, and the funny breathing he heard coming from the stall.

"Mike, you OK?"

"Doug!" Mike answered with an unmistakable trace of alarm. "W-what are you doing here?"

"I forgot the damned schedule book." Doug was immediately worried. Things didn't add up.

The toilet flushed and out walked Mike, a huge smile plastered on his face. "Can't keep you away from this place," Mike said, his eyes dancing about the room.

Doug didn't return the smile. He was stunned by what he saw. Mike's face was slightly flushed and his pupils were absolute pinpoints. The conclusion was inescapable, but Doug's mind refused to believe it.

"What's with the tourniquet?" Doug asked.

"What're you talking about?"

"I saw a tourniquet on the floor."

"It dropped out of my pocket, I guess." Mike abandoned his smile. "Geez, Doug. What's your problem?"

"You are, Mike. Your pupils are goddamned small enough."

Mike hesitated, then said, "It must be this cold medicine I've been taking."

"Cold medicine!" Doug's mind clung to denial, but he commanded it to accept the truth. "You don't have a cold." Now it all made sense, the haggard appearance, the euphoria. "You think I'm stupid, Mike?"

"What're you saying, Doug? C'mon, just say it!"

"Cut the crap, Mike!" Doug said, his voice rising swiftly. "We both give this shit to people all day long. I know what it looks like."

"You think I'm using!"

"Show me your pockets!" Doug shouted. "Show me your arms, if you're clean!"

"No, I won't. Listen, I gotta get back to my case." Mike tried to maneuver around Doug, who was blocking the exit.

Doug grabbed his arms, squeezed hard and shook him. "Show me your damned arms!" Doug screamed.

"No, I won't!" Mike pleaded. "You're my friend, Doug. Can't you trust me?"

Before he could finish his sentence, Doug pushed up the sleeves to Mike's scrub jacket.

"There, Mike. What the hell's this!" Doug said, exposing a fresh puncture wound on his left arm. "I suppose you're taking your damned cold medicine by injection."

He threw Mike's arm down and turned his back on him in disgust. "I can't believe it, Mike."

"Doug, listen to me." Mike touched him on the shoulder. "You gotta listen. It's not what you think," Mike said, his voice breaking up.

Doug turned and faced Mike. It was hard to see his friend in such agony, to see the tears. He took several deep breaths to calm himself and spoke in a lower tone. "How long, Mike?"

"I just started, Doug." Mike sat down on the bench and stared at the floor. He tried to wipe away the tears. "This morning was the first time, I swear. I was gonna tell you."

"Why Mike? What about Colleen and the kids?"

"I know, I know," Mike said, shaking his head. He looked up. "It's stupid, but I did it for them, Doug."

"That's crazy!" Doug said and put his hand to his forehead. He took a few steps away and paced about in a small circle. He couldn't believe this was happening. Not Mike. It just wasn't possible.

"I just needed a little help through this malpractice shit," Mike said. "That's all. They're counting on me, Doug. I can't let them down." Mike buried his face in his hands, his body wracked by sobs.

Doug walked over and put his hand on his back. "Mike, there are better ways to get help."

"I guess. Doug, you can't turn me in," Mike said, choking back the tears. "Listen, I swear that was the last time. I'm not hooked yet. I can stop like that." He looked up, met Doug's eyes for the first time, and snapped his fingers.

"I don't know, Mike." Doug's anger was dissipating, being replaced by concern and pity.

"Doug, listen. You just can't tell anybody yet. If the lawyers get wind of this, they'll crucify me. You know how it goes— drugged up doctor kills patient. If this gets out, I don't know what I'll do."

"I'll have to think about it, Mike, OK?" Doug turned and exited the locker room, his mind a tangled mess of emotions. The schedule book was no longer a concern.

CHAPTER ELEVEN

"Are you sure?" asked Laura Landry as she punched buttons on the microwave. She shuffled her slippers on the vinyl brick kitchen floor.

"Yes, no doubt about it," said Doug. He was slouched forward in his chair at the large oak trestle table, his back to her.

"I'm making coffee. Want any?" she asked.

"Sure, decaf." His tired gaze roamed around the room, but the familiar details of the rustic country decor didn't register. Lots of pigs and cows in all shapes and sizes peeked out from shelves and countertops. Antique implements, some of long-forgotten function, hung from the walls and wooden ceiling beams. Doug sighed and said, "He had no reason to lie. Besides, I saw the needle mark on his arm."

"Wow," she said above the hum of the microwave.

"I didn't want to talk about it until the kids were in bed."

"This is just horrible," she said. "Mike always seemed so happy, so stable. I can't believe it."

He heard instant coffee being scooped into mugs. "I can't either. I'm sure it must have to do with his case. He really took it hard." Doug massaged his temples, his elbows resting on the table.

"And you said he got sued over it too?" she asked.

"Right," he said. The microwave beeped and was opened. He heard sounds of pouring water, followed shortly by a spoon clinking. The aroma of freeze-dried coffee drifted over to him. She appeared with the two steaming cups and placed his on the table.

"Here, give me a hug," he said, standing up.

"Sure."

She set her mug on the table, stood on her tiptoes and embraced him tightly. Even though she was wearing flannel p-j's, slippers, and wore no make-up, he found her very attractive. He always had. Her thirty-nine years and three pregnancies had done nothing to change that. He buried his face in her long black hair and breathed in her fragrance; it was a muted floral scent that arose from her favorite shampoo and bath soap. They fit together perfectly, so comfortably, he couldn't tell whether it was just good fortune, or if their bodies had molded themselves somehow into an exact match over the years. He felt closer to her than he had in months.

She looked up into his eyes and said softly, "You'd never take drugs, would you?"

He returned her gaze and looked into her dark brown, liquid eyes. "No way. I've got too much to lose."

"Colleen's gonna be devastated," she said, turning her eyes away.

"Yeah, I just can't figure out what to do."

"What do you mean?" she asked.

"Well, Mike pleaded with me not to tell anyone. You know, that he just started, and he could stop like that." He felt her body stiffen ever so slightly.

"Do you believe him?" She withdrew from his arms and backed up a step. Her voice had lost its soft tone.

"I don't know." Doug missed the warmth of her body. He sat down and picked up his coffee cup. He noticed she had given him his favorite mug, the one with three little cubs crawling all over the big papa bear. When he felt how hot the ceramic was, he set the mug down without taking a sip.

"Doug, you've got to tell someone."

He could almost hear Laura's mind shifting on the fly. "What do you mean?" he asked and looked up at her.

"You've got to tell the chief of the medical staff, Doctor, uh—"

"Nichols."

"Right. You've got to tell him." She started to pace.

"Well, I figured I'd sleep on it. If this got out, it would ruin Mike," Doug said tiredly. He wasn't in the mood for a long discussion.

"It's not *Mike* I'm concerned about."

He recoiled a bit from her stern tone. "What's that supposed to mean?"

"Doug, you can't let him in the OR anymore. What if he kills someone else?" "What!" He felt the peaceful mood slipping away like the steam escaping from the coffee mugs.

"Someone else might die because he's on drugs and not paying any attention." Laura's eyes were now on fire, and she appeared to be brimming with energy.

"That's not what happened, Laura. I was there." He smiled at her in an attempt to offer an olive branch, but she wasn't paying attention.

"Were you there from the beginning?"

"No—"

"So, you don't know what really happened." Her jaw was set, and he knew her mind was likewise set, in concrete.

"Look, Laura, the guy had a massive MI. Shit happens. I was with Mike during the resuscitation. He seemed fine."

"It doesn't matter, Doug. This isn't something to take lightly. You've got to tell Nichols."

Her authoritative tone always rankled him. Where did this come from? "And just what do I tell Mike? Sorry pal, best friend, I just can't trust you. You're a junkie. It's time to give your career the old heave-ho, but don't worry, it's all for the best." Doug felt himself heating up.

"Don't get sarcastic," she said and gave him a withering stare.

"Look, how about if we talk about this thing tomorrow. I've had a long day, and I'm pretty beat." Doug stood up and eyed the hallway to the bedroom stairs.

"I've had a long day, too, with the kids."

"The point is, Laura, if I tell Nichols, it'll all be over. They'll suspend his privileges—"

"No," she interrupted hotly, "the point is, you don't have a choice!"

"You mean, you're not giving me one," he countered. They traded glares briefly. He noticed her fists were clenched, a sign he had become all too familiar with recently, one that heralded an imminent meltdown.

"You're so good at figuring things out," she said. "Why can't you figure out this one? If you don't tell someone, and some innocent person gets hurt, it will be just as much your fault as his! Don't you get it?"

Her raised voice and pointing finger completed his slow burn. He felt his face flush with anger. "Yeah, I get it all right! You really don't care about Mike. You've written him off already. And I'm next!"

Tears welled up in her eyes, and she squeezed her hands so tight her fingers blanched. Her voice worked although nothing came out but high-pitched squeals.

"Cut me a break," he said to himself. He couldn't stand it when she got so emotional. "Do you have any idea what you're asking me to do? He's my best friend," he said trying to sound reasonable even though he knew he wasn't anymore.

"And Colleen's one of *my* best friends! Her pain will be far worse than Mike's! *I'll* have to deal with that!"

"Always the martyr," he said with disgust.

"I hate you!" she screamed.

Judging from the intensity of her expression, he believed her. "Likewise!" He whirled and stalked out of the room, passing by the untouched coffee mugs, which were no longer steaming. "I've got to go to bed, so I can go to work tomorrow!" he called back over his shoulder.

CHAPTER TWELVE

Doug finished giving report about his patient, thanked the recovery room nurse, and washed his hands with some Betadine. It was 10:30 Saturday morning, and he had just finished the fractured hip case for Dr. Clark. He left the recovery room and headed for the anesthesia on-call room. For the moment, he didn't have any other cases scheduled; he'd cleared the decks. Many a call day saw cases stacked up like planes at O'Hare jockeying for a place to land. He should've been happy, but he still felt like shit.

Doug had gone to bed last night buffeted by a wide range of emotions. He was sick over Mike and angry with him at the same time, and he was furious at Laura for telling him what to do. But mixed in was genuine sadness about their latest fight and confusion over why it was happening. When he went to bed, his stomach was tied up in knots, and his neck and back muscles were locked in spasm. Sleep had not been in the cards.

He passed the cysto room on his left and the anesthesia workroom to his right. Walking further, he came to the surgeon's lounge, and the smell of fresh-brewed coffee caused him to veer from his course. Even though he'd already gulped two cups earlier in the morning, he couldn't resist a third.

He walked into the lounge and realized why there was a new pot of coffee. The two X-ray techs who had helped with the fractured hip case were standing by the coffee machine, cups in hand, waiting for it to finish brewing.

Now that their surgical masks were down, he could see their entire faces, not just their eyes. He thought it was interesting to note how wrong one could be in predicting someone's face from just a view of the eyes. Doug remembered being surprised on more than one occasion after meeting a new scrub nurse or sales rep whom he'd never seen before. After talking to them for a while with masks up, he'd be forced to paint a mental picture of their face. When he finally saw them outside the OR, masks down, he was sometimes shocked to find that the girl with the pretty eyes and nice voice was actually unattractive, or that someone with plain eyes might be beautiful when their whole face was revealed.

Doug immediately recognized the bigger tech. Her name was Tammy or Tanya or something, and she was a veteran who had been there over twenty years. She had obviously been teaching her companion the finer arts of C-arm technique, and the ever-important skill of dealing with an orthopedic surgeon without being reduced to tears.

Doug had never seen the other girl before. She was much younger, probably right out of tech-school, and Doug couldn't help but notice she was striking. Her long brown hair, previously tucked in her surgical hat, flowed freely over her shoulders.

Why should he even look at her? He was a married man after all, a father. She'd be lucky to be half his age. Still, her beauty tugged at something, some archetypal hardwiring of his brain. He wondered whether other men had the same problem.

The coffee machine ended its brewing cycle, and the X-ray techs both helped themselves. As Doug poured himself a generous cup and added some milk, he couldn't help but steal some glances at the new tech. He was only partially successful and spilled a bit of milk on the table in the process. The older X-ray tech gave him a reproachful "That's what you get for staring" look and exited the room with her baby duckling in tow.

"Damn it," Doug cursed silently. He wiped up the spill with some paper towels and threw them into the trashcan with more force than he'd intended, sending the plastic hinged lid spinning out of control. Wow, a bit testy this morning, he noted.

Doug couldn't get the picture of Mike's flushed face and pinpoint pupils out of his mind. He couldn't get Laura's angry face and tears out either. All night he'd wrestled with Mike and Laura, arguing over and over about the drugs, wondering what to do.

He walked back to the on-call room and sat down sipping his coffee. He glanced up at the pictures on his desk. He had upwards of fifteen snapshots of Laura, the boys, and himself in every combination strewn about. Some of the older photographs had actually acquired frames, but most of the more recent ones were propped precariously on various knick-knacks on his desk. The large bottle of Advil was a favorite propping device.

He looked at last year's Christmas picture of Laura and himself seated by the fireplace. God, she looked pretty when she smiled. She of course hadn't been smiling last night when he told her about Mike. Strange, he thought, how easily they fought these days. They seemed to have lost the ability or desire to abort fights in the early stages. Now every argument, no matter how trivial, escalated to a full-scale fight. The braking mechanism was faulty.

Doug was very uncomfortable with their fighting. He had been raised in a relatively fight-free household. In fact, Doug's only childhood memory in this area was of his mother sobbing, sitting on the staircase when he was five years old. He remembered trying to comfort her. Doug had never seen her cry, and to this day the vision had visceral impact on him. He recalled vividly fearing the loss of his nice safe world and didn't want his kids to have similar memories. So consequently, Doug believed early on that good relationships were fight free. Each time Laura and he tangled over the years, he would sulk away fearing the worst about his own marriage.

Over the twenty years they had been married, they had had their sporadic fights, and Doug had gradually come to accept that occasional spats didn't equate with a bad marriage; sometimes he realized they were even useful to resolve sticking points in the relationship.

Now, however, things were worse. Doug couldn't shut up the voice in his head: "See, I told you so. Fighting like this means something is fundamentally wrong with your marriage. Mom and Dad never fought. Maybe you've grown apart. It happens. Something is wrong."

Doug was truly perplexed. He knew some of the problem lay with Laura and her workaholic syndrome, but what really bothered Doug, was trying to figure out just how much *he* was responsible for the hurt to the family. Why was *he* becoming less tolerant of Laura and her ways? Was this his subtle, passive/aggressive way of signaling his dissatisfaction with the marriage? Doug hadn't dated much before Laura, and he wondered if this was coming back to haunt him. Was this all a manifestation of some mid-life crisis where he kept asking himself what might have been, or what would it be like with another woman?

Doug reflected on last night's fight again. She was, of course, right about telling Dr. Nichols. Doug almost always agreed with Laura on big moral issues such as abortion, capital punishment, etc. This was one of the reasons they had been so compatible over the years. Opposites may attract, but nobody ever said they stay married. Deep down, Doug knew this, and it infuriated him all the more. He hadn't wanted to call Dr. Nichols last night. He needed time to explore all options, see if there was any way to spare his friend the disgrace.

It wasn't that they had disagreed so much; they differed in their style of thinking. He liked to think things through, mull them over, analyze the problem from every angle. He knew this was just the opposite of Laura's approach. She was usually able to make snap decisions or determine if something was right or wrong in a flash, and then stuck to her guns with the tenacity of a pit bull. He sometimes resented not having enough time to arrive at his own conclusions.

He took another sip of coffee and glanced at Mike's desk. He shook his head, got out a piece of paper, and started writing. "Dear Dr. Nichols—"

Didn't she mind being right all the time?

But he would wait a little to mail the letter. In fact, he would hand deliver it to Dr. Nichols next Friday at the Executive Committee meeting. He would have to tell Mike, and this was a conversation he dreaded.

After he finished the letter, he folded it up neatly and tucked it in the envelope. He stared at the envelope for a while. Strange, he thought, how this little envelope had the power to destroy a man's career and ruin a friendship. He shook his head to dispel these thoughts and put the envelope in his briefcase.

Now, Doug's thoughts roamed to where they went every chance they got over the last three days—Jenny Stuart. He knew she was here somewhere. She said she'd be working today. Just knowing she was in the same building made it hard to concentrate. How could he just sit here and read or do paperwork when she was so close?

He resisted an almost overwhelming urge to run over there. He knew it would be a mistake. He had vowed to himself that he would never cheat on Laura. Getting to know Jenny better could only unleash powerful temptations that could wreak havoc in his life.

He didn't want to see Jenny today. The hospital was a big building; surely, he could avoid her. He was even mad at Jenny because he blamed her in part for last night's fight.

Isn't that what really happened Doug? Is it a coincidence you fought last night? I suppose it had nothing to do with the fact that you knew she'd be here today, that you knew she wanted to talk to you.

He honestly didn't understand his motivations; they were buried somewhere beyond reach. But it didn't take Sigmund Freud to figure out that Jenny's interest in him was undoubtedly a contributing factor.

So his plan was simple, do nothing and thwart his subconscious desires. He reasoned they might make him fight, but fights can be smoothed over, forgiven. He didn't have to be unfaithful. Who was in control anyway? He would make rational decisions. No emotions here—No *la petite tete sur la grande tete* at work here. Besides his plan called for no action; it was easy.

He laid down on the sofa, closed his eyes and tried to rest.

* * *

Laura maneuvered her Plymouth Voyager minivan skillfully through the light Saturday morning traffic as she sped home. She had just finished dropping the kids off at her sister's, who lived in Lebanon. Laura's sister was single, and every other month or so she took the boys, usually when Doug was on call. Laura had a busy day planned, helping out at the church's Christmas giveaway to the poor. She pulled into the local Texaco to fill up. She thought about last night, and tears immediately welled up. She hadn't meant for them to fight. She knew she was right about Mike, but was just realizing how tough it must be on Doug. She knew she probably could've handled the discussion better. What really scared her and had fueled her reaction last night, was her fear that Doug would fall victim to a similar problem. She knew work was getting more and more stressful with all the changes brought about by managed care. Health care delivery was now in the hands of big business and government, and stability was a thing of the past.

She pulled out her wallet to get her credit card. As she opened it, she was struck by the wedding picture she kept there. She looked at the picture and saw the two of them with looks of such unadulterated joy radiating from their youthful faces that she couldn't help but smile. Nonetheless, it was a sad smile as she recalled earlier times.

She had been swept away ever since she had looked into Doug's steel-blue eyes and fallen under the spell of his charm. He was different from anyone she had ever known. Within days, she understood the definition of "soul mate." She didn't believe in love at first sight, but figured this was about as close as it got. He was carefree, had an amazing sense of humor, and was great fun to be around. But he was also a dreamer and had a sensitive streak a mile wide. He made her feel so special and loved.

They had been married after Doug had completed his first year of medical school at the University of Pittsburgh. She had transferred to Carnegie-Mellon from Cornell to complete her pharmacology degree. The wedding was lovely, and the honeymoon in Aruba even nicer. Doug's dad, weakened and ravaged by the chemotherapy, had not missed the wedding. He put on a good show of smiles and laughter despite the pain, and she knew it remained a special, bittersweet memory for Doug. They spent three blissful years at Pitt, marred only by his dad's funeral, before Teddy came along toward the end of Doug's fourth year.

What Laura remembered most about those early years were the long walks they took in the evening. She and Doug were deeply in love and shared everything; they talked of their hopes and dreams, and confided their fears to each other. She remembered those years clearly, but now they seemed to be someone else's memories. She couldn't quite connect them with the present. What had changed?

Clearly, the years in between had been hectic, a fast-paced blur of raising three children. She had focused on the children and their school and activities while Doug was at work. He was great with the kids while at home, but was basically clueless about the logistics of running a busy household. She couldn't remember the last time they had had a long discussion about their future life together. She thought back to Doug's difficult residency days.

He had stayed at Pittsburgh to do his residency at Allegheny General. As he dealt with the pressure of residency, Laura sensed that some of his beliefs underwent a subtle change. He began to feel that loving and caring for people led to vulnerability and pain. When Teddy got croup and had to be hospitalized, Doug was beside himself with fear and dread. She didn't know if he could've coped, had anything happened to their precious son. Then there was the unfortunate incident with Stephanie in obstetrics. His dad's death also resurfaced. Doug began to say strange things like, "You can care too much." He became more withdrawn and less willing to talk to Laura. He said he didn't feel right burdening her with his problems and fears. Laura knew he wasn't the macho type; he was too sensitive for that. Nevertheless, she wondered if he was trying to be the strong guy, the protector, like his father.

"I said that will be twenty-five dollars, mam," the gas station attendant said impatiently, shattering Laura's thoughts.

"OK, sorry," said Laura and hastily handed him her credit card.

When she got home, Laura decided to page Doug at the hospital and apologize. She knew exactly what would cheer him up; it had been a long time. They could make plans for tomorrow. She felt bad that he hadn't sleep well last night and was probably having a rough time at work today. She dialed his beeper number and punched in their home phone number.

* * *

Doug's beeper went off, and he opened his eyes. Now what, he thought. He pressed the button and saw his home phone number. What does she want? Before he could complete the thought, the hospital PA system crackled to life.

"Anesthesia STAT! Surgical Intensive Care Unit!"

"Anesthesia STAT! Surgical Intensive Care Unit!"

Shit, the damned SICU!

He rolled off the sofa right onto the floor, before getting to his feet. Still groggy and disoriented from his brief sleep, he grabbed his tackle box and hustled over to SICU, which was on the same floor.

"What do you need?" Doug shouted a bit too roughly as he cleared the automatic doors into the SICU. STAT pages always made him on edge because he never knew what disaster awaited him. The unit secretary looked up from her work and said cheerfully, "Mr. Jones, the post-op craniotomy needs re-intubated. He's in twenty-four."

"Thanks." Doug figured he had a good idea what had happened. He knew Mr. Jones had a highly malignant brain tumor and had undergone an extensive debulking procedure yesterday. It wasn't unusual for these patients to wake up disoriented and combative. Wrist, ankle restraints, and round-the-clock sedation were the norm.

Doug trotted over to room twenty-four to see what prize awaited him. One good look at the situation was worth twenty minutes of poring over the chart. On his way, he glanced briefly about the SICU for any sign of Jenny, but didn't see her. Doug entered the room and saw Mr. Jones thrashing about on the bed, his right arm free, clutching his endotracheal tube. His left arm was still held fast by a wrist restraint. He was struggling to breathe. Doug realized he'd have to put Mr. Jones to sleep just to get the tube back in him. Traces of a familiar scent taunted him, but he couldn't identify it amidst the strong hospital smells.

Where was the nurse taking care of him? The respiratory therapist was at the head of the bed ineffectively mask-ventilating the patient. Still no Jenny in sight.

"What happened?" asked Doug accusingly, knowing full well that Mr. Jones had gotten loose from the restraint and pulled his own tube.

"I don't know how that bugger worked his arm free," the therapist replied defensively. "I just checked his restraints a few minutes ago, and they were snug."

"Hmmm," Doug said and gave her a doubting look. If you had to re-intubate him, you'd be more careful with those restraints, he thought. He opened his tackle box, drew up the appropriate drugs and readied a tube and laryngoscope. "Hold his arm still and I'll give him something," Doug ordered sternly.

The respiratory therapist held the patient's arm semi-still while Doug injected the drugs into the bobbing IV port. Within seconds, Mr. Jones stopped thrashing and soon stopped breathing as well.

Doug took over ventilation and had more success with the immobile patient. As he bent down to do the laryngoscopy, he noticed the familiar scent again, only now much clearer.

"Can I help you with that, Dr. Landry?" Jenny asked. She had materialized in the room and was standing right next to him.

Doug practically jumped. "Uh, sure," he said. A tug of war immediately began to rage inside him; he had strongly divided feelings about seeing her. She wriggled up tight to him, so close he could feel the warm swell of her breast pressed against his right arm as he exposed Mr. Jones's vocal cords. He took his eyes off his patient to see she had picked up the endotracheal tube. He paused to marvel at the way she handled the tube, her long delicate fingers wrapped around it, bright fuchsia nail polish gleaming in the light. He took the tube from her, but had trouble refocusing on Mr. Jones.

"Do you need help putting it in?" Jenny whispered in his ear.

Doug still didn't move; he was too absorbed feeling her push up against him, seeing her slender hands, and breathing in her perfume. The room seemed very hot, and he felt himself becoming aroused.

The alarm from Mr. Jones' pulse oximeter went off when his oxygen saturation dipped below ninety percent. Doug regained his senses, pushed the tube home and started to ventilate Mr. Jones through it. He broke off bodily contact with Jenny and took several deep breaths. He turned to the respiratory therapist who was eyeing them curiously and said gruffly, "He'll need a blood gas in thirty minutes. And please tie that arm down better. I don't want to be called back here tonight!"

"Yes, Doctor. I'll be leaving now." She turned and exited the room smartly.

"Thanks for saving the day, Doctor Landry." Jenny was standing several feet from him, all smiles, face aglow. "He's my patient. I just don't know how he got his arm free."

From the way she said it and the way her eyes twinkled impishly, Doug knew what had happened to the wrist restraint. However, his anger seemed to melt away. She came over to him and touched him gently on his arm. She lowered her voice and said, "Thanks so much for coming to see me, Doug."

Doug recoiled when he felt her hand on his bare skin; the electricity of her touch was a physical force. He took another step back, banging into the ventilator. He was afraid to get too close to her again; irrationally, he had visions of white-hot sparks arcing from her body and burning him. He could see from her face that she had felt the surge between them as well. Except she didn't look the least bit concerned about it, rather that she'd expected it.

He had never felt anything as strong as this before; well, maybe he and Laura had experienced this kind of electric touch way back when, when they were engaged, but that was twenty years ago. His memory wasn't that clear. Besides, he thought the circuits responsible for this phenomenon had burned out long ago.

While he pondered these things, another part of his brain managed to keep up his end of the exchange. He returned to the conversation already in progress just in time to hear himself say:

"Next weekend I'm going down to Baltimore to the Inner Harbor. I have a meeting there."

"Where are you staying?" she asked.

"The Hyatt—the one right on the water, that's all glass."

"Oh, I love that one. Does your wife like it too?"

Alarm klaxons ripped through his confused brain. My wife!? How does she know? "Uh—yeah—but, she's not going. She can't because the boys have Christmas pageants at school." No need for secrets now.

"Oh, that's too bad."

Yeah, too bad. He grimaced slightly.

"How many boys do you have, Doug?" she asked sweetly.

Doug paused, feeling very self-conscious. He looked around to see where the other nurses or respiratory therapist were. No one in sight. He knew the last thing he wanted was to be seen having a long, personal discussion with Jenny. He was nervous that everyone would see through him and realize the extent of his desire. Camouflaging feelings of this magnitude was undoubtedly beyond him. And he knew that gossip spread like wildfire throughout the hospital.

"I—we have three—twelve, seven, and three."

"Wow, I just love kids—boys especially." She looked at his eyes, waiting for him to meet her gaze.

"Me, too." He looked around again, this time possibly for help. Still no one around. He was drawn irresistibly to her eyes and reluctantly surrendered to their power.

Jenny reached out with her hand again and touched his arm. More electricity. She lowered her voice and said, "I could meet you down there for lunch, or something, Saturday. It might be easier to talk there than here." She tossed her head about to indicate the surroundings and her blond hair danced playfully.

"Yeah, you're right about that—hmmm lunch—let me think."
Think about the 'or something'.
Just say no!
Don't you feel it?
Are you crazy?

The tug of war was going badly. The home team seemed to have been electrocuted by some unknown force and was being dragged pell-mell through the mud, past the centerline.

"I'd like that," he heard himself say.

CHAPTER THIRTEEN

Bob Lehman rolled over in bed, luxuriating in the fact that on some deeper level, he knew he was sleeping late. Sunday mornings were glorious. He bobbed over the threshold of consciousness only to sink down again into the warm, peaceful womb of dreamland. He imagined himself frolicking in the surf off the southern shores of Bermuda. He was no longer a sixty-year-old widower inured to a hard life, but a young man of twenty-six on his honeymoon again with his pretty bride. Worries didn't exist in this timeless domain. Mistakes had not been made. Their life together stretched out in front of them, not behind, with an intoxicating array of shiny new dreams and possibilities unspoiled by the harsh realities of life.

The fresh ocean breeze gently caressed his face. He lingered at the edge of the water, eyes closed, to take a deep breath, savoring the saltwater scent. Suddenly, the air was flooded with a pleasant coffee aroma carried on the breeze. The young man did not find this strange, even though they were on a deserted beach; in fact, he thought this was the most natural of meteorological phenomena. Just as dark clouds presage rain, gentle ocean breezes often smell of coffee.

* * *

April walked into the bedroom and saw that her father was sleeping. She paused to look at him and smiled when she realized he was probably in the midst of a dream. He was a bear of a man, well over six feet tall with enormous shoulders and thick hairy arms. His face was angular with rough-hewn features, most notably a large flat nose and jutting chin, but his appearance was marred by the numerous lines that zigzagged across his face. They were cut ravine deep, a testament to the hard duty they had seen channeling all the pain and sorrow from his face. This morning a small smile softened his usual careworn features.

She hated to wake him, but couldn't wait any longer. "Daddy, Daddy, Happy Birthday!" she squealed with delight. "Look what I've brought you!" She carefully set down her heavily laden tray on the nightstand by the bed. "It's ten o'clock. Wake up sleepyhead. Here's your favorite breakfast, and fresh brewed coffee." The favorite breakfast consisted of scrambled eggs, slightly gooey, laced with melted Monterey Jack cheese and mushrooms. Fresh sausage, pan-fried to a delicious golden-brown, rounded out the meal.

Bob Lehman opened his eyes, and his smile broadened as he saw April and the breakfast tray. "April, is it really ten o'clock? You shouldn't have let me sleep so long." He sat up in bed and stretched his massive arms. "I *was* having a really nice dream though."

April was clearly excited about her father's birthday. She had good reason to be. Just six months ago, she wasn't sure there would be another birthday to celebrate. Bob Lehman had undergone emergency coronary artery bypass grafting just before the Fourth of July.

He had been at the office when he developed crushing chest pain and was rushed to the local community hospital, Our Lady of Mercy. April had taken the call at home and had raced to the emergency room just in time to see her father being wheeled to the cardiac catheterization lab. She remembered her father's ashen complexion and perspiration-soaked gown. But these were nothing compared to the thinly veiled look of terror in his eyes. She kissed him and gave him a quick hug in spite of the tangle of EKG leads, IV tubing, arterial line, and oxygen hoses crisscrossing his body. She told him she loved him and would see him shortly, when this was all taken care of. *Oh please, God, pull him through. I swear I'll do anything.*

The emergency room physician had told her they would try to dissolve the offending clot with a new drug called "tissue plasminogen activator," or "tpa" for short, but they also needed to obtain some pictures of the blood vessels feeding the heart—the all important coronary arteries. Unfortunately, they only had about four hours before the damage to the heart muscle became irreversible. A myocardial infarction would be the result. This translated into death of a portion of the heart muscle and could be fatal.

April remembered the agonizing wait while her father was in the cath lab. When one of the interns came out and told her he was being rushed to the OR for emergency bypass surgery, she was beside herself with fear and dread. Only last year she had watched her mother die in this hospital; it was a horrible, suffering death as only metastatic cancer can provide. Now she was to lose her father. She quickly made more promises to God, not holding back anything.

Her father survived his surgery and actually did quite well. He had only one minor complication—an incisional hernia that was scheduled to be repaired the following day as an outpatient. He appeared to thoroughly enjoy his birthday, and April marveled that he spared little energy worrying about the upcoming surgery. She only wished she could be so relaxed.

* * *

It was late Sunday night, and Rusty Cramer knew he should've been in bed. Instead, he pored over his computer screen. He had finally received the e-mail he had been waiting all weekend for. He read it and reread it. Rusty shut down his computer and ran his fingers through his hair. Things were coming together. He got up from his chair, paced around the room for a few minutes, and then made his decision. He would skip the Visiting Professor lecture series tomorrow. Perhaps Wednesday, he would take a trip to Philadelphia. He had more business to attend to.

CHAPTER FOURTEEN

It was 11:45 a.m. Monday morning, and Melissa Draybeck was dutifully setting up for a noontime lap choley in OR#2. She was a conscientious OR scrub nurse with considerable experience built up over twenty years of service to Mercy Hospital. Melissa prided herself on her rigid, sterile technique and extensive knowledge of surgeons' operative techniques including the vast array of surgical instruments involved. This was no mean feat, considering virtually every surgeon had a rather large laundry list of likes and dislikes for everything under the sun, including which gown to put on (Gore-Tex or regular), which gloves (latex, rubber, non-allergenic, orthopedic, Vaseline wipe before gloving), which surgical instruments, which OR room, which OR table, which suture, which dressings, etc. And of course, each surgeon believed his technique was the only logical choice and therefore expected the nurses to anticipate his needs or there would be hell to pay.

Thank God most ORs, in an effort to pander to the surgeons and preserve the sanity of their staff, made up a card for each surgeon and his individual operations. A general surgeon might have ten cards—one for his laparoscopic cholecystectomy, one for his bowel resection, one for his herniorrhaphy, etc. This gave the poor scrub nurse some degree of protection from the wrath of God when the demanded instrument was not immediately on hand. Melissa knew how the conversation went:

"I'll need a thirty-degree scope for this part."

"We'll get you one in a minute, Doctor. We just have to run down the hall and get it from Central."

"What! You don't have it in the room? Damn it! I always use a thirty-degree scope. That's gotta be on my card. I never have this problem at Poly."

"Let me see, Doctor. Sorry, it's not on your card. Would you like us to add that?"

"Yes of course, damn it! I don't ever want to have to wait for that again. I could've sworn I've told you to add that before."

She shook her head and wondered what had led her to this tough job. She remembered a time when she had had different plans for her life. As a young woman, newly graduated from nursing school, she had envisioned herself married with children someday, but the proper relationship never materialized for reasons she cared not to examine too closely. She knew she was no beauty, but it was more than this. Although she continued to date sporadically, deep down she knew she was not marriage material. She was so set in her ways that she couldn't imagine giving up her relaxed, if somewhat dull, free, if somewhat lonely, lifestyle for some man. Or more correctly she believed, for some man who would be interested in her. She had long since given up on the idea, and now appreciated the freedom of no children or husband. Melissa's life was reasonably simple, and she was reasonably content with it, although she might have defined content as resigned.

She realized what gave her life meaning was her job. At work, she could put her lonely existence of making rent and cooking meals for one on hold and participate first hand in real-life drama more exciting than any of the soaps she watched. Although many of the physicians, especially surgeons, fell into the love-to-hate category, she would never characterize them as boring. Flamboyant, rude, obnoxious, egomaniacs, prima donnas, greedy maybe, but not boring. On some deeper level, Melissa was vaguely aware that she came to work each day not solely for a paycheck, but to fill a void in her life.

Halfway through her suture count, she noticed she was missing some 3-0 Vicryl on a P-3 cutting needle. She knew Dr. Alfonse was a stickler about these things and would whine unmercifully if she didn't have it. She started across the hall toward OR#1 where a large supply cabinet of suture material was located. Halfway across the hall, she noticed that the lights were out in OR#1. She didn't give it much thought, as it wasn't that unusual. She simply assumed they must've broken for lunch and turned the lights off when they left.

As she approached the door, she stopped and hesitated a moment. Through the small window in the heavy wooden door, some motion caught her eye. She thought she could make out a shadowy figure at the opposite end of the room where the anesthesia equipment was. The shape seemed to be moving quickly towards the other door at the far end of the room. Strange, she thought, that someone would be in there working in the dark.

She shook her head briefly to dispel the growing fear, pushed the door open, and entered the room. As she turned and groped for the light switch, she distinctly heard the creaking of the far door as it closed. The lights blazed on and bathed the room in bright white, hospital-approved light. The room was empty.

Melissa walked over to the suture cabinet, opened the doors and retrieved her missing suture. She had the unmistakable sensation that someone was watching her through the window in the far door. The window shade was pulled down, so she couldn't see, but she was convinced someone was on the other side. It gave her

an acute condition of "cutis anserina" or goose bumps. She considered for a moment walking over and opening the door, but she
couldn't summon the proper courage. All she could manage was
a long stare. Soon she turned around and rapidly exited the room
with her precious suture in hand.

CHAPTER FIFTEEN

Doug hated Mondays, especially those following a call week-end. Only halfway through the day and he already felt bushed. He summoned some additional energy and went to meet his noontime patient. There were seven patients awaiting surgery crammed into the small holding area. The scene frequently reminded Doug of a busy stockyard where the patients were the cattle. He squeezed in between two of the litters to get to his patient. Doug extended his hand to the big man lying on the litter in front of him.

"Mr. Lehman, Hi I'm Doctor Landry. I'll be helping you go off to sleep today, so we can fix your hernia."

"Hello, Doctor Landry. Nice to meet you." Bob Lehman grasped Doug's hand and pumped his arm hard with a grip some-where between firm and crushing.

"How are you doing today?" Doug asked, extricating his hand quickly to avoid injury.

"Just fine," Mr. Lehman replied. "That shot really helped me relax. I'm kinda hungry, though."

Doug glanced at his watch—12:05 p.m. "Yeah, I agree—that's the worst part. So, nothing to eat or drink after midnight, right?"

"Not a thing. And let me tell you, just between you and me." Mr. Lehman lowered his voice conspiratorially and Doug leaned closer. "I don't miss many meals." Mr. Lehman patted his ample midsection and grinned. "I'd settle for a cup of coffee right now. It doesn't help when they wheel you right past that coffee machine over there." He pointed across the hallway to the surgeon's lounge. "Smells great."

"Yeah, pretty cruel, I know. But you want your surgeon to be awake, right?" Doug paused and glanced at Mr. Lehman's chart. The only thing that really stood out in his history was his recent bypass procedure. Doug hoped Mr. Lehman's heart was in as good shape as the rest of him seemed to be. "I've read through your chart and everything seems to be in order. Any questions for me?"

"No, let's get it over with."

"Left-sided hernia, correct?" Doug asked.

"Right—I mean yes, left."

Both men chuckled, and Doug wheeled the litter down the hall toward OR#1. Doug instinctively liked the big man although he knew it was a mistake to become too chummy. Always better to keep the relationship professional.

Once inside the room, Mr. Lehman transferred himself from the litter to the OR table with help from the circulating nurse, Sue Hoffman. Doug was impressed that he moved so adroitly for such a big man.

"Just when I got that one warmed up you make me move to this cold bed," Mr. Lehman complained, although he had a smile on his face. "Not very comfortable either."

"I'll get you a warm blanket in a minute," said Sue Hoffman. "First, we must put this strap on so you don't fall off this narrow table." She snugged a six-inch-wide leather strap that meant business around Mr. Lehman's upper thighs, effectively fixing him to the table. Doug often wondered what patients must think of this strap; it seemed to be a direct descendant from the days of the Inquisition.

"Bed's kinda small," Bob Lehman commented as he looked around the room.

"Yep," Sue said, placing the blanket over him. "Not designed for comfort, are they?"

"I'm gonna be hooking you up to some monitors here, Mr. Lehman," murmured Doug as he fell into his pre-induction monologue. "Just routine." He had long ago hit upon what he considered the best combination of phrases to help inform and relax the patient. He knew very well that this was a particularly stressful time for most patients, pre-op medication notwithstanding. He remembered being in this position himself several years ago and literally shaking as he climbed onto the OR table. He also knew his monologue helped to relax himself as well and couldn't help but notice that he felt strangely on edge.

"I need your right arm out here." He ripped Velcro and wrapped a blood pressure cuff around Mr. Lehman's arm, hoping it would fit. "This is a blood pressure cuff. It's going to pump up and squeeze your arm. It'll let go in a minute." He activated the automatic blood pressure machine. "These are sticky EKG patches, so we can monitor your heart." He placed the first two. "And this last patch goes on your left side, and it's the coldest of all."

"Yikes," said Mr. Lehman. "First you warm me with the blanket, and then you freeze me."

"Now put your left arm out to this side. I have a little clip that goes on your finger and tells me how well you're breathing." Doug placed the pulse oximeter finger sensor.

"It feels like I'm being crucified," Mr. Lehman remarked, wiggling his outstretched arms.

"Well, it *is* a Catholic hospital, Bob," Doug said with mock seriousness, then added quickly, "Just kidding."

"Thank God it's not Good Friday," Mr. Lehman said and laughed.

"Yeah, right," Doug said as he quickly glanced at the monitors to get some baseline numbers. BP was 145/90, pulse was 78, and O2 sat was 96% on room air. The EKG trace showed normal sinus rhythm. Everything looked good.

"I'm going to give you some medicine to help you relax while we get you set up here." Doug administered two cc's of Fentanyl, a potent narcotic used to blunt the patient's response to pain. He couldn't help but think of Mike; Fentanyl was the same drug Mike was abusing. He had a vision of Mike sitting in a bathroom stall injecting himself. He forced himself back to Mr. Lehman. "Here's some oxygen I want you to breathe." He placed the mask, which was hooked up by plastic hoses to his anesthesia machine, on Mr. Lehman's face. Doug dialed the oxygen flowmeter to five liters-per-minute. Doug watched the pulse oximeter reading rise from 96% to 100% as Mr. Lehman's lungs filled with 100% oxygen. "Are you feeling any of that medicine yet?" Doug asked.

"Yes, I believe I am," came Mr. Lehman's muffled response from under the mask.

"OK, now it's time to pick out a pleasant dream. You'll be going off to sleep in about a minute."

"OK, Doc. I'm on the beach in Bermuda," Mr. Lehman said smiling. "On my honeymoon."

Doug thought of Aruba and his own honeymoon. He and Laura had been so happy. Where in God's name had they gone wrong? Just yesterday, Laura had tried to make up to him. He hadn't realized it at the time; he had been too busy projecting coldness. By the time he figured it out, the fragile moment had passed. Perhaps his encounter with Jenny had blinded him to Laura's intentions?

Mr. Lehman's voice brought him back to the present. "I'm in your hands, Doc."

Doug hated it when they reminded him of that. He turned around to get the necessary induction drugs. About twelve syringes filled with the basic anesthetic meds of his trade lay at the ready on top of his anesthesia cart. He reflected briefly on the fact that here before him was a deadly arsenal of drugs. Each syringe was potentially lethal if given in the wrong amount, wrong combination, or wrong order.

Doug shook his head to break this destructive line of thought and hooked the Diprivan syringe to the IV set and injected the entire contents. "OK. Here we go. You're going to drift off to sleep in about thirty seconds."

All twenty cc's of the thick, white emulsion snaked through the IV tubing toward Mr. Lehman's hand, where it buried itself in a vein. Doug could feel his own heartbeat quicken and his senses snap into focus as he pushed the Diprivan. Whenever he induced a patient, he was keenly aware of taking several irreversible steps— the first being the administration of the induction agent.

Very quickly Mr. Lehman's jaw sagged, his eyes closed, and he stopped breathing. Doug checked for the absence of a lid reflex by gently touching his eyelids to assure himself that Mr. Lehman was unconscious. He then grasped the mask with his left hand, tightly applied it to Mr. Lehman's face to effect a seal, and squeezed the breathing bag on the anesthesia machine. He gave Mr. Lehman a couple of quick breaths by forcing air into his lungs. After checking to make sure he could ventilate his patient, Doug moved on to the next irreversible step—this one bigger than the last.

He injected 160 milligrams of Succinylcholine, a muscle relaxant that temporarily produces a muscular paralysis necessary for intubation. A strange wave of muscle rippling traveled through Mr. Lehman's body as the Succinylcholine exerted its effect and rendered his muscles completely flaccid.

Doug took his laryngoscope, a barbaric-looking metal device with a bright light on one end, in his left hand and opened Mr. Lehman's mouth with his right. He slid the laryngoscope blade in and hunted for the glottis, which is the opening to the trachea. The laryngoscopy triggered a strong déjà vu. Doug imagined he could feel Jenny pressed up against him, and he could even smell her perfume. He suppressed the memory angrily and glanced around to see if anyone had noticed his hesitation. Sue was busy filling out her paperwork, and the scrub nurse was counting her instruments.

He refocused on Mr. Lehman's vocal cords, which were asleep on the job, paralyzed by the Succinylcholine. With his right hand, Doug carefully inserted the endotracheal tube through the opening between the vocal cords and pushed it several inches down into the trachea. He removed the laryngoscope blade from Mr. Lehman's mouth, inflated the cuff at the end of the endo tube, and hooked it up to his breathing circuit. As he squeezed the bag, Doug watched Mr. Lehman's chest rise and fall. He quickly listened to both sides of Mr. Lehman's chest with his stethoscope to check for equal breath sounds. Hearing good sounds bilaterally, Doug flipped on the ventilator and dialed in two-percent Isoflurane gas and some nitrous oxide. This would keep Mr. Lehman asleep as the Diprivan wore off.

Doug barely had time to tape the endotracheal tube in place before all hell broke loose. Doug heard the EKG monitor alarm sing out first, and he snapped his head to look at it.

"V-tach! Shit!" he mumbled to himself. "Where the hell did that come from?" He paused for an instant and then said loudly, "Sue, get some help in here stat and bring the crash cart! Got trouble!"

Doug rarely called for help. He had confidence in his abilities to solve most problems, but he recognized true emergencies when he saw them and knew calling for help early was sometimes key; the first five minutes of a crisis were critical. The malpractice records were replete with stories of bad outcomes related to delayed diagnosis and treatment of emergency situations.

"Think, Think," he muttered to himself. "Must've been playing possum." Doug figured that Mr. Lehman may have appeared to have been adequately anesthetized just prior to intubation but actually wasn't. He knew that intubation is a very stimulating procedure. It can cause a grossly elevated BP and a dangerously rapid heartbeat and/or V-tach in a sick heart.

Doug didn't wait for his BP machine to cycle. He quickly turned his anesthetic agent to the max and in rapid succession administered as much Fentanyl as he had, injected one syringe of premixed emergency Lidocaine, and gave some Labetalol. In so doing, Doug went way out on a limb. His clinical instinct told him his patient had an exaggerated sympathetic response to the intubation; an outpouring of adrenaline from his adrenal glands in a classic flight or fright response. Doug didn't have all the facts in yet, but sometimes waiting the extra thirty seconds to be sure of the diagnosis could cost thirty seconds of treatment time and push you over the edge into irreversible damage. He had just given enough drug to dangerously lower a normal person's BP. But, it may have been lifesaving in a hypertensive crisis.

Funny thoughts ran through his head. He heard Kelly McGillis from the movie, *Top Gun* saying, "That's a hell of a risk with a thirty-million-dollar airplane lieutenant. What were you thinking?" To which he responded in Tom Cruise fashion, "You don't have time to think up there. If you think, you're dead."

230/110! *I knew it!* The V-tach had persisted and quickened. The crash cart rolled through the door with Dr. Kim Burrows, Dr. Patterson, the surgeon and several OR personnel in tow. Stat pages for the crash cart had a way of attracting people.

"What's the problem, Doug?" Kim asked.

"V-tach on induction. Out of the blue. Gotta shock him quickly before it gets worse. Pressure went sky-high, but I think I got a handle on it—mix me some Nipride though." Doug was happy to have Kim's help; she was good in these situations.

"Landry, what'd you do to my patient?" bellowed Dr. Patterson.

"I'm kinda busy right now, Tom. If you wanna help, bring those paddles over here." Doug knew Patterson didn't like to relinquish control, what with the surgeon being captain of the ship and all, but he knew that in these situations the anesthesiologists were actually far better qualified to render emergency treatment. He pushed the defibrillator unit up to the OR table and handed the paddles to Doug.

"Charge to 200 joules," Doug ordered. "Set to synchronous."

"Synchronous set—charging—ready, Doug," said Kim, who'd pushed the fumbling Patterson out of the way.

Doug applied the paddles, shouted "Clear," and fired them into Mr. Lehman's chest. God, he hoped this would turn around.

"No good!" shouted Kim. "Nipride's ready. I'm plugging it in. What's the pressure?"

On cue, the Dinamap beeped with the newest blood pressure, 220/100.

"Still up there," said Doug, but he was thankful to see a lower pressure. "Give me three hundred. Run the Nipride wide."

"Paddles ready," said Kim.

Doug applied the paddles a second time and let the electricity loose. Everyone held their breath waiting for the electrical interference to die down so they could make heads or tails of the EKG.

"Sinus! Doug, you got sinus!" shouted Kim. Respirations resumed collectively in the room with an audible rush. "Better watch the pressure with all that pride on."

"Yeah, I'm cutting it back, Kim." Doug regulated the dangerous Nipride drip.

Doug and Kim stared at the Dinamap waiting for the next BP. The machine beeped and showed, 190/90.

"Nice going, Landry," said Patterson. "You just saved the patient from yourself. Now can we proceed with the surgery?"

"Yeah, yeah," Doug said. "Thanks a lot. You can forget about surgery today—"

"Now, wait just a minute," Patterson interrupted. "He's my patient and—"

"Surgery's canceled, Tom," Doug snapped back. "Get it? Canceled!"

This stopped Patterson momentarily and he gave Doug a puzzled look. The rest of the people in the room were also looking at him. Doug was pleased; he knew they were surprised to hear him tell off the surgeon.

"I'm gonna take him to the SICU," said Doug, "and let the cardiologists evaluate his heart. Something's obviously not right." Doug took a couple of deep breaths and tried to urge his own heart to slow down. One patient with V-tach was enough.

Patterson huffed out of the room, muttering something about not having these problems at Poly.

"You OK, Doug?" asked Kim.

"Yeah. Thanks for your help, Kim."

"Sure," she said. "Way to tell Patterson off. He's such a pain in the butt." She paused for a couple of seconds and looked at him. "I've never heard you raise your voice before. I didn't know you could."

"Yeah, I know it's unusual."

"You save the guy's life, and all Patterson's concerned about is having his surgery canceled." She walked out of the room shaking her head.

Sue Hoffman came over, put her hand on Doug's arm, and squeezed gently. "Nice going, Doug." He met her eyes and could tell she was smiling beneath her mask.

Doug stared out of the window in the OR complex, far down at the end of the hallway. He had just returned from tucking Mr. Lehman safely in the SICU. Snow flurries swirled about outside. He imagined their delicate, individual shapes being whipped thoughtlessly by the rough December wind. He had come down here to try to collect his thoughts after Mr. Lehman's case. He had to pull himself together; he still had two cases to go. He took several deep breaths, closed his eyes, and focused on the crystalline snow and ice—pure and simple. What was the point of emotions anyway? They just got him into hot water. Doug tucked his feelings back into the freezer of his mind and headed down the hall to meet his next patient.

CHAPTER SIXTEEN

Bryan Marshall couldn't get Karen McCarthy out of his mind. She had always been a favorite of his. Except now, he wasn't focusing on the good times. Here he was, sitting in his office Monday morning supposedly preparing for a big meeting with Pinnacle and hospital administration. Instead the door was locked, the metal box in the drawer was open, and her pictures were strewn about the desk. He kept thinking about their conversation that stifling hot night in August so long ago; it had been the last time they had ever spoken. God, his head hurt. He leaned forward and cradled his throbbing head in his hands. Was it really possible to develop a conscience after twenty-five years? He only did what he had to do. He could still hear her voice, quavering but full of determination.

"May I come in," Karen McCarthy asked, standing in the doorway to his office.

"Of course," Marshall answered. He was seated at his desk and motioned for her to enter. "What a pleasant surprise," he said warmly; he was always pleased to see her. The two were on call together, but the OR was quiet, and the last thing he expected was for her to drop by. "It's kind of late for a meeting." He checked his watch. "It's past midnight. What will people think?" he asked and chuckled.

Karen ignored him. "I have something to tell you," she said. Her face held a grim expression. She looked past him, avoiding direct eye contact.

"Ah, you've made a decision regarding your, uh, problem?"

"Yes, I have."

"Good girl." He had never doubted Karen was a bright girl. "I know just the place in Chambersburg." He reached forward to consult his Rolodex. "Friend of mine runs it and—"

"I'm not going there," she said firmly.

He paused for a moment and raised his eyebrows with surprise. "You prefer some other facility?"

"No, I'm not going anyplace. I'm going to have this baby!"

"Are you now?" Interesting, he thought. This girl was feistier than he had given her credit for. He had been taking advantage of her regularly for six months, and by some stroke of bad luck, she had become pregnant. But so far, she had shown no sign of backbone. He slid out of his chair and rounded the desk. "What about your career? What about your baby at home? Are you forgetting all this, dear girl?" he asked smoothly, as he narrowed the distance between them.

She began to tremble, but held her ground. "We'll manage. I'll get another job." She locked eyes with him, and through the fear, Marshall thought he saw some strength, some determination, he wouldn't have thought possible. But he wasn't about to be cowed by anyone, let alone a young woman with a big problem. He had plenty of experience bending people to his will. He adopted a menacing tone. "Don't be so sure. I have contacts all over. You'll never set foot in another OR!"

She appeared to cringe at his voice, but amazingly continued to hold his gaze. He felt his face flush with blood; his anger, simmering always just beneath the surface, threatened to erupt. He took several deep breaths to calm himself and played his trump card. "Karen, no one will believe your little fantasy of coerced sex. There was no gun to your head; you put up no struggle." She tried to protest, but he continued, louder. "What they *will* believe, is that you came on to me, and in a moment of weakness, I acquiesced. It'll be your word against mine. Remember though, you're the one with the credibility problem. You lied on your application—you *do* have an out-of-wedlock child."

Marshall studied her pretty face; his words had the desired effect. Her head drooped, and he saw the determination drain out of her face. "We'll work it out Karen," he said soothingly and began to stroke her shoulder. "We always have. No need for rash decisions." He became aroused seeing her helplessness and reached out with his other hand to fondle her.

Suddenly, her head snapped up and she glared at him. Before he could react, she coiled her arm and let loose a vicious blow that connected solidly with the side of his head, sending his glasses flying. Marshall reeled backwards in total shock. Pain reverberated through his skull, and his face stung miserably. He sucked in several large ragged breaths, as he rubbed his face. He took a step toward her and stopped. His anger burned hugely through him, and he was shaking. Only a Herculean effort on his part stopped him from strangling her on the spot. "Get out of here, you whore!" he bellowed, pointing at the door. "You're finished here! You're finished!"

"No, I'm not," she said, as she made for the door. "One more thing." She turned to face him. "I'm going to tell everyone who the father is!" She slammed the door in his face.

Marshall's watch beeped on the hour—10:00 a.m. His heart was pounding from the memory of his encounter with Karen. Stupid, idealistic girl. What a waste.

Marshall rocked back in his chair and wondered what was taking Sister so long to summon him to the meeting? Pinnacle, with their army of arrogant consultants and high-powered lawyers, must already be there, poisoning the well. Marshall hated the ever-increasing intrusion of big business, law, and politics into medicine. He smiled with the realization that if Karen and he had tangled nowadays, she would've slapped him with a sexual harassment suit so fast his head would've spun. And she would've easily prevailed. Luckily, things were different back then. He remembered the way Karen had looked as she had left the hospital that morning—the morning after she had hit him. He walked over to the window overlooking the parking lot, the same window he had watched her leave for the last time twenty-four years ago.

Karen was all smiles and looked light on her feet as she made her way out to her VW beetle. Her recent defiance made his blood boil all over again. Marshall absently stroked the side of his face where she had whacked him last night. He'd teach her a lesson or two about who was boss around here. She reversed her car out of the parking space and then pulled smartly away, windows rolled down. He knew she would head home to Halifax via Route 225. The road was a treacherous, two-lane affair that snaked over Peter's Mountain. The lanes were narrow, shoulders were often absent, and it had numerous hairpin turns, a carryover from road design of bygone years. Old, rusted guardrails offered only illusory protection from several hundred-foot drop-offs.

Marshall believed he could see her singing, probably to the radio, as she pulled out. She obviously hadn't noticed the greenish fluid underneath her car. He couldn't see it from here, but he knew it was there—little puddles of brake fluid that had dribbled onto the asphalt from the brake lines he had cut several hours ago. Sing Karen, go ahead and sing.

* * *

Karen was very proud of herself as she made her way out of the hospital. Her night shift was over, and she was headed home. She laughed out loud for the first time in months.

They'd make it. Marshall had underestimated her strength when he had targeted her. She turned on the radio and started humming along with the Bee Gees as she headed out of the parking lot.

She had a good twenty-five mile drive over Peter's Mountain to get home. Normally she minded the commute, but today she knew she'd enjoy it. Not even the gray, clumping storm clouds could dampen her spirits. She was free of him.

As she braked for the first stoplight, the Beetle lurched a bit, but the engine rumbled happily as it idled. She was in such a good mood, singing aloud with the blaring radio as she planned her new life, that she ignored the odd feel of her brake pedal. Soon she was climbing Peter's Mountain and had no need for the brakes.

Rain let loose with a fury on top of Peter's Mountain. Karen turned on her lights and windshield wipers and tried to pay more attention to the road. She was coming up on the first and sharpest of the hairpin curves, going about forty mph.

She touched her brakes, intending to slow down. Nothing happened. She pushed harder on the pedal, and it slid all the way to the floorboard with sickening ease. Again, nothing happened to slow the vehicle. The Beetle even accelerated from the downhill grade of the road.

"Oh shit!" she said, jarred completely out of her daydreams. Something's horribly wrong. She mashed on the pedal with all her strength. Nothing. The guardrail loomed ahead, perhaps thirty feet and getting closer all the time.

I'm not going to make it! The Beetle was now going forty-five mph and still accelerating.

She quickly downshifted to first gear and popped the clutch, gears grinding loudly. Even the Bug's renowned synchromesh transmission was not up to this abuse. The engine howled in distress when the gears finally engaged. The car shuddered, and she was thrown forward by the force of deceleration. The car slowed, but it still didn't seem like enough.

The guardrail was fifteen feet away. She grabbed the emergency brake lever and ripped it with all her might. The car slowed further. *Please God, help me!*

The Beetle plowed through the rusted guardrail at twenty mph, retaining just enough momentum to send it over the steep embankment. It rumbled and rolled like a toy, bouncing off rocky ledges and stunted trees before coming to rest on a gentle slope wedged up against two larger trees. Amazingly, Karen still clung to consciousness. She felt no pain, although she could feel something warm running down her neck and soaking her shirt. She looked down and saw dark blood mingle with her strawberry hair and thought the colors were beautiful. She lifted her head with effort and had trouble focusing her eyes. Finally, she made out an exquisite spider web pattern in the front windshield. My head made that, she thought giddily. So pretty. Sadly the shattered glass wouldn't stay in focus and began to dim. She was so tired, so weak, all she could do was listen to the rain drum heavily on the crumpled metal roof. Time for a quick nap, she thought and closed her eyes.

* * *

The office intercom buzzed. Julie, the group's secretary, said, "Doctor Marshall, Sister's calling for you now."

"OK, thanks." He hastily scooped up the photos and replaced them in the box. A single newspaper clipping was left on his desk.

He unfolded the old, yellowed paper carefully and read the head-line—"Nurse dies in accident on Peter's Mountain." He shook his head, folded the clipping and put it back. He locked the box and closed the drawer.

The intercom came to life again. "Doctor Marshall, I just got word from the OR," Julie said. "They had another cardiac arrest down there. It was Landry's case."

CHAPTER SEVENTEEN

Melissa Draybeck spun the dial hard on her combination lock. "Damn it!" she muttered to herself. Finally, on the third try, the lock yielded to her nervous fingers. She tugged her scrub top over her head.

"Hey, Melissa," Sue Hoffman said. "Heading out?"

Melissa startled from the question; she hadn't noticed Sue's approach. "Yeah, I'm going home," she replied. She thought her own voice sounded high and squeaky.

"Didn't mean to scare you, there," Sue said. "You OK? You look a little pale."

"Yeah, fine," Melissa said halfheartedly as she stripped off her pants. Sue was a comfortable work friend, and they occasionally socialized outside of the hospital. "You leaving?"

"Naw, I'm taking Bonnie's evening shift. I need the OT," Sue said, as she opened her locker several rows over. "I'm just getting some dinner money." She clanged her locker shut and turned to leave. "See ya."

"Take care." Suddenly, Melissa was struck by an idea and called to Sue excitedly, "Hey Sue, wait. You were there."

Sue stopped and turned, a puzzled look on her face. "What're you talking about?"

"I heard Landry's guy cased and all, but what went on?"

"Oh, that," Sue said. She took on a thoughtful expression. "Well, it was a little odd. He was a real big guy, not really fat, just big. Right after Doctor Landry intubated him, he went into V-tach out of the blue."

"Did Landry have trouble with the tube?" Melissa asked.

"No, didn't seem to."

Melissa ignored her clothes for the moment and just stood there in her underwear. She stared at Sue and asked, "Sue, did you notice anything funny when you set up the room?"

"No, what do you mean?"

"I don't know—anything weird or out of place?"

"No, I don't think so. What're you getting at?" Sue asked, frowning. She seemed to be tiring of the twenty questions.

"Oh, nothing, forget it." Melissa decided not to tell Sue what she had seen in OR#1. She knew it sounded odd—kinda crazy, seeing shadowy shapes and all. She didn't want to appear like a frightened child. And Sue had a pretty big mouth.

"The only thing I remember was that Landry was his usual cool self."

"Thank God it was him," Melissa said as she slid her jeans on.

"Can you imagine if Ayash or Raskin had been in there?" Sue remarked, shaking her head.

"Oh my God," Melissa said and pulled her ski sweater on. "That would have been a real mess."

"Yeah, I like it when Doctor Landry's in the room."

"We all know that, Sue." This was what irked her about Sue. Sue always had a soft spot for Dr. Landry.

"No, I mean you can relax about the anesthesia." Sue paused and added dreamily, "He does have a soothing voice, though. And his eyes—they're bedroom eyes, if I ever saw them."

"For crying out loud, girl—he's married with a bunch of kids." Melissa put on her boots.

"Yeah, but rumor is he's not so happily married," Sue said, her eyes twinkling.

"Oh, get off it. Doctor Landry's a real family man. He'd never run around."

"Well, not according to my friend, Liz, the respiratory therapist. She saw Landry getting pretty cozy with one of the nurses at a Case One."

"That's hard to believe," Melissa said, but couldn't stifle her curiosity. "Who was it anyway?" she asked, trying to sound nonchalant.

"Jenny Stuart."

"Who's that?"

"The new blond over in SICU." Sue stuck her chest way out and primped her hair for effect.

"Oh, that one." Melissa's heart sank.

"Remember Melissa, men think with their dicks," Sue added matter-of-factly.

"You're disgusting." Melissa grabbed her ski jacket and headed for the door.

Melissa walked out of the locker room and made for the elevators. She fumbled in her pocket for her keys and noticed her hands were still shaking badly. "God, I need a cigarette!" *Someone was probably in that room, and I should tell somebody.*

The elevator chimed, and she walked on and pressed "L." The elevator chimed again, the door whooshed open, and she emerged into the lobby. Although Melissa was usually comforted by the religious statues, especially the Virgin Mary, now they had little calming influence. She paused on her way out and stopped at the bank of pay phones in an alcove just off the main lobby. She glanced around. None of the phones were being used. Melissa searched in her pocket for some change. Abruptly she turned from the phones and took several steps away toward the exit. She stopped in mid-stride and wheeled about to return to the phones: her mind was made up. She would call Dr. Landry and tell him what she had seen. He would know what to do. He wouldn't make fun of her either.

She quickly glanced around again. The phones were still deserted.

"Oh shit," she said when she realized she didn't know his number. *This thing really has me spooked.* She quickly pulled out the dog-eared phonebook and started to look up Landry's number. *What if it's unlisted? What if he's not there? What if his wife answers?*

"Shut up," she commanded her bothersome mind. "Look, here it is." She put in her quarter and dialed the number, while preparing to speak. Melissa was so engrossed arguing with herself, that she barely noticed the man coming out of the lavatory just around the corner.

"Hi, this is Laura," came Laura Landry's happy voice over the line. "You've reached seven-six-three-two-one-two-eight. Doug and I can't come to the phone right now. At the beep, please leave a message and we'll get back to you. Thanks." BEEP

"Hi, uh—this is Melissa Draybeck. I'm calling for Dr. Landry . . ."

* * *

He walked as close as he dared, not wanting to appear suspicious. He had been watching Melissa closely all day. He was nervous about how much she had actually seen earlier. Now, she was behaving erratically—this worried him more. He needed to get close enough to hear some of her conversation, but he didn't want to frighten her, especially if she had recognized him earlier. He stopped at a nearby phone, turned his back to her, and hid behind the divider. There. He could just make out bits of her speech.

". . . Landry . . . need to . . . you . . . call . . . tonight . . . urgent . . . I talk . . ."

The man waited for Melissa to leave and quickly walked off in the opposite direction. He had heard enough. "Shit," he muttered to himself. "Trouble."

CHAPTER EIGHTEEN

He craned his neck to get a better look at the street sign he had just passed. "Where the hell is it!" he muttered in disgust. "Locust Lane—Shit! That's not it. Need Birch Street." He tromped the accelerator, and his Saab Turbo growled and leapt forward like a beast of prey. "Light's fading fast. Gonna be hard to see the fucking street signs." It was only 4:20, but being mid-December, the sun was sinking fast. "All these seedy neighborhoods with their duplexes, apartment complexes, and row homes look alike. How do they ever find their way around? Wait, there's one—Cherry Street—Shit!"

He was agitated and he knew it. *Damn bitch.* He slammed down his car phone. She was forcing him into action; he had to get to her before she talked to Landry. He'd planned to confront her directly, but had just called and found out she wasn't home. He thought for a moment, then smiled. Just getting into her apartment would freak her out. Perhaps this was better. He knew a thing or two about locks from his days in the service; he had some tools in the trunk. A threatening note would do the

trick. Maybe a good ransacking was in order? He'd figure it out
when he got there. He cranked up the car's heater a notch; he
couldn't seem to get warm.

He went over what he knew about her again, looking for some
angle of attack, some leverage. She was in her mid-forties, never
married, and lived alone. Unfortunately, that was about all he knew.
Whenever he thought of her, the only image that came to mind was
her standing outside the hospital back entrance, huddled and shivering in a corner with the other die-hard smokers, braving any degree
of winter's severity to light up. He shook his head. Some people just
had no self-discipline. He jammed on the brake to slow down; he
almost missed the next street sign—Oak Street. Damn tree lovers.
He ignored the stop sign and roared down the road.

She seemed to have a thing for Landry, but then so did half of
the OR nurses. Goddamned playboy. He'd heard the scuttlebutt—
Landry getting it on with that new SICU bitch. Whatever happened
to family values? Landry had a slew of kids for Chrissakes. No
morals. That was what was wrong with this hippie generation—
free love and all that crap. Landry deserved what he got; in fact, he
wasn't through with him yet. He felt himself getting heated up. This
was good. It would make it easier to carry out his plan.

The sun sank below the horizon, and the sky took on an eerie
luminescence peculiar to cold December evenings. The few clouds
on the western horizon were strongly backlit, appearing dark purple, almost black, against the pinkish sky glow. The clouds stood
out sharply, as if cut by a knife. The wind howled outside the car,
as if it too were bothered by the unnatural appearance of the sky.

"Birch Street! About fucking time!" He jerked the wheel hard,
and the Saab squealed around the turn. Up ahead was the sign for
Tree View Terrace Apartments. He quickly parked on the street,
barking his front tire on the curb. As he opened the driver's door,
the wind threatened to rip it from its hinges. Climbing out onto
the frozen ground, the cold, slashing air took his breath away and
was truly bitter. He searched a bit before finding Apartment IIA.

Her name was printed in bold, black letters on the buzzer/mailbox arrangement—DRAYBECK, M.

He pushed on the buzzer, heard it ring inside, and waited. Nothing. He pushed it again. Still nothing. Luckily, as he had hoped, the lock was one of those cheap jobs that matched the flimsy metal door. He pulled out his toolkit and picked it with ease.

He stepped into the narrow hallway, which posed as a foyer and was immediately struck by the stale cigarette odor that hung heavily in the air. He closed the door behind him and locked it, interrupting the wind in mid-howl. He froze; he heard a television in the living room with a newscaster droning out the early edition of the evening news. *Oh shit.* He had thought she was out. What should he do?

"Hello," he called out. "Anybody home?"

No answer.

"The front door was open," he said, "so I let myself in." He glanced down the hallway again—there was a single overhead light fixture, and an opening to the kitchen, five feet down on the left. The hallway emptied out in ten feet into what appeared to be the living room. No windows in sight.

He walked quietly toward the living room. As he passed the empty kitchen, he smelled something cooking, probably from the meatloaf family, he guessed. He continued forward, the TV getting louder as he went.

The living room was also deserted. The room was poorly lit by a single lamp on a little table; he couldn't tell if the bulb was just inadequate or if his vision was hampered by the smoky haze. The remaining furniture consisted of a small sofa and one sitting chair and a portable TV resting on a metal cart with wheels. One window at the far end of the room overlooked the parking lot. He saw a framed photograph of Melissa on top of the TV and walked over to it. She was a plain woman with long, straight brown hair. The photo was close enough to show she had a generous supply of wrinkles, no doubt courtesy of her beloved cigarettes. They made her look much older, he thought. He could see another hallway, presumably leading to the bedroom, but the door was shut.

He called out again. "Hello, Ms. Draybeck. Are you here?"

No reply.

He headed toward the bedroom. He passed a little bathroom that was also empty. His heart began to pound. Was she here? Why didn't she answer? Maybe this wasn't such a good plan? Maybe he should leave? He opened the bedroom door. A loud hissing noise stopped him in his tracks, and his heart banged painfully in his chest. A large tiger tomcat squirted out of the room bumping his leg on the way by.

"Jesus Christ!" He sucked in some big breaths, clutched his chest, and leaned on the doorway. Thank God, the bedroom was empty. She must've stepped out for something, but she'll be back soon. Need to hurry. The fucking cat gave him an idea, and he smiled. "Here, kitty, kitty."

* * *

Melissa came through the front door carrying her milk, bread, and *People* magazine. *God, it's cold out there.* As soon as she closed the door, she thought she could detect an unfamiliar odor. Strange, she thought. Perhaps the meatloaf is burning? She walked into the kitchen, set her grocery bag down on the table, and slung her coat over one of the kitchen chairs. She opened the oven and checked the meatloaf. Everything was OK. Where was Tony? she wondered. Normally he'd be all over her at this time of the day, impatient for his dinner. "Tony," she called. "Mommy's home. Want some din-din?"

She opened the pantry, pulled out some Meow Mix, and poured it into his plastic bowl. The cat food clattered distinctively, and she knew it was a sound Tony couldn't ignore even if he was playing aloof.

Still no Tony. This was definitely strange. She walked into the living room. The five o'clock Pennsylvania lottery drawing was on the TV, but no sign of the cat. Again, she caught a whiff of some unfamiliar scent. Immediately her anxiety skyrocketed and threatened to overwhelm her. She tried to calm down, telling herself her nerves were just shot today. A cigarette was in order, she quickly decided. Melissa backtracked to the kitchen. She lit up despite her shaky hands and inhaled deeply. Ah, that was better. She saw the phone on the wall. Perhaps she should call Dr. Landry now? No, she had to find Tony first. This was too weird.

She headed toward the bedroom. She thought she could make out Tony's shape on her bed, but the room was dark; maybe it was just a trick of the shadows or some clothes. She entered the room and flicked on the light switch by the closet.

There was Tony on the bed all right, but his head was bent back in an unnatural angle and some drapery cord was wrapped tightly around his neck. His tongue stuck out grotesquely, his eyes bugged out, and he was motionless. Melissa stood there shaking violently from head to toe and screamed.

Before she got much more than a peep out, she felt a gloved hand clamp over her mouth and nose and a large arm encircle her neck. She panicked, screaming all the louder. She managed to get several muffled bursts out.

"Stop screaming for Chrissakes!" he yelled at her.

The voice was familiar. She felt herself being propelled to the wall by his massive body. Suddenly her head was accelerated and collided savagely with the wall. She actually heard her skull make a horrible cracking sound when it hit, like a baseball bat smacking a line drive.

She didn't lose consciousness completely. She flopped to the floor and felt her attacker straddle her and begin to throttle her with both hands. She stared up at him but the image was blurry. Her brain reeled to grasp what was happening.

Finally her eyes focused, and she recognized Dr. Raskin, his face contorted with exertion and suffused with blood. Things clicked into place. He had been the shadowy figure in OR#1, no doubt doing something terrible. He had killed Tony, and now she was next. She must free herself and tell Dr. Landry. She clawed at him with her hands but could inflict little damage through his winter parka. She saw that Tony had scored several deep scratches across his cheek. Her air hunger was becoming unbearable.

* * *

Raskin watched as her eyes bulged out first, then her lips became increasingly cyanotic, then her struggling dwindled and ceased and her pupils dilated. It all took less than five minutes.

Raskin slumped over her body, sucking in ragged breaths. He felt sick. He hadn't meant for it to turn out this way. He had just wanted to scare her. Now this. He looked at her face, mottled and blue in death, and felt another wave of nausea.

It wasn't his fault, though. She had to come home when she did. He had just about finished his work. And then she had to scream. Jesus, why did women always scream? He couldn't let her do that. Anyone could see that.

He stood up and staggered to the living room on stiff legs. His hands still ached, but his breathing had evened somewhat. Damn nuns! Damn Carlucci! It was all their fault. That fat Polish bastard wasn't supposed to die either. Could he help it if Carlucci screwed up the resuscitation? Even the great Dr. Landry himself couldn't pull that one out of his ass. He knew he had done a better job with Danowski and his patient; monkeying with the vaporizers—now that was clever.

Raskin reached a gloved hand to his face. "Ow!" The glove came away bloody. "Fucking cat!" He looked around the apartment to make sure he hadn't left anything. The nausea had left him.

The phone rang and Raskin jumped. After four rings, Melissa's answering machine clicked on loudly. "Hi, this is Melissa. I can't come to the phone right now—"

"Ain't that the truth," Raskin murmured.

"—I'll get back to you as soon as I can—"

"Don't hold your breath, asshole." He began to cackle. For a moment, Raskin wondered about his sanity. He had just killed somebody, by accident of course, but nonetheless she was dead, and here he was laughing. His thoughts were cut short, however, as he recognized the voice coming through.

"Hi, Melissa, this is Doctor Landry. I'm returning your call. Uh, you said it was urgent. Please give me a call whenever you get in tonight. Otherwise, I'll talk to you tomorrow at the hospital. OK, bye."

"Sakes alive! Douglas fucking Landry!" God, that guy really burns me up. "Too bad you'll never know what she wanted," he said to the phone as he prepared to leave. "Better get the fuck out of here!"

CHAPTER NINETEEN

"Two V-tachs in one week! That's pretty unusual isn't it?" Rusty asked and then stuffed the remains of a poppy seed bagel into his mouth. He paced back and forth in the confines of the small anesthesia on-call room, his sneakers squeaking noisily.

"Absolutely," replied Doug, who was sitting on the sofa also working on a bagel. "I've been here twelve years, and I can't recall ten episodes." It was Tuesday morning, and Doug still felt drained from his on-call weekend and ordeal with Mr. Lehman yesterday. He gulped down most of his second cup of coffee, hoping the caffeine would kick in soon.

Mike appeared at the doorway with his own cup of coffee. He hesitated briefly and entered the room. "Morning, Doug," he said sheepishly. "Hi, Rusty."

"Hi, Mike. How are you?" Doug asked. He was still torn up about his friend's drug use, and their confrontation Friday remained fresh in his mind.

"Fine," Mike replied and walked over to his desk. He didn't look so fine; he looked as if he hadn't slept in days. Mike picked up a framed picture of Colleen and the girls and gazed at it with a pained expression. Doug studied Mike looking for subtle clues. Is he still using? Nobody said anything further, and the silence became awkward, interrupted only by the sound of Rusty's sneakers.

Suddenly, Rusty stopped in his tracks, his face brightening. "There're bagels in the front office, Dr. Carlucci," Rusty said. "The Pfizer drug rep is pushing Zemuron. Do you want me to get you one?"

"No thanks, Rusty," Mike said. "I'll get one myself in a minute."

Rusty looked disappointed and continued pacing. Mike sat down at his desk, began sipping his coffee and playing with the styrofoam cup.

Doug debated whether to continue the V-tach conversation now that Mike was here; he knew it would be a sensitive subject. He decided it would probably be okay; it might even make Mike feel better. Besides, in the past, the two had always loved to exchange war stories. "You should've been here yesterday, Mike," Doug said. He knew Mike had been off-call Monday and had the day off.

"Why?" Mike asked. He continued to decorate his coffee cup in earnest with fingernail carvings.

"You, too, Rusty."

"We had a visiting professor," Rusty said quickly, "and I had to stay at the med center to hear his boring lecture." With genuine disappointment he added, "What'd I miss?"

Before Doug could answer, Mike looked up and said, "I heard the nurses talking about it in my room this morning. What happened, Doug?"

"Well, not much to tell," said Doug. "Really strange. I induced the guy, intubated him, and boom, his pressure went sky high. Next thing I knew, I had V-tach."

"That sounds just like Dr. Carlucci's case," Rusty said excitedly. He pulled a second bagel out of his scrub jacket pocket and also produced a mini-container of cream cheese and a plastic knife.

"Yeah, I know," said Doug. "I was there. Pretty weird, huh?"

Mike stopped playing with his coffee cup all of a sudden and became rigid in his seat. "Doug, did you have fib?" he asked.

"No, I was lucky," Doug said. "I got the pressure down and shocked him out of V-tach before it got bad. He's still in the SICU."

Mike looked lost in thought.

Rusty said, "What d'ya make of it, Doctor Landry—"

"It's Doug, Rusty."

"OK. The cases being so similar and all?"

"I don't know," Doug said. "Bizarre coincidence, I guess." Doug didn't really think much of the experience. Twelve years in the OR had taught him to be a frank pragmatist. He was a firm believer in the expression that had been drilled into him as a resident: "When you hear hoofbeats, don't think zebras." Perfectly logical explanations abounded for the mishaps. Perhaps he had gotten a little sloppy with his induction. He knew intubation itself was a very powerful stimulation. If the patient isn't deep enough prior to intubation, a large sympathetic outflow may be triggered and send the pressure very high. He'd seen it before. Although he had to admit, he'd never seen it progress to V-tach, but he figured that was just bad luck.

"Doug, did you hear about Ken's case?" Mike asked impatiently, sounding almost agitated. He met Doug's stare for the first time.

"I heard he had an awareness case last week—"

"Yeah," Mike interrupted, "the lady, Mrs. Lubriani, remembered half of her surgery. Her lawyer's going through her medical record now."

"That's too bad."

"Too bad? Is that all you can say?" Mike was glaring at him. "Ken feels like shit—did you talk to him?"

"No, I haven't run into him yet. Why, what's up?"

"He thinks somebody tampered with his machine beforehand." Mike was on his feet, his voice becoming shrill. "There was Suprane in the Forane vaporizer!"

"Get out of here. How did he know that?" Doug asked incredulously.

"He smelled it."

"He's probably just mixed up," Doug said. "They don't smell all that different, Mike." Rusty had stopped eating his bagel and was following the conversation intently.

"No, really Doug. He drained the vaporizer after the case and had it analyzed by the lab with their mass spec. It was Suprane all right."

"The techs probably got mixed up and filled the wrong vaporizer." Doug chugged the remainder of his lukewarm coffee. He felt more tired now than when he had come in.

"Doug, you're the one who's mixed up!" Mike said heatedly. "You know how hard that would be to do. Ken thinks someone did it deliberately."

"What!? Is Ken here today?" Doug was on his feet, heading for the door. "I'll go talk to him right now." He passed close by Mike on his way out.

"Doug, wait." Mike reached out and put a hand on Doug's shoulder. "He's not here. He took the day off—he's still kinda shaken up by the whole awareness thing."

Doug stopped, turned and said quietly, "Hmmm, seems like a lot of people are getting shaken up around here, Mike." Doug met Mike's eyes, but Mike quickly dropped his gaze.

"Doug, what if somebody did sabotage his machine?" Mike lifted his head slowly and met Doug's stare. "Maybe there's a connection with *our* cases."

Doug saw the sincere, almost pleading look in his friend's eyes, and for a moment, as if a door had opened and slammed shut, he caught a glimpse of the enormity of Mike's anguish, his private living hell. Doug shuddered. Unfortunately, he also saw enough to convince him of Mike's continued narcotic usage.

"Yeah, Doctor Landry, uh, Doug—maybe someone messed with your syringes—I saw it in a movie once," Rusty said eagerly.

"Sounds pretty far fetched," said Doug, shaking his head. He believed Mike was clutching at straws, looking for any excuse to exonerate him from Rakovic's death, and thereby put an end to his torture.

Before Doug could leave, Bryan Marshall entered the room. He didn't look too happy. He cleared his throat, looked directly at Doug and said, "I need to talk to you two, alone." He nodded toward Mike. Wonderful, thought Doug. What could he want now?

Marshall shot a glance at Rusty that said, "Get out."

Rusty headed for the door, mumbling, "I was just leaving."

Strangely enough, Marshall continued to stare at Rusty while he made his way out of the room. It looked like he almost did a double take when Rusty walked by him. Doug thought, what in the world was that about?

Marshall continued, however, without missing a beat. "I just finished getting reamed out in Sister's office. What the hell is going on down here?" Marshall's face was characteristic beet red and his eyes bored into Doug. "First, Carlucci's patient dies."

Out of the corner of his eye, Doug saw Mike wince and look at the floor.

"And yesterday," Marshall went on, "I hear your patient almost bought it. What the hell is going on?" He paused to catch his breath, and the redness in his face eased up a bit.

"Look, Bryan," Doug answered sharply. "This is an operating room. Shit happens. We work on older and sicker people every day." He knew it was never a good idea to argue with Marshall, but couldn't help it. He had been stung by Marshall's callous treatment of Mike and also felt a certain amount of guilt about his own case.

The redness flooded back into Marshall's face with a vengeance and darkened to an ugly purple. Neck and temple veins bulged dangerously. Undoubtedly, he hadn't expected any back talk. "Don't you guys get it!?" Marshall screamed. "The timing couldn't be worse. Pinnacle is breathing down our necks. We can't afford any screw-ups now!" He pounded on the desk as he said this, and Doug's empty coffee cup toppled over.

Doug picked up the cup slowly, trying to get a handle on his own emotions. He was determined not to get into a shouting match. "Nobody screwed up, Bryan," he said as evenly as he could manage. "It could've happened to anyone." He paused to glare at Marshall. "These patients had bad hearts—ticking time bombs just waiting to go off."

"Don't give me that crap, Landry!" Marshall fired back. For an instant, a slight grin appeared, but just as quickly it was gone. "I suppose you're gonna tell me the lady who was cut open awake had a bad heart too!"

This caught Doug by surprise; he had no answer and felt his face start to burn. He'd definitely have to talk to Ken. He looked at Mike, but he was busy studying his Nikes. He looked back at Marshall. If he didn't know better, he'd swear Marshall was enjoying this scene. *Bastard.* However, Marshall's smug smile soon gave way to a troubled expression.

"You'll have to deal with this someday when you're chief," Marshall said and eyed him curiously.

"Yeah, I guess so." It was Doug's turn to smile. He knew Marshall was always paranoid about other people assuming the chief-ship. He worried particularly that Doug's main ambition in life was to replace him as chief. Nothing could be further from the truth, but it felt good to play into Marshall's fear at this moment.

"My break's over," said Doug, glancing at his watch. "I gotta get back." He gave Mike a nod that said, "See you." Marshall looked like he wasn't quite finished, but Doug pushed by him.

"Remember, Landry. No more fuck-ups!" Marshall shouted at his back.

Doug headed down the corridor and out of the OR complex. He actually had ten minutes left on his lunch break, so he took the elevator up to the twelfth floor. Here at the top of the hospital was a spacious patient solarium with huge plate glass windows on three walls, overlooking the Susquehanna Valley. The room was empty. Doug came here from time to time to collect his thoughts. He rested one foot on a low magazine table and took in the view.

The winter sun shone painfully bright, and high wispy clouds floated in light blue. He could see the Susquehanna River, half sheathed in ice, as it sparkled and wound around like a giant serpent through the Appalachian mountains. The city and surrounding communities were all abuzz with activity, reminding him of his miniature train layout he had loved as a boy.

A lot of things swirled through Doug's mind, and he needed some time to be alone and think. Unfortunately, the nature of his work did not allow this; the next case to do, the next dire emergency, the next on-call night was always right around the corner. Everything moved so fast. Time to think, like in the old days, was a luxury.

He wasn't ready to buy into Mike and Rusty's imaginative sabotage theory. He had real concerns like Laura, and what to do about Mike's drug use. And what the hell was eating Marshall?

He also couldn't get Jenny out of his mind. *Should I really meet her this weekend?* He couldn't deny the chemistry between them. Wait—no—chemistry was the wrong word. Too cold, analytical, pertaining to beakers and Erlenmeyer flasks. Rusting iron was chemistry. He needed some term to convey the heat, the incendiary intensity, the out of control nature of his feelings. Napalm. Now that was better. Napalm was dangerous. It was likely to scorch everything in sight—sometimes more than was intended.

What would it be like to hold her in his arms, caress her silky blond hair, kiss her willing mouth, bury his face in the warm softness of her breasts? He could see himself slowly undressing her in some room where sunlight streamed through partially closed blinds. Her tanned skin, so smooth and tight, shimmered almost iridescent in the shafts of light. His senses were all sharpened, heightened. The tiny blond hairs on the nape of her neck were clearly visible against her golden skin. He breathed in her natural scent, which blended deliciously with her light perfume. He felt her hungry hands on him and her warm breath tickled his ears. The scene was intoxicating to him as he stared off into space.

He also hated himself for it. He couldn't help thinking about Laura and the kids. The soft fuzzy scene dissolved. In high-contrast black and white was his wife of twenty years looking at him with tears streaming down her determined face. She fixed him with an expression of such hurt and betrayal, that he squirmed like a bug under a boy's magnifying glass on a sunny day. His three kids were there with bewildered looks on their innocent faces. *Can I actually do this to them? Is it worth risking the marriage?*

He stopped short. This line of questioning sounded awfully familiar to him; it was just like what he had said to Mike on Friday in the locker room. "What about Colleen and the kids?" He had ridden his high horse so much with Mike that his butt hurt. Was adultery any better than taking drugs?

Then the damage control part of his mind kicked in: Adultery? Whoa pardner. Who said anything about adultery? We're just gonna meet for drinks. No biggee. "Yeah, right, dad—su-ure," he could hear his seven-year-old son say.

The problem with Mike also continued to haunt him. *Should I turn him in?* He had the letter in his briefcase. All he needed to do was mail it and Mike's career, not to mention their friendship, would be finished, but he felt his real obligation was to the unsuspecting patients. He couldn't knowingly subject them to Mike. Yeah, that's right—true blue Doug Landry here, alias Mr. Morals.

But something else even worse gnawed at the foundations of his mind—a large developing sinkhole that threatened to swallow him up whole. Maybe Marshall was right. Maybe he did screw-up in the OR yesterday because of his preoccupation with Jenny, Mike, and Laura. He had always been extremely careful to separate his personal problems from his professional conduct. Anesthesia demanded vigilance if nothing else, a single-minded focus. He likened it to a laser cutting through the morass of insignificant data, false positives, and boring redundancies, to bring to light the essential facts upon which someone's life rested. Jenny had blurred his mind; Mike had robbed his laser of its coherence. He, himself was impaired. *Am I just as dangerous as Mike? Maybe I should remove myself from the OR, too?*

The hospital overhead paging system crackled to life, inter-rupting his thoughts. "Doctor Landry, two-four-oh-oh. Doctor Douglas Landry, two-four-oh-oh."

He knew he had been gone too long, and the OR was looking for him. Back to work. God, what a mess!

As he picked up the phone, he suddenly recalled Melissa's message on his answering machine. She had said it was urgent. He punched in 2400.

"Operating room."

"Hi, this is Doctor Landry—I'll be there in a minute."

"Doctor Goldsmith's waiting. We couldn't find you, and he's getting upset."

"Yeah, yeah. I said I'd be right there." Always in such a god-damned hurry. "Oh, which room is Melissa Draybeck in today?"

"Hold on, let me check." He heard muffled talk in the back-ground. "She didn't show up for work today," came the reply.

"You mean called off sick?"

"Well, not exactly. She just didn't show up."

"Hmmm—thanks." What the hell does that mean?

CHAPTER TWENTY

"Sorry, it took me so long, Doctor Carlucci," Rusty said. "I had to make an important phone call."

Mike studied him for a second. Rusty was grinning as usual, and his red hair stuck out around his ears in contrast to his blue surgical cap. He looked excited about something. "I still took a couple of wrong turns on the way back, though," he said.

"No problem, Rusty," Mike said. He liked Rusty; he helped take his mind off his own problems. "Look, maybe I can help you with the layout. Basically, the OR complex is arranged in a cross shape. Here, I'll show you." He drew a diagram on his scrub pants. "The control office, where we are now, is the nerve center of the department. It's here at the center of the cross." He pointed to the appropriate place on his pants. "The anesthesia on-call room, where we had out little discussion over bagels this morning, is at one end. The recovery room is at the other end. The OR's are here." He slid his finger down the long part of the cross.

"Thanks," said Rusty. "That helps."

"Here, have a seat." Mike gestured to one of the other four chairs in the room. "I just started reviewing our next patient's chart. He's the one sawing wood out there." They both paused to listen. Loud snoring could easily be heard coming from the holding area across the hall.

"Yeah, I noticed him on the way in," Rusty said. "He must've had some good pre-op medication. What was it?"

"Midazolam."

Rusty reached for one of his pocket pharmacology handbooks and started to page through it. "What kind of drug is it?"

"Midazolam is in a class of potent tranquilizer, anxiolytic drugs in the benzodiazepine family of Valium fame."

"Geez, I guess I don't need this," Rusty said and put the book back. "You're a walking encyclopedia."

"Wake him up and ask him how sleepy he is."

A bewildered look appeared on Rusty's face that Mike found amusing.

"OK, you're the boss," Rusty said and dutifully got up and walked out. Moments later he returned smiling. "It's weird." Rusty leaned his tall frame against the doorway. "The patient says he's relaxed, but not sleepy. Then he closed his eyes and started snoring again."

"That's exactly what I wanted you to see," Mike said. Midazolam is incredibly insidious in its effect. Many patients deny feeling any effect whatsoever, even though they are obviously impaired—slurred speech, loss of short term memory, and marked drowsiness."

"That's pretty cool."

Mike frowned. "It's also dangerous in the wrong hands." Mike lowered his voice. "Maybe you've heard of "Easy-Lay?" It's a date-rape drug with a chemical structure similar to Midazolam."

"Oh," Rusty said, erasing his smile. He hesitated for a moment and asked, "What's up with Doctor Landry today?"

"What do you mean?" Mike replied and went back to studying his patient's EKG.

"He seemed kinda upset." Rusty shuffled his sneakers on the floor and looked at them intently. "I just saw him in the locker room getting ready to leave. It's only four o'clock. Why is he going home so early?"

"He's pre-call," Mike answered. "He's on call tomorrow."

"Oh—didn't you think he was upset?" Rusty asked, looking up directly at Mike.

Mike was surprised that Rusty had picked up on the tension between them this morning. Although, on second thought, maybe it wasn't that hard. "He must have his reasons." Mike quickly broke eye contact and resumed reading his patient's chart. He hoped Rusty would let it drop.

"Don't you know?" Rusty pressed. "I thought you guys were buddies."

Mike paused from reading the lab values, sighed, and met Rusty's gaze. His initial irritation quickly subsided when he saw that Rusty's concern was sincere; Rusty wasn't just being a meddlesome, pain-in-the-butt kid. A rare quality in a med student. He decided to answer him. "I'm not so sure—"

A loud, electronic screech, followed by the blaring of the OR-wide intercom interrupted him. "Anesthesia! STAT! PACU!"

"Let's go Rusty!" Mike said, jumping to his feet. He felt his heart slam into action; STAT pages always had that affect.

"PACU? What's that?" Rusty asked, his body visibly tensing.

"Follow me," said Mike, breaking into a run. "It's the recovery room—post anesthesia care unit or some bullshit like that."

"Oh."

STAT pages to the recovery room were rare. The recovery room nurses at Mercy were generally experienced, so when STAT calls were made, they tended to be legitimate. Mike was slightly out of breath when the pair got there. He noticed Rusty was breathing fine.

The PACU was a large narrow room with twelve bays, complete with monitors and oxygen setups, for surgical patients to shake off the effects of general or spinal anesthesia. "Bay" was a nice term for a space on the floor to park the litter. There were no cubicles or walls. Slidable partitioning curtains hung from the ceiling giving one the illusion of privacy, but these were used only to hide the prison patients and their shotgun-toting guards from the public.

"Doctor Carlucci!" yelled a stocky fireplug of a woman, identified by her nameplate as Peg Vargas, R.N. She was clearly upset. "My patient's having a hard time catching his breath—it's getting worse!" She quickly motioned them over to the struggling man's litter.

Peg Vargas had over fifteen years experience in the recovery room. Perhaps because of this, she felt entitled to be brusque, although Mike would've called it rude. He got along well with most of the recovery room nurses, but Peg Vargas wasn't one of them. Interestingly, Mike watched her calm down right before his eyes. She had just fulfilled her primary nursing responsibility and had summoned help. Now it was out of her hands and up to the doctor to do something. She could relax and play her favorite game of armchair anesthesiologist.

"Who is he?" asked Mike, as he scanned the patient and his monitors. Most troubling was the pulse oximeter reading of 82%. Rusty looked back and forth between the patient, Mike, and the nurse. His eyes were wide, and his hands twitched about. Mike gave Rusty credit for appreciating the gravity of the situation.

"Mr. Tompkins, seventy-five," Peg answered sharply. "He had a radical prostatectomy. Dr. Marshall brought him in about half an hour ago." She was no longer flustered at all.

"How long has his sat been in the 80s?" Mike fired back, stalling to get his bearings. Oxygen saturations below 90% were considered dangerous. The patient was obviously struggling to breathe, and Mike knew he'd have to do something quickly. Oddly, he reflected that he was the only one who truly felt the pressure of the situation. Although Rusty most likely realized how serious it was, they all expected Mike to know what to do. Just once, he thought, he'd like to see Peg Vargas in his position; see her snooty, know-it-all facade crumble in a panic.

"It's been falling just in the last couple of minutes—that's why I called," Peg said somewhat defensively.

"He was OK when he came in?" Mike asked. Jesus, he looks dusky.

"Yeah, he seemed fine." Peg had no trouble returning his glare.

Mike wondered how he went from fine to respiratory distress in minutes. He doubted she had kept a close enough eye on him, but now wasn't the time to cast aspersions. "Put him on a hundred percent rebreather," he ordered.

She just stood there for a moment, looking at him. Was she questioning his judgement? Or perhaps she didn't trust him after Mr. Rakovic's death in the OR. He knew they all talked about how he had cracked under the pressure behind his back. "I'll have to get it," she finally said and wheeled from the bedside.

"What do you think's wrong with him, Dr. Carlucci?"

Mike put up his hand to shush Rusty. "Hang on Rusty."

Mike knew he didn't have the luxury of time to expound upon medical diagnostic theory at the moment; the situation demanded immediate action. He was acutely aware that he didn't have a working diagnosis yet. He turned to the patient. "Mr. Tompkins, how's your breathing?"

"Not—so—good," the patient managed to get out, in a cross between a whisper and a gasp.

Good question, Mike. Now that we got that clear, can we move on to make a diagnosis? Mr. Tompkins was sitting bolt upright on his litter and laboring mightily to breathe. He was a tall, gaunt man with white, patchy stubble adorning his hollow cheeks. Mike whipped out his stethoscope and listened to his chest. He didn't hear much air moving. The oxygen sat had fallen to 80%.

"C'mon Peg! I need that mask!" Mike shouted in the direction she had headed. He was oh-so-thankful he had dosed up this morning. The Fentanyl was the only thing standing between himself and decompensation. *Be cool. Gotta think.* God knew he couldn't handle another catastrophe.

"Rusty, hear that noise?" Mike asked. Mr. Tompkins was making a faint squeaking noise as he struggled to suck air in; breathing out seemed to be OK.

Rusty leaned in close to the patient, and a puzzled look came over him. "Yeah," he said unconvincingly.

"It's all upper airway—the chest is clear," Mike said as much to himself as anybody. He needed to make a diagnosis—his patient was heading south quickly. The scene was horribly reminiscent of Mr. Rakovic's case. *Please, no V-tach.* He shot an accusatory glance at the EKG monitor. It was OK for now, but he knew time was running out.

"Do you need a chest x-ray?" Rusty asked, interrupting his thoughts.

"No time."

"Are you going to intubate him?" Rusty asked excitedly.

"Not sure yet."

The sat monitor beeped loudly as the alarms announced the sat had dipped below 80%. It continued to fall: 79, 78, 77.

"Here, hook up that Ambu bag to the oxygen," Mike said. He handed a long green tube to Rusty and motioned to an oxygen nipple outlet on the wall. He turned to the patient and said, "I'm going to help you breathe, Mr. Tompkins."

Mike grasped Mr. Tompkins's bony shoulders and pulled him back down to the bed. 76, 75, 74.

"I . . . can't . . . breathe . . . Need . . . to . . . sit . . . up."

Mr. Tompkins tried feebly to get up, but Mike held him down. He began to manually assist Mr. Tompkins's breathing with the Ambu bag. It was difficult to get a good mask seal on his face; his lips caved in because he had no teeth, and his skin was oily. 73, 72, 71.

Mike knew it wasn't pleasant to have someone force air into your lungs, but it beats suffocation. "Relax and don't fight me," Mike said. "Everything's going to be all right." A faraway corner of his brain registered that this last expression was generally reserved for when things were far from all right. "Rusty, go get some intubation stuff—tube, laryngoscope—hurry!" Mike said without looking up. He saw some fog in the mask and knew he was getting some air in, but it didn't seem like enough. *Shit! Running out of time!*

Just then, Peg came back with the rebreather mask. She stared at the sat monitor a little too long, as if to say: "What did you do to my patient?"

"Never mind the mask now!" Mike barked at her. "We're beyond that." He concentrated all his effort on mask ventilating the old man.

"What's wrong with him?" Peg demanded. "Can't you do something?"

He stopped ventilating for a second to glare at her. "Can't you see I'm trying." He had trouble thinking with her badgering him.

70, 69, 68.

Mr. Tompkins began to thrash about. His face continued to turn deepening shades of blue. Mike felt bad for the man and tried to reassure him. "You're going to be fine, Mr. Tompkins. You're going to be just fine." But again, he couldn't help thinking: hospital lingo for you're in deep shit.

Even with Mike's skilled hand on the Ambu bag, the oximeter continued to plummet. Mike saw the horror of airway hunger, one of the most dreadful of all human sensations, grip Mr. Tompkins. Panic glazed his eyes, and his thrashing intensified.

64, 63, 62.

The pulse ox continued to make its horrible, low-pitched beeps. If he had a free hand, he'd turn the damned thing off. Peg just stood there staring at him. "Peg, turn the alarm off!" Where was Rusty? What was taking him so long? Mike could almost feel Mr. Tompkins's life slipping away between his fingers. He glanced again at the EKG monitor. The rhythm had begun to become irregular. *Oh shit! Not again!*

"Do something!" Peg shouted at him.

Suddenly a bit of inspiration flashed through his mind. "Get respiratory here STAT with a racemic epi treatment!" Mike had made his diagnosis; he only prayed it was right and not too late.

Peg flung the mask down and headed for the phone.

Just then, Rusty ran back up to the bedside, breathing hard now, his hands full of intubation equipment. He looked scared to death as he fumbled with the laryngoscope and tube, trying to get them ready. The heavy metal laryngoscope fell on the floor making a loud racket. Before he could do or say anything further, Mike held up his finger. "Wait, Rusty. I have an idea."

Moments later, the respiratory therapist, a heavyset man in his twenties, waltzed in, seemingly without a care in the world and asked, "Is this the patient who needs the breathing treatment?"

"Yes, it is!" Mike shouted. Bonehead! How many other patients do you see here being bagged with a sat in the 60s? "Hurry and hook it up, please," Mike said, barely controlling his fury.

"How much epi?" said the therapist, unfazed.

"Point three cc's in three cc's normal saline!" Mike thought it was an asinine question because the adult dose was always the same. "Hurry, damn it!" Mike roared. "Can't you see he's dying!"

"No need to yell." The therapist methodically hooked up the nebulizer. Steam hissed out from the mask in a large plume. He strapped it tightly to Mr. Tompkins' face.

After several minutes of breathing the racemic epinephrine, the result was almost miraculous. Mr. Tompkins's breathing eased dramatically, and his O2 sat climbed into the 90s.

God, that was close. Mike allowed himself a couple of deep breaths as well. "How's that, Mr. Tompkins?" he asked.

"Better. Thank you," said Mr. Tompkins in a relieved voice.

"Feel better now, doc?" the respiratory therapist said and smirked. He packed up his bag and left the room shaking his head and muttering, "Dying—yeah right."

"Hey, I don't hear that noise anymore," Rusty said.

"Yeah. That was inspiratory stridor," said Mike. "We were dealing with a partial laryngospasm, but I'm not really clear why yet."

"What's rasimic epi?" Rusty asked.

"Racemic epi. It shrinks down swollen laryngeal structures allowing him to breathe easier. I think we saved him from being re-intubated and spending the night on a blower." *And saved me from another man's death.*

Peg Vargas returned to the bedside and shot Mike a "You-got-lucky-this-time" glare and moved on down the line to tend to more pressing matters.

CHAPTER TWENTY-ONE

"Wow, that was some fancy piece of diagnosis back there," Rusty said and meant it; he was not engaging in any med student/attending brown-nosing. They were back in the anesthesia control office taking a breather while waiting for the next case to go. He flipped the top on his Pepsi and took a long swig. He admired Dr. Carlucci's quick thinking; he wondered if he would ever have the skill and nerve to deal with similar situations. "How exactly does that epinephrine work?" Rusty asked. "I've never heard of it."

Dr. Carlucci smiled and took a large gulp of his Coke. "Epinephrine is another name for adrenaline. It's a powerful vasoconstrictor."

Dr. Carlucci continued to smile, and Rusty realized he hadn't seen him this happy since he'd met him. "What's the racemic mean?"

"That's an organic chemistry term. Surely, you remember your O-chem, Rusty. You're a lot closer to it than I am."

"Well . . ." Rusty felt himself blush. Here we go again.

"It refers to a compound that's optically active," said Dr. Carlucci.

"Huh?" What the hell does that mean?"

"Actually, it means a fifty-fifty mixture of two mirror image molecules." Dr. Carlucci put his hands together fingertip to fingertip to demonstrate. "You know, it's like a spider doing push-ups on a mirror," he said and laughed as his hands pumped up and down.

"What's the point?" Rusty asked, baffled.

"In the body, epinephrine is produced by the adrenal gland. Only the levo-isomer, or left-hand molecule, is actually made. The dextro-isomer, or right-hand molecule, isn't made because it's physiologically inert. A racemic mixture contains 50% L-isomer and 50% D-isomer."

Rusty struggled to follow the explanation. "But you said the D-isomer is inactive as far as the body's concerned, so why put it in the mix?"

"Good question. When the compound is synthesized in the laboratory, both forms are produced in equal quantity owing to some physical chemistry property that I really don't remember. It would be very expensive to extract the L-isomer, since chemically the two molecules function identically. Only in a complex biological system, such as an animal or human with stereo-specific receptors and enzymes is there any difference. So they just don't bother."

"Oh," said Rusty woodenly. Then he added with more life, "Wow, I'm impressed. How do you know all that?"

"I was a chem major in college." Suddenly, a strange look came into Dr. Carlucci's eyes and his smile vanished.

"Where'd you do your under—"

"Jesus!" Dr. Carlucci shouted and jumped out of his chair, propelling the wheeled thing backward to crash against the wall.

Rusty startled, almost spilling his Pepsi. "What is it?" he called to Dr. Carlucci's back. He was puzzled—he had never thought organic chemistry was that exciting. He had to run to follow him out the door.

"Tell Raskin to start my next case with a nurse," Dr. Carlucci called from halfway down the hall. "I'll be in the library."

Minutes later, Rusty walked into the hospital library. He was surprised to see how small it was compared to the sprawling layout he was used to at the medical center. An elderly lady with a volunteer button manned the front desk. He quickly spotted Dr. Carlucci at one of the carrels paging through some big reference books. Otherwise the room appeared to be empty, but he couldn't see behind all of the bookshelves. Rusty flashed the old lady a smile and made his way over to Dr. Carlucci.

Dr. Carlucci looked up, the strange light still burning in his eyes. "It's the perfect murder, Rusty!" he whispered vigorously.

"What are you talking about?" asked Rusty.

Dr. Carlucci immediately grabbed Rusty's shoulders and squeezed hard. "Don't you see?" he asked and a look of such anguish crossed his face that Rusty was shocked. Before he could answer that he didn't have a clue, Dr. Carlucci continued. "Maybe I didn't kill him. Maybe I didn't."

Rusty wriggled free and backed up a step. "Kill who?" he managed to get out. He was worried that Dr. Carlucci had gone off the deep end.

"Sorry, Rusty," Dr. Carlucci said. He seemed to get a grip on himself and relax a bit. The anguished look was gone. "Let me back up some. Let's say someone slips epinephrine into one of your syringes—it wouldn't take much—only a milligram or so. You push the doctored syringe, pardon the expression, into a patient, and blammo, the pressure goes ballistic, and the heart goes haywire—V-tach, V-fib, you name it."

"Wow! But wait a minute, I thought you *gave* epinephrine at codes to save people, not kill them."

"Epinephrine, or adrenaline, is a strange drug, Rusty. A milligram of it is life-saving to someone in cardiac arrest or anaphylactic shock, but give that same milligram to you or I, and you'd likely kill us."

"Be-zarre!" Rusty exclaimed a bit too loud. The librarian, who had been staring at them all along, cast them a fresh look of disapproval.

"But getting back to murder." Dr. Carlucci paused and quickly glanced around the room. "The beauty of it is, epinephrine's a natural compound. That means, A, it's already supposed to be there and B, it's quickly degraded by natural enzymes. It would be virtually undetectable, and even if it was, you couldn't separate it from normal levels."

"Amazing. So you're saying someone sabotaged your and Doctor Landry's syringes—added epi to them?"

"Yes, and both our patients had coronary histories—mix that with high dose epi, and it's a sure-fire recipe for disaster."

"Yeah, the perfect murder, all right," Rusty said. He couldn't believe he was hearing this.

"Unless . . ." Dr. Carlucci stared off into space.

"What?" Rusty asked anxiously.

"Maybe there is a way—"

"But, you said there's no way to detect it, didn't you?"

Dr. Carlucci began to furiously flip the pages of one of the large reference books he had piled up helter-skelter on the table. "Look! Right here!" he practically shouted. He stabbed his finger repeatedly at the page.

Compound		B t1/2
Epinephrine	{ L-isomer -	55 sec
	{ D-isomer -	23 hrs

"The B t1/2 is the half life elimination time of a drug from the body. The physiologically active L-isomer is degraded on the order of minutes, but the D-isomer is relatively inert and relies on the much slower hepatic conjugation and renal elimination pathway for the body to clear it."

"What're you saying?"

"Doug's patient from yesterday, Mister what's-his-name, is still in the SICU. He probably still has some D-isomer in his blood!"

"Holy batshit! Let's go!"

"How long will it take the lab to run the analysis?" Rusty asked, referring to their newly acquired blood specimen. They were sitting in the doctor's charting area in the SICU. Dr. Carlucci had two blood tubes in his hand and was writing orders in Mr. Lehman's chart.

"I'm not sure," he answered, frowning. "Come to think of it, they'll probably have to send it out to a more sophisticated lab. Might take a week."

"That long," Rusty said. "What should we do in the meantime? Shouldn't we call Doctor Landry?"

"I'll call Doug tonight if I get the chance—I'm late-man and all. Otherwise, we'll talk to him tomorrow."

A blond nurse glided around the corner. "Did I hear you mention Doctor Landry?" she asked. "Is this about his patient?"

Rusty was surprised by her sudden appearance. He looked at Dr. Carlucci, who had a worried look on his face. He looked back at the nurse. God, she was gorgeous. Her nametag read, Jenny Stuart, R.N. What should they say?

"Just some routine bloodwork," Dr. Carlucci said and smiled nervously.

She looked skeptical. "I didn't see any ordered."

"I'm ordering it now," Dr. Carlucci said.

She appeared satisfied and then lightened her tone. "Doctor Landry made quite the save, I hear," she said, eyes sparkling. Rusty noticed she had a killer body too and couldn't help but stare. Her perfume drifted over to him, and he thought it was quite nice.

"Yes, he did," Dr. Carlucci replied evenly. He played with his pen and looked hurt.

"Doctor Landry—miracle worker," she said and sighed. Dr. Carlucci frowned at this but she didn't seem to notice. "Is it true they call him the Iceman?" she asked.

Dr. Carlucci hesitated a second. He put his pen back in his pocket and looked up at her. "Yes, and his wife and kids think the name's a riot."

She didn't say anything but made an irritated face back at him.

Dr. Carlucci stood up to leave and said, "We'll take the specimen to the lab ourselves. C'mon, Rusty."

"Tell Doctor Landry I said 'hi,' if you see him," she said.

Rusty would've preferred to stay a while longer and watch Jenny Stuart, but he obediently got up and followed Dr. Carlucci out of the SICU. He glanced back in time to see her pivot lightly on her feet and return to her work; the rear view was equally rewarding.

The two men walked down the corridor toward the lab in silence. Finally, Rusty's curiosity got the better of him. "Did you hear the way she said 'Doctor Landry'?"

"Hard to miss," responded Dr. Carlucci.

"What's up with that?" Rusty prodded further.

Dr. Carlucci stopped walking and looked at Rusty. "Look, Rusty, let's not add to the rumor mill. Anyway, Doug's too smart to get mixed up with the likes of her."

They continued walking. Rusty decided to drop it. He didn't really think Dr. Landry seemed like the fooling around type—he was too nice—but you never knew. Besides, thought Rusty, he'd seen pictures of Mrs. Landry. She was quite attractive. Up ahead, Rusty saw the sign for the lab.

"Are you here tomorrow?" Dr. Carlucci asked.

"Actually, no. I gotta take care of some, uh, stuff." Rusty knew he had plans of his own tomorrow.

"Don't tell anyone else about this, OK?" Dr. Carlucci stopped several yards from the lab drop-off window and said softly, "We really don't know who, if anybody, is behind this."

A chill went through Rusty. "This could be dangerous, couldn't it?"

"Well, if my theory proves correct, we're dealing with a pretty nasty individual."

Dr. Carlucci had a talent for understatement, Rusty thought. Seemed like an attempt at cold-blooded murder. Rusty got another chill and felt both nervous and excited. "Shouldn't we go to the police?"

"I don't think so," Dr. Carlucci said. "All we have here is some guesswork on my part, and I'm starting to have some second thoughts. Maybe Doug's right—maybe this sabotage thing is crazy." The fiery light had left his eyes. "If the sample tests positive, that's a different story."

"Okay," said Rusty. "I'll sit tight."

"I must get back to the OR. Raskin surely has more work for me to do before I can leave." He glanced at his watch. "It's after six, Rusty. You go home. I'll take care of this." He held up the blood tubes.

"All right, thanks." Rusty heard his stomach growl. "I am getting hungry."

"Listen, Rusty—keep your eyes and ears open. Trust no one, and watch your back."

"OK, you too."

CHAPTER TWENTY-TWO

Patti Lubbock was not in the best of spirits tonight. Several things were annoying her at present, although if truth be told, this was not an unusual state of affairs. She set down her bag and flung her coat on her desk. *God, why did it have to be so cold out there!*

Tonight, what topped the annoyance list was punching in late for work. She had been on the phone with her stupid ex, arguing about child support again. Tom, who had been in and out of jail for as long as she had known him, never seemed to generate any excess income. He invariably explained to her he was broke when she was lucky enough to get him on the phone, but somehow he always managed to drive his dates around in a nice new Ford pickup. She had also heard through the grapevine that he'd outfitted his bass boat with a new 200 horsepower Merc outboard. God, she'd like to choke him!

She glanced at her watch and then looked at the daunting pile of work in the IN basket over at the lab drop-off window. Although she was late, she didn't feel like jumping in just yet—one of the benefits of working alone on nightshift. She needed something to cheer her up first.

She fished through her bag and pulled out a Devil Dog. She got up, went to the lab refrigerator, and grabbed a Diet Coke from her personal stash. She knew it was against the rules to store food items in the fridge, but she also knew that not many people dared to cross her.

She sat down again at her desk and flipped the top on the soda. The pictures of her two teenage boys on her desk caught her eye; they seemed to be jeering at her. They were just like their father. Of course, she had to have had boys, dripping as they were with testosterone. They were constantly bucking her authority, driven by their hormonal storm, but she would keep them in line, by God, one way or another.

Patti noisily peeled the cellophane wrapper off the Devil Dog and bit in. She leaned back in her chair and reflected on her life as it should have been. She often imagined herself a physician or pharmacist, instead of a lab tech working night shift. If only her life hadn't been derailed by that miserable excuse for a man.

She was a victim, pure and simple, a casualty of the evil male and his insatiable sexual appetite. When she'd eloped at eighteen with her drug-using, ex-con boyfriend, she had been duped. The butterfly and dragon tattoos that seemed so cool twenty years ago, no longer looked so good. They had probably been Tom's idea, though if pressed, she would admit she had been shit-faced at the time, so she really couldn't remember whose idea it had been. Two children later—again deceived. All the weight she had put on was a natural consequence of the depression she suffered because of her miserable life.

Victim status had its perks, however. Gone was the weighty responsibility of just about anything in her life, and she was free to be as nasty and crabby as she felt like. The world owed her this much.

Feeling better, she strolled over to the lab window. Something caught her attention in the IN basket. Here's something odd—a blood tube for a D-epinephrine assay. Don't see one of those everyday. Patti had to admit to herself that she didn't know what D-epinephrine was, so she looked it up in one of her lab manuals.

Hmmm, I wonder if the goddamned doctor knows his precious specimen has to be sent out. He might have to wait a couple of days. She knew how impatient doctors were and smiled at the thought. The smile quickly faded as she wondered if evening shift had told him there would be a delay.

Probably, she reasoned, but if they hadn't, he'd be pissed off and guess who would shoulder the blame, as always. She knew Missy Swintosky on evenings was such an incompetent ditz, she might have forgotten. She was so busy reading her romance novels and fiddling with her acrylic nails. *I better call to make sure.* She sauntered back to her desk and dialed the number for the anesthesia department.

"Anesthesia," a male voice replied.

"Is Doctor Carlucci in?"

"No, may I ask who's calling?"

"It's the lab with a message for him," Patti said impatiently.

"Oh, okay. Give it to me—I'll make sure he gets it."

"I just wanted to let him know that the blood specimen he dropped off earlier will have to be sent out to Wyeth Labs," Patti said. "We don't run that kind of assay here."

"What kind?"

Damn, he must be another pain in the ass doctor. "Optical assay," she said with disgust.

"Optical? What on earth is that?"

Stupid, too. And they let these jokers prescribe medicine. I'll have to spell it out for him. "It's for the stereo isomer D-epinephrine—you know—dextro-rotated. Although what he wants it for—"

"Did you say epinephrine?" he interrupted.

"Yeah, D-epinephrine."

"Who was the patient?"

Nosy bugger. "Robert Lehman—and what's your name, sir?"

Click.

Patti slammed down the phone uttering, "Buttfucker!" She added another straw or two to the poor camel who had long since seen his spine fractured and now was being crushed under a tremendous pile of man-hatred straws. She reached into her bag for another Devil Dog.

* * *

Joe Raskin hung up the phone, feeling suddenly light-headed and nauseous. Carlucci, that son-of-a-bitch! D-epinephrine assay—too smart for his own damned good. Raskin nervously paced back and forth in the anesthesia on-call room. Now what should he do? He hadn't really meant to hurt anyone. The patients were just poor slobs with bad tickers. They didn't have long to live anyway. And that hypochondriac bitch—well, no harm done there. She got her gallbladder out, didn't she?

But this was different. He couldn't just go around killing people in broad daylight. That would be murder. He eyed the crucifix over the doorway and shook his head. How had they forced him into this? He couldn't afford to let Carlucci expose him. Not now, after all he had done. And he couldn't afford to lose his job—he had expenses, obligations, a family for Chrissakes. What was he going to do? Suddenly he stopped pacing. "Midazolam," he said softly and smiled. "That's the ticket!" He reached for the phone.

CHAPTER TWENTY-THREE

The phone rang, jarring Mike Carlucci awake. He had been dreaming of demons prancing about in operating rooms, choosing patients to torment and equipment to sabotage. He glanced at the digital clock on his dresser—1:20 a.m. "Shit," he cursed to himself as he climbed out of bed to get the blasted phone. Colleen moaned and rolled over.

Mike had the ability to quickly go from a semi-comatose state to being reasonably alert, thanks to years of practice. He knew before he picked up the phone that the call was from the hospital, and he was being called in to work. Joe Raskin was on call and Mike was his backup man; he was the first to be called back in case of an emergency.

Mike picked up the phone. "Hello," he got out hoarsely.

"Mike, Raskin here. Sorry to bother you, but I'm in the middle of this bad bowel obstruction—you know, septic as hell—the internists sat on it too long. Well anyway, she's going down the tubes. OB calls and says they have a labor epidural—some screaming twenty-one-year-old. They say it can't wait. I hate to call you, but I just can't leave this case."

"Yeah, okay. I'll be there shortly." *Damn it!* Mike felt sick because he had just left the hospital at 11:00 p.m. after finishing a grueling carotid endarterectomy. By the time he'd gotten home, he was too exhausted to call Doug. He had gone straight to bed, figuring he'd tell Doug about his theory in the morning. He'd found Colleen in bed, slumped over her book with her glasses on and the light still on. He hadn't seen any point in waking her; she'd probably had a rough day with the kids. He had taken her glasses off, helped her lay down, and kissed he gently on the forehead.

Mike hung up the phone and thought it could have been worse. He knew he could slip in the epidural in no time and turn right around. He was actually relieved to find out it wasn't a more difficult case. Shouldn't need any pharmaceutical assistance for this one. He smiled grimly and got dressed; his clothes were still strewn about the floor where he had left them several hours ago.

Mike said goodbye to his unconscious wife, grabbed his coat, and went downstairs to the cold garage. He fired up the Suburban, which he noted ruefully was still warm, and pulled out of the garage. Once on the road, he called the hospital to tell them he was rolling. "God, this job sucks!" he muttered.

He arrived at the hospital twenty-five minutes after he had taken the call at home. Raskin was in the locker room when Mike trudged in. Strange, thought Mike. He hadn't expected to see him there, with his big case and all.

Joe flushed the urinal as if in response and walked over to Mike.

"Don't bother to change, Mike. The stupid bitch delivered about fifteen minutes ago. Listen, I'm sorry to run you in here."

"Just my luck."

"That's OB for you," Raskin said. "Me, I can't stand it. A bunch of wimpy women screaming in pain—and it's always in the middle of the fucking night!"

"Yeah—well, look if you don't need me, I'm gonna go home. I've got a shitty day tomorrow and I need to get some sleep."

"You've had a rough week or two here, Mike. Stretch of bad luck." Raskin smiled thinly and shook his head. "I heard they sued." He looked curiously at Mike.

"That's right. See ya, Joe." Mike headed for the door. He didn't particularly care for Raskin, and two in the morning did nothing to improve their relationship.

"Don't you just hate those fucking lawyers!" Raskin exclaimed and followed him out the door. "Greedy bastards!"

"Yeah, see ya." Mike zipped up his coat and headed for the stairwell. He didn't relish the cold trek home.

"Mike, wait! I just brewed some fresh coffee," Raskin said, sounding worried. He quickly added, "Better have some for the drive home. You look like you could use it."

Mike hesitated, his hand poised on the door handle. "Yeah, you're right. I am still half asleep." He turned and walked back.

A look of relief washed across Raskin's face. "I'd feel awful if something happened to you tonight," he said. Raskin grinned a little strangely, but Mike didn't make much of it.

Raskin led Mike into the surgeon's lounge where a full pot of coffee was brewing. He poured a cup for each, and then produced a pint-sized milk container from the refrigerator. "Milk?" he inquired of Mike.

"Sure," Mike responded absently. Raskin carefully added some milk to Mike's cup, but neglected his own. He put the container away.

"I like it black," Raskin said.

Mike drained the coffee in several minutes and left the lounge. "See ya Joe," he called from the hallway. "Thanks for the coffee. Try not to call me back." *Asshole.*

CHAPTER TWENTY-FOUR

Mike's Suburban sped down the on-ramp and merged onto Interstate 283 heading north. The only good thing about driving at this time of night was that traffic was light. He should be able to make good time. *Thank God. I'm especially tired tonight and can't wait to crawl into bed. That coffee sure hasn't kicked in yet.*

Something was bothering Mike, but he couldn't put his finger on it. His tired brain turned over the events of the last hour. He certainly wasn't thrilled to be on this particular wild goosechase. He was angry with Raskin even though if the circumstances were reversed, he probably would've called in his backup too. But that wasn't what was bugging him.

Maybe I should tell Colleen about the drugs? Mike felt bad he had kept this secret from her. He had always believed neither of them would ever keep secrets from each other. *Perhaps I should get help? Colleen will understand.* But then thoughts of his children and how they looked up to their strong daddy flooded his mind. *God, I hate being a failure.* He stepped on the accelerator, anxious to get home. *What will Doug do, I wonder? Turn me in? And what exactly was going on between him and that SICU nurse?* Faint lights in the rearview mirror caught his attention. He made out the characteristic running lights of an eighteen-wheeler in the distance. He decided to tell Colleen. She would support him and help him figure out what to do. *I could call her now.*

He glanced down at his car phone, screen glowing in the dark, and a new thought struck him: *Why didn't Raskin call me in the car and tell me the lady delivered? Why did he wait until I got to the hospital?* Mike couldn't think of a good answer and realized this was what had been bugging him. He was disturbed by it, but too tired to muster more than: *I'll have to keep a close eye on Raskin.*

He yawned and tried to concentrate on the road. He was approaching the construction zone where both directions of traffic were carried on the northbound route. The lanes were separated by cattle chutes—five-foot high, preformed concrete barriers on all sides. They were difficult enough to maneuver through in broad daylight when you were wide-awake.

Driving while tired reminded Mike of an incident when he was in medical school. He had been coming home from the library late one night after a particularly exhausting study session. He had fallen asleep at the wheel on a wooded back road. Luckily, the gravel on the shoulder had crunched noisily under the tires when his car failed to negotiate the curve. He had awoken just in the nick of time to swerve back on the road, avoiding several waiting oak trees.

He had vowed that night never again to ignore the warning signs of sleepiness at the wheel—eyes closing momentarily, car drifting slightly, daydreaming, visions of bed, etc. Thereafter, whenever sleep beckoned, he would roll down the windows, turn the radio way up or try to stop for some coffee or soda. One time on the turnpike, he even pulled over and took a short nap until the wave of irresistible sleep had passed.

But tonight Mike would've sworn on a stack of bibles that, yes, he was tired, but nowhere near the dangerous point of sleeping at the wheel. As his head slumped forward and his hands relaxed their grip on the steering wheel, Mike wondered if he heard an air horn in the distance. He groaned but did not open his eyes.

* * *

Trucker Marty Johnson bellowed along with Merle Haggard as he nudged his rig up past seventy-five mph. He knew he couldn't carry a tune, so he made up for it with volume. Marty loved driving at night—not much traffic or many cops—so he could make good time. Of course, he frequently fudged his records, so his time didn't look too good. Tonight, he had the road all to himself—except for that damned Suburban up ahead. He'd been trying to catch and pass the bastard for the last couple of miles. Just his luck to get stuck behind the guy through the one-lane construction.

There was something wrong with that guy, too. Marty had been watching him swerve all over the road for the last mile. That candy-ass in his fancy SUV is probably going nighty-night. Marty hated SUV's. His faggoty boss drove one. Whenever he passed one on the highway, he made a point to creep over the line and scare 'em just a bit.

Marty's irritation soon gave way to anticipation as an idea struck him. After all, Marty knew how to wake people up. He goosed the gas and soon was riding the Suburban's bumper. He didn't let the fact that they had entered the cattle chutes bother him. The jerk didn't even seem to be aware of him. Marty grinned as he gave his air horn a tremendous long blast. "That'll either wake the dead or give 'em a heart attack," he said and chuckled.

Much to Marty's surprise, the two-and-a-half ton Suburban traveling at sixty-five mph continued to inch closer to the center concrete barrier. What the hell was going on? The left front bumper hit first, a glancing blow that sent the truck careening toward the outer concrete barrier. *Holy shit!*

Marty quickly realized his mistake. He took his foot off the gas and applied the brake; he now craved some distance between the two vehicles. As his rig begrudgingly slowed, Marty watched in horrid fascination as the Chevy truck impacted the outer barrier at roughly a 45-degree angle—no glancing blow this time. The passenger side front end crumpled hideously, exploding the right front tire in the process. The truck fishtailed and spun on impact, until the left back end made contact with the center concrete barrier. Having turned almost completely sideways, it continued to skid, quickly bleeding speed as it scraped along both concrete walls. The twisted Suburban came to rest completely blocking the road barely thirty feet away.

Marty jammed on his brakes as hard as he could and hit the horn again, but knew it was hopeless. He had slowed to about forty mph, but didn't really have a prayer of stopping his twenty-ton baby in time. And the damned barriers prevented him from avoiding the Suburban. "Shit!" His eighteen tires screeched in unison, a horrible racket that was outdone only by the sickening sound of the collision.

* * *

As the flames licked over his left hand, Mike's brain flickered into consciousness. He felt searing pain, smelled the burning rubber, plastic and skin and heard the roaring flames. Slowly his comprehension gelled; he knew he was in his truck and that there had been a horrible accident. He tried to move but only managed to produce waves of pain from the mangled pieces of bone and muscle that had once been his legs. He was hopelessly trapped in his burning truck.

"What happened?" He'd dreamt that he had safely arrived home and was snuggled up in his warm bed. And then it dawned on him. Mike knew with astounding clarity what had happened. "That son-of-a-bitch! Raskin must've drugged me. I was right!"

The flames, encouraged by the strong night breeze, engulfed the whole vehicle. The truck filled with thick smoke, obscuring Mike's vision and causing him to breathe in short, choking gasps. He groped for his cellular phone, but it was gone. The impact of the collision must have jarred it loose from its floor mounting. His hand closed on some wires, and he followed them a short distance. The phone was wedged under the dash. He couldn't free the handset from the cradle. *Shit! No voice message.* He doubted the thing even worked. He couldn't see the keypad but this didn't matter, as he had long since memorized it anyway. He punched in RCL 04 and was rewarded by normal sounding beeps from the phone. *It takes a licking and keeps on ticking.* He pushed SEND and heard one last beep. He hoped to God that someone would understand his message. He clutched his gold crucifix and began to pray. The pain of the fire was becoming unbearable. Just then, he heard a noise above the roar of the flames. He looked out the window and thought he could make out the Angel of Death swooping out of the darkness to collect his soul.

CHAPTER TWENTY-FIVE

Doug Landry drove down the road on his way to work practically in a trance. He had one more call day to get through before the weekend. Deep down somewhere he realized that this weekend would be a crossroads for him. He had never before even considered meeting someone secretly, let alone set the plan into motion. What in the world was he doing? Didn't Laura and the boys deserve better? Then he saw Jenny standing there, posed in some silky nightgown, smiling seductively, beckoning him. He squeezed his eyes tight and shook his head. If only he could get her out of his mind.

His daydream was penetrated by the news on the radio. ". . . and in local news—this just in—area physician Doctor Michael Carlucci was killed when a tractor trailer collided with his vehicle late last night on Interstate 283, just south of the Hershey exit. Let's check with Chuck in the Traffax Command Center to see what affect this is having on the morning rush hour commute. Chuck . . ."

Doug almost plowed into the car ahead of him as he listened horrorstruck. He didn't believe it at first—he thought he'd obviously heard wrong. He switched to the all news station, and his fear was soon confirmed. When he got to work, the nightmare continued.

"Doctor Landry, did you see the paper?" Julie Miller, the group's secretary asked. Her eyes were red with tears, and her voice quavered badly.

Doug just nodded his head in response; he didn't trust his own voice. He left her and ran to the surgeon's lounge, not bothering to change. Morning papers would be found there.

Five or six surgeons were hovering around the coffee pot, most with newspapers in their hands, all talking loudly. Kim Burrows, Omar Ayash, and Bryan Marshall were chatting with the surgeons. The numerous conversations stopped almost immediately when Doug burst through the doorway. All eyes were upon him; they knew that Doug and Mike were close friends. Nobody moved.

"Bad news, Doug," said Marshall, the first to recover. He walked over and handed Doug the front section of the paper as explanation. "Read this."

"Doug, I'm so sorry," said Kim. She reached out and stroked his arm.

"Those truckers are a menace!" Ayash said angrily. He banged his fist in his palm repeatedly. "If I say it once, I say it tousand times."

Several surgeons offered their condolences, but most became absorbed in suddenly pressing paperwork and telephone calls.

Doug didn't say anything but quickly looked at the paper. There was a large color picture of the fiery wreck. The headline read, "Doctor Falls Asleep At Wheel." His eyes blurred with tears. He scanned the article, only able to focus on bits and pieces of it.

"Trucker Marty Johnson, who was uninjured in the crash, had this to say: 'I couldn't stop in time. There was just no way. He was just sitting there crossways blocking the road. Must've had a heart attack or fallen asleep—I seen him swerve. Happens more than you think.'"

Doug paused to wipe his eyes. He continued to read.

"Dr. Carlucci had been on the way home after doing emergency surgery at Mercy Hospital, where he worked as an anesthesiologist for six years. He is survived by his wife, Colleen, and two children Emily, five, and Christine, two."

Doug was completely numbed by the news. His best friend cut down in his prime. What a waste! Colleen must be a basket case. He knew he should call and offer his support and comfort, but he couldn't face it right now. He envisioned the upcoming funeral and couldn't bear the thought of seeing Mike's two little kids there.

Intense grief was not the only emotion Doug wrestled with. He was also stricken with guilt. He believed he knew why Mike had fallen asleep at the wheel. Surely it had to do with the fact that he was abusing drugs. It was their little secret. He should've mailed the letter, should've gone right to hospital administration, should've spilled the beans on Mike's drug use. Laura had been right. Mike's career would've been ruined, but at least he'd be alive, maybe in a rehab program right now. At least his kids would have a father. Another bad decision, Doug.

Doug was completely miserable as he headed to the locker room to change. The hospital-wide intercom sparked to life: "This is Sister Emmanuel from Pastoral Care Service with our morning prayer, taken from the gospel of our Lord Jesus Christ . . ."

As Sister Emmanuel prayed, Doug said his own prayer. He prayed for Mike and Colleen and the two girls. Finally, he prayed for himself. He wondered how he was going to make it through the long twenty-four-hour call day ahead. His life was unraveling before him, and he was felt he was responsible.

All morning, Doug practically ran from one operating room to the next. As call man, he supervised four CRNA rooms, which meant he had to interview, induce anesthesia, and wake up all the patients and arrange for breaks and lunches for everyone. There were labor epidurals and steroid epidurals to do in between. He was horribly distracted; more than once he caught himself almost giving the wrong drug.

Doug wondered where Rusty was this morning. He had taken a liking to Rusty, after working closely with him for the past week. He smiled thinly when he thought of how Rusty's personality and mannerisms conjured up images of a golden retriever puppy in his mind. Rusty was cheerful, smart, eager to please, and followed him everywhere. All that he lacked was a big, furry tail. And Doug badly needed a friend to talk to.

Doug knew he didn't make friends easily himself. He had never been able to have anything other than superficial conversations with Marshall, Ayash, or Raskin; usually these centered on corporate finances or anesthetic issues. He got along well with Kim, but certainly wouldn't consider it a deep relationship. He felt most of the problem wasn't even his fault. All his life, people had shunned him because of his intelligence and success. Ken Danowski and Mike were the only ones he really confided in, besides Laura of course. Ken was still taking some days off. And Mike, his one, true best friend, wouldn't be coming in today. Or tomorrow. Tears returned to his eyes. He wiped them away roughly and attended to his next duty.

CHAPTER TWENTY-SIX

Rusty Cramer finally crawled out of bed after beating the snooze button senseless. He had trouble getting up because he knew he didn't have to; he had already called in sick yesterday. Also, his sleep had been interrupted by wild, unsettling dreams of botched surgery. He could only recall one, but the vividness of the memory shocked him. He had been the patient, and they had been cutting him open awake. The surgeon's face had been hidden by his mask but was somehow familiar. The pain of the sharp blade had forced him out of his body until his spirit hovered above the OR table. Blood had been spattered everywhere—his own. Finally, when it seemed he could bear no more, someone had appeared to comfort him, wrapped their arms around him, and whispered soothing things in his ear. He had stared up into the eyes of his mother.

Rusty shuddered and shook his head. The dream was so weird because he had no recollection of his mother or, for that matter, his father. He had been told that his parents had died in some horrible accident when he was a baby; no more details were provided.

On his way to the bathroom, Rusty tripped over his sneakers and stubbed his toe. He hoped a nice hot shower would calm him down and erase some of his mental fog.

The hot shower felt good indeed, and Rusty languished there, enjoying the unaccustomed freedom of a day off. He stood there, eyes closed, and let the force of the pounding water on his skull drive the tiredness out of his brain. He reminisced back to his days in the Milton S. Hershey Home for Boys, where he had been placed by the state.

Milton Hershey of Hershey Chocolate fame was a renowned philanthropist whose first act of charity was to set up a school for orphaned boys in the early nineteen forties. Rusty admired the man Hershey, and hoped to one day emulate him after he made his own fortune. Rusty felt he owed the man double because one of Hershey's trust funds had also allowed for the creation of the Medical Center in 1968, where Rusty was currently a med student.

His memories of the orphanage were mostly pleasant; he had known no other home, so it wasn't bad, like a blind man not missing sight. His family was the boys who shared his house and the counselors who provided love and guidance. Perhaps his lack of a real mother or father had led to his difficulty relating to people genuinely and had helped "Plastic-man" to emerge. He always had trouble trusting people enough to let down his guard and show them his true self. Rusty found it interesting that he felt closer to Dr. Landry and Dr. Carlucci then he had to anybody in a long time. It would've been nice to have had a father like one of them.

While in the orphanage, Rusty developed a love of comic books that he shared with many of the boys. Superheroes appealed especially to boys without mothers or fathers. To this day, he couldn't bear to part with a certain banged up footlocker that housed his cherished collection of comic books. His speech was still laced with trademark expressions from his childhood buddies, Spidey, Torch, and the Caped Crusader.

Only later as he grew up and saw what families were all about did Rusty begin to sense an absence in his life. And so had begun his search for his missing past. After years of frustrating dead ends to the point where he had all but given up hope, he finally hit pay dirt.

A med school buddy tipped him off to a serious Internet missing persons search site. His friend, an antique car buff, told him it had helped him locate some very obscure people on a car title for his sixty-nine 'Vette. Rusty was dubious at first. When he heard about the fees involved, he figured it was just another scam. He reluctantly typed in his credit card number and anted up the twenty dollars required to access the site. It cost ten dollars thereafter for every query with no guarantee of return. But much to Rusty's surprise and delight, he got closer to the truth than he ever had been—all for under sixty bucks. This is what had led him to Mercy Hospital. Unfortunately, his new information raised some troubling questions, but he had also gotten some fresh leads to track down.

Rusty got out of the shower and toweled off. He felt much better; he of course wasn't really sick. He quickly threw on some jeans and his favorite sweatshirt, the blue, University of Florida one with the green gator on the front. He ran a brush through his damp red hair and went over his course of action. He planned to drive to Philadelphia to visit the large Municipal Court Building where he could search through birth and death certificates. He also intended to visit the Philadelphia Public Library and read through some microfilmed newspapers. He grabbed his watch from the dresser and checked it—9:15 a.m. *Shit! The day's a-wasting.* He'd hit McDonald's on the way and grab an Egg McMuffin for the turnpike. As he bolted out of his apartment, notepad in hand, he stepped over his neighbor's newspaper lying upside down on the doormat.

CHAPTER TWENTY-SEVEN

Doug walked into the anesthesia call room and flopped down on the sofa. He was exhausted already. It was only lunchtime, and this was his first opportunity to sit down and collect his thoughts. After spending several minutes steeling himself, he called Colleen. In between her pitiful sobbing, he managed to tell her that he and Laura would help in any way possible with the kids and that they would pray for them. He was in tears himself by the time the call ended.

Doug didn't feel much like eating. He couldn't stop looking at Mike's desk, where there was a recent picture of Mike and Colleen with the two kids at Disney world. Everyone was smiling, and it looked like they didn't have a care in the world.

He walked over to Mike's desk and grasped the picture to take a closer look. As he lifted it up, a little piece of paper fluttered out from behind it. He would've ignored it, but a familiar name caught his attention—Bob Lehman.

He picked up the slip of paper and saw Bob Lehman's hospital ID number also stamped on it. What would Mike be doing with Bob Lehman's hospital ID number? Doug was baffled. He finally decided Rusty might know; he had been working with Mike yesterday. He called the Medical Center Anesthesia Department and asked to speak to Rusty. "He's attending the visiting professor lecture series, I think," Doug added helpfully. He tapped his foot while waiting and glanced over at the photograph again. Colleen's arm was wrapped around Mike's waist with the girls tucked in front and Goofy towering over them from behind. He could almost hear Colleen giggling and the girls squealing. Even Mike looked relaxed. Doug's eyes threatened to blur again, and he forced himself to look away.

"Uh, the Visiting Professor series is only on Mondays, sir," the voice on the phone said. "There are no lectures today. Let me see—ah, yes—Dr. Cramer called in sick last night, sounded bad with the flu."

"I see. Thank you." That's odd—Rusty seemed fine yesterday.

Doug called and paged Rusty at the hospital. No answer. It wasn't like Rusty to play hooky. Doug wondered what Rusty was up to, but his thirty-minute lunch break was over, and he had to get back to work.

Later in the afternoon, the call day grinding on, Doug decided to play a hunch. He knew that Mike had a habit of using his car phone on the way home from work to attend to business matters. Mike had a thirty-minute drive and prided himself on always putting the time to good use. Doug picked up the phone and dialed.

"ConTel phone company. How may I help you?" asked a bored female. Doug envisioned a relatively young employee judging from her high-pitched voice.

"Hi, uh, this is Doctor Landry from Mercy Hospital." He rarely identified himself as doctor unless he was desperate. "I need to check the phone records for Doctor Carlucci."

"That would be highly unusual—we don't give out that kind of information," she said. The words came out in a clump, slurred together, suggesting it was a well-worn phrase.

"No, you don't understand," Doug said, working to keep his voice calm. "He works for Keystone Anesthesia in the corporate account. You send us the monthly bill all the time. I need to check to see where he called yesterday." Doug hoped he didn't sound too pleading.

"I'm afraid I still can't help you sir," she said cheerily.

"Well, can you find someone who can?" Doug asked, beginning to lose his patience.

"I'll have to check with the manager," she said huffing and sighing so, it sounded like she had been asked to scale Mount Everest.

"That would be fine."

"Can you hold?" Click. She didn't wait for an answer.

Doug drummed his fingers on his desk; he commanded himself not to look at Mike's desk. He glanced at the TV. MSNBC was on with the afternoon Street Sweep; the NASDAQ was in record territory again. Great—Mike and he always dreamed of riding the tech wave and retiring early.

"Hi, Doctor Landers—"

"Landry."

"Doctor Landry. This is Mister Jenkins, and let me just say that we do appreciate your business, and I'll help you any way I can. Now, what can we do for you?"

Thank God—that's more like it. "I need to check some phone calls on one of our corporate mobile phones," Doug said.

"We can fax over the corporate billing statement, if that would help?"

"Yes, great. Our account is Keystone Anesthesia Associates. Thanks a lot."

"You're welcome—"

"Is this record up to date?" Doug interrupted. "I mean will it show calls made as late as yesterday?"

"Oh, yes! Here at ConTel we employ the latest in computer tech—"

"Great! Thanks! Just send it." Doug hung up. While waiting for the fax, Doug grabbed some Advil to dull the pain in his head and swallowed them dry. He didn't think he was over his self-imposed daily limit of six yet. He sat down at his desk and massaged the back of his neck and his temples. Shortly, the fax machine hummed to life and spewed out several sheets. Doug jumped up and ripped off the flimsy paper, still warm to the touch. He quickly located Mike's car phone number near the bottom of page two.

Mobile Phone Number 763-2108

December 17th

| 2250 | 731-5431 | Elizabethtown | 13 min |
| 2302 | 1-215-439-8700 | Malvern | 6 min |

December 18th

| 0130 | 763-2121 | Lancaster | 2 min |

cont'd on next page
- 2 -

The first number was Mike's home phone. He must've called when he was leaving the hospital as late man.

Doug didn't have a clue about the second long distance number, but he would call it shortly. The third listing was Mercy Hospital OR. Doug knew Mike had been called in last night; it had been in the newspaper. He figured Mike must've been telling the hospital he was on his way back in—standard procedure.

He dialed the second number.

"Hello, Wyeth Labs," came a pleasant female receptionist voice. "How may I direct your call?"

Wyeth Labs? What the heck? Doug thought fast. "Uh, this is Doctor Landry from Mercy Hospital in Lancaster. Did you receive a specimen yesterday on a Bob Lehman?"

"You want the clinical lab department, sir. I'll transfer you."

"Thanks." What in the world would Mike have sent to Wyeth Labs?

"Lab," came a male voice. Not so pleasant.

"Hi, I was wondering whether you received a specimen on a Bob Lehman from Mercy Hospital?" Doug asked politely.

"Hospital number?"

"Uh, wait a minute." Doug cradled the phone between his ear and shoulder and rummaged through the disorganized pile on his desk, searching for the missing scrap of paper. He located it and read off the number.

"Please hold." Click. Doug drummed his fingers in time to lousy elevator music. "Yes, just arrived this morning."

Bingo! "What was it for?" Doug realized his mistake as soon as the words left his mouth.

"Sorry, sir. That's confidential."

Oh shit, here we go again. "But, it's a matter of great importance!"

"I'm sorry, sir," replied the male voice, sounding anything but sorry. "Just following policy," he added, the delight over these three words plainly evident in his voice.

Doug slammed the phone down. Obnoxious twerp! He punched the redial.

"Hello. Wyeth Labs—"

"Laboratory, please." He had a new idea and fervently hoped for a different, less officious lab tech.

"Lab," answered a female voice.

Thank God a different voice, although she didn't sound much friendlier. "Hi, uh, this is Doctor Carlucci. How are you today?"

"Fine. How may I help you, sir?"

"I need to check on that blood specimen I sent you yesterday on a Mister Robert Lehman."

"Hospital number?"

Doug repeated the number again.

"Yes, I see it."

"Your form was a little complicated, and I'm afraid I may have screwed it up." Doug smiled as he laid it on thick with his best absent-minded professor voice. "Did I remember to check the plasma pseudocholinesterase box? I really need that."

"No, sir," she said impatiently. "You just have D-epinephrine checked."

Gotcha! "Damn! I knew I forgot." Doug smiled again and couldn't resist adding, "Do you think you could run them both?"

"I'm afraid not. That would be against policy. You'll have to send us another order form."

"That's what I thought. Thanks anyway." There's more than one way to skin a cat. "You've been most helpful," Doug said and believed he could almost see her face pinch into a bewildered frown.

D-epinephrine! What the hell was that for? Doug knew what D-epinephrine was and also understood that D referred to a dextro-rotary optical isomer, but beyond that he was lost. He couldn't recall ever hearing of D-epinephrine being a useful clinical lab value. He picked up the phone fax again while he pondered the D-epi mystery.

He turned to the next page and realized with a jolt that there was one more phone entry under Mike's number and it was for December 18th—today!

Mobile Phone Number 763-2108 (cont'd)

December 18th
0216   737-2456   Marysville   1 min

This last call must've been made right before Mike's accident! The paper had said 2:30 a.m., but this was close enough. The number looked familiar, but he couldn't place it. He dialed rapidly.

"You've reached the residence of Doctor J. Raskin. At the sound of the tone, please leave your name and message . . . BEEP . . .

Raskin! "Hi, uh, Joe. This is Doug Landry. I, uh—" He stopped when he heard the receiver being picked up.

"Hello, Doug," Raskin said. "I'm here. What the devil are you calling me at home for? You know I'm off-call."

"Sorry—hey, did you hear about Mike? Have you seen the news?"

Raskin paused, then asked slowly, "No, what happened?"

"He's dead. Killed in a car wreck driving home last night," Doug said. "Paper said he fell asleep at the wheel."

"You don't say. Tragic. Dammit, I told him he looked tired. Had to call him in for a fucking epidural. Tried to get him to drink some coffee, but he wouldn't have it—said it would keep him up the rest of the night. God, I feel awful."

"Not your fault, Joe. Well, listen I won't bother you anymore. I'll let you know if we hear anything about funeral arrangements."

"Thanks for calling, Doug. Tragic, simply tragic. See you later—"

"Uh, Joe, one more thing," Doug said before Raskin could hang up. "Did Mike call you at home late last night?"

Raskin again paused. "I was in the hospital working all night, Doug—you know that. Why would he call here?" There was silence for a moment. Doug could make out Raskin's wheezy breathing; he sounded somewhat out of breath. Raskin worked through a coughing fit and continued. "But I know of no call. Phyllis would've told me if anyone had disturbed her sleep."

"OK. Thanks." Doug hung up the phone, mystified. He wondered why Mike had called Raskin at home last night. Doug had heard about Raskin's bad case and knew he had stayed in the hospital until at least four or five in the morning. Mike clearly would've known this. He would've had no reason to call Raskin's home at two in the morning and wake up his bear of a wife, Phyllis. It didn't make any sense. Maybe it was just a phone malfunction caused by the accident.

The intercom squawked again.

"Doctor Landry—induction room 2."

"Doctor Landry—pre-op room 4."

"Doctor Landry—recovery room needs a patient evaluation."

Doug reluctantly put his growing concerns away. Maybe tomorrow he could give them some more thought. He groaned as he hoisted himself out of the chair and headed toward the OR.

CHAPTER TWENTY-EIGHT

Joe Raskin hung up the phone and felt like he was going to vomit. He staggered over to the kitchen table where the newspaper was spread out and sat down hard. He ran his trembling fingers through his hair several times and took in some deep breaths. He reread the article to see if he had missed anything. Phyllis *had* complained to him that someone had disturbed her precious beauty sleep. His mind raced and his heart pounded in his chest. Could it actually have been Carlucci? He played with his beard, twirling sections of it into tight little knots. How could Landry have possibly known about a call to my house made by a dead man? It doesn't make any sense.

No, no, that's absolute bullshit. Landry, that asshole, must be bluffing. He's trying to flush me out. Raskin got up and began to pace. His shoes clip-clopped loudly on the Grecian ceramic tile in his spacious, Mediterranean-style kitchen. Thank God, Phyllis was out this afternoon at one of her silly Ladies' Auxiliary meetings. He needed time to think, plan his next move. He went over what he knew.

He had never liked Landry from day one, that much was clear. Landry was so goddamned confident, never made a mistake—Mr. Perfect. People were always making special requests for Landry to do their anesthesia. It was disgusting. Joe used to get lots of requests, well some anyway, before Landry and Carlucci came.

He walked into the expansive dining room and had to shield his eyes. The large crystal chandelier appeared to be on fire, as it caught the rays of the setting sun streaming through the two large bay windows. The entire room was bathed in bright orange. It reminded him of Carlucci in his burning truck and he frowned. Not a pretty way to go.

He felt bad about Carlucci. People thought he didn't care, but they were wrong; he had feelings too. Except, nobody cared about his feelings—Phyllis certainly didn't. Raskin felt his stomach churn and his nausea intensify. Carlucci reminded Raskin a little of himself. He wasn't perfect like Landry; he was always too goddamned nervous —should have been a dermatologist or something.

Raskin eyed the doors to the study; he was being drawn there. He walked over and reached out to open the door. The door was halfway open when he stopped, struck motionless by a powerful thought. What about King David from the Old Testament? Wasn't he, himself just like King David, who's practically a saint? He recalled the story of how King David, lusting for Uriah's wife, Bathsheba, had put him on the front lines. Uriah was immediately killed in battle.

The point was, that King David didn't actually kill him—the Ammonites did. Likewise, he hadn't killed Carlucci—that dimwit trucker, Marty Johnson had. Why, he never even intended for him necessarily to die. A good crack-up, a good scare would've been just fine by him.

He walked all the way into the study and closed the door. Framed photographs of his three children, now grown or in college, immediately caught his attention. He remembered that

Carlucci was a family man, too—the paper had said two girls. Raskin felt a stab of remorse. Blessed are the little children for they shall inherent . . . something. He shook his head and took in several deep, cleansing breaths, letting the odor of incense and candle wax wash over him. This was where he came for comfort.

Raskin knelt down and turned his gaze toward the exquisite oil painting taking up half of the far wall. He remembered when he had first laid eyes on the painting at some stupid art exhibit Phyllis had dragged him to. He just had to have it. It didn't matter that the painting was an original and outrageously expensive. The painting had spoken to him then as it continued to do so now. It embodied the central philosophy of his life, ever since he was a young boy.

He studied the anguished face of Jesus on the cross. Jesus was looking toward a man to his right, the thief, who was also being crucified. The man appeared to be pleading with Jesus. The expressions were so lifelike, the lines and detail so perfect, the colors so vibrant that Raskin thought he was staring back through a window in time.

Raskin closed his eyes and stilled his breathing. He believed he could hear Jesus speaking. "Your sins are forgiven. Today, you shall be with me in paradise." He opened his eyes and made the sign of the cross. He smiled and felt his nausea subside. After the unfortunate accident with Melissa, he had visited the study several times—the painting had worked its magic then, too. It was simple, really. You could do all this bad stuff, anything actually, and as long as you asked for forgiveness before you died, you would wind up in heaven—just like the thief.

There was only one catch, however—you couldn't die too quickly. But what were the odds of that? He'd seen lots of people die over the years. Normally they had time—it would only take a couple of minutes for Chrissakes to say a quick prayer. He figured he'd take his chances. Even Carlucci probably had time to make it right with his maker before he roasted. Raskin felt much better; he always did when he knelt at the foot of the cross. He decided he was wrong to get all broken up over Carlucci—he was a friend of Landry after all. And Landry was the real evil one.

Landry was probably in league with the nuns. They had no doubt cooked up this whole merger thing along with the Pinnacle deal to force him out. They would throw him out on his ear in disgrace after all he had done for Mercy. It just wasn't right. Besides, what really galled him was that Landry was such a sleazebag—*he* should get the axe. Didn't they know Landry was shacking up with that SICU bitch? Whereas, in contrast, he had never cheated on Phyllis in thirty-five long years of marriage. Well, maybe once or twice, but he had been drunk, so they didn't count.

So, Landry thinks he can call here and play his little game of mind-fuck. Well, it was time to get even, settle the score. No more Mr. Nice Guy. His hands were clenched and he was breathing hard as he stood up, knees creaking. The painting looked ordinary now and no longer captivated him. He left the study and closed the door.

Raskin walked back to the kitchen and sat down at the table, the newspaper picture of the burning wreck in plain sight. It occurred to him that he had been lucky with Carlucci; Midazolam was metabolized slowly and might easily have been detected in Carlucci's blood. Lucky for the fire. He needed something better—he closed his eyes again and rested his head in his hands, hoping for inspiration.

His mind wandered back to his days at State College, and he saw himself seated in a large lecture hall, noisy and crowded with students. Professor Herbrandson was droning on about some aspect of organic chemistry; Raskin couldn't quite make out what he was saying. The professor's head dodged in and out of the powerful light beam coming from the overhead transparency projector; it reflected in bursts off his spectacles and shiny, bald head. Herbrandson wrote the words "Hoffman elimination" in big block letters, and then wrote it again and again. Raskin could even hear his felt-tip pen squeaking over the vinyl sheet.

What the hell does Hoffman elimination have to do with anything? The answer came to him in a flash—Atracurium. He smiled. Atracurium was a devilishly clever molecule. He became excited and quickly ran through what he knew of the drug. Atracurium was of a class of short-acting, non-depolarizing muscle relaxants. Muscle relaxant was a nice way to say it induces a full-blown muscular paralysis. Death by asphyxiation occurs quite rapidly, in the order of three or four minutes, following a paralyzing dose of Atracurium.

But the beauty of the drug wasn't its neuromuscular blocking qualities; other drugs paralyzed equally well, if not better. Raskin remembered the drug rep, the skinny blond with platform shoes and a short dress, telling them, in her New York accent, why Atracurium was worth such a premium price. She had called Atracurium a "pharmacologic time-bomb." It was specifically designed for use in people with impaired liver or kidney function. The drug wears off entirely by itself, not relying on any organ function, in about thirty minutes. As the drug heats up to body temperature, it undergoes what's known in organic chemistry parlance as spontaneous Hoffman degradation. That translates into a heat-sensitive, molecular self-destruction.

Raskin felt his smile stretch wider: even a corpse, at room temperature or above, would clear Atracurium from the blood. He took the stairs down to his office in the basement where he kept his medical bag and some supplies.

CHAPTER TWENTY-NINE

Brrring!

Doug stared at his watch as he picked up the phone, but his eyes were too blurry to make out the small numerals. "Hello. Doctor Landry here."

"Is this anesthesia?"

Doug yanked the receiver away from his ear—the caller's voice seemed way too loud. "Yes, I'm the anesthesiologist on call." He hated when they referred to him as anesthesia.

"We need a labor epidural up here."

Super. "What's up?" His stubborn eyes finally deciphered the little lines on his watch—11:00 p.m.—eight hours to go. Might as well have been an eternity, the way he felt.

"We have a twenty-two-year-old, Mrs. Concepcion, who's about four CMs and on pit."

"OK, I'll be up. Man, you guys have been busy up there at night. Can't you give it a rest?" Doug reluctantly threw off the thin, scratchy hospital blankets.

"Whatd'ya mean? Last night we were empty."

"No, they called down for an epidural last night too. I'm sure of it." Doug sat up on the lumpy pullout sofa bed and shivered. Normally, he wouldn't have bothered to argue, but tonight, he felt especially irritable.

"Well, I don't know who told you that, but I worked last night and I did cross-stitch the whole night long. Quiet as a mouse."

Doug hung up the phone, again perplexed. Why the hell would Raskin lie about the epidural? The conclusion seemed inescapable, but Doug still didn't want to believe it; it just seemed too bizarre. Already overwhelmed by the events of the recent days and blunted by the rigors of the call day, he just couldn't complete the circuit. He was exhausted—he'd go put the epidural in, and then maybe he could catch a couple hours of sleep.

* * *

Raskin snuck into the surgeon's lounge. Good—empty. No cases were going on. It would not be disastrous if anyone saw him—anyone but Landry. He would be incredibly suspicious.

He reasoned Landry must be asleep in the call-room; the door was shut. He pondered his course of action as he patted the special syringes he had brought from home. Should he sneak into the call-room and inject him? What if he was awake? He didn't relish the thought of taking on Landry physically; he preferred to finesse it somehow. *How shall I do this?*

Just then the phone rang. Raskin jumped and realized how on edge he was. He went over to look at the phone and saw incoming Labor & Delivery on the caller ID. He noted this call was going to Landry's call-room. He gently picked up the receiver and listened.

"Hello," came Landry's voice thick with sleep.

"Is this anesthesia?"

"Yeah."

"Sorry to bother you. I know it's one-thirty, but Mrs. Concepcion's hurting again. Could you come up and re-inject her epidural?"

"Yeah, sure," Landry replied with resignation.

Perfect, Raskin thought as he hung up the phone. Ask and you shall fucking receive. The plan formed instantly in his mind. He quickly emptied his syringe into the full pot of coffee. He knew Landry was a sucker for a fresh pot and being the caffeine addict that he was, he'd almost certainly stop here before he went to OB.

He waited just long enough, hiding behind the OR scheduling desk to see the weary Landry emerge from his sleeping quarters and head for the lounge—not the most direct route to OB. He could only be heading there for one reason—the coffee. Vengeance is mine, saith the Lord.

Raskin left silently and headed up the stairs to obstetrics, since he figured Landry would never make it.

* * *

It was a clear, moonless night; countless stars appeared frozen in the hard, black sky. Rusty zoomed down the Pennsylvania Turnpike passing the Downingtown interchange, halfway back to Harrisburg. He was listening to the eleven o'clock news on the radio when he heard: " . . . the partially decomposed body of Melissa Draybeck was discovered today in her apartment. Neighbors became suspicious when they hadn't seen her for a couple of days and began noticing a bad odor coming from her apartment. Police are saying she was strangled to death but aren't revealing any details. They have no suspects at this time. . ."

Rusty recognized Melissa's name, but didn't make too much of the murder. Other thoughts occupied his mind. The Municipal Court had been mostly a waste of time. Rusty had only managed to find one bit of useful information. After hitting a deli and ordering several Philadelphia hoagies, Rusty had proceeded to the Center

City Public Library; this had proved to be much more fruitful. After scanning hundreds of major local newspapers for accidents occurring within a specified time frame, he had finally struck oil. He relived the excitement. Although he had been sitting in the same uncomfortable chair for hours and his eyes had throbbed miserably with strain, he had suddenly sat erect and stared at the microfilm reader's screen with rapt attention and shouted, "Eureka!" Things had finally begun to fall into place.

Two hours later, Rusty arrived back at his little apartment in Hershey. He was tired of fact-finding and glad to be home. He knew he should go to bed soon so he would be able to function tomorrow when he returned to Mercy. But first, he couldn't resist the Philadelphia hoagie he had brought back with him. They were legendary after all, and three didn't seem out of line for a long day. He sprawled on the sofa in his tiny living room, opened a Rolling Rock, and clicked on the TV. He had eaten about three-quarters of the sub and finished the beer when he decided to rest his eyes for a second.

Rusty was in and out of a fitful sleep when something on the news jolted him wide-awake. " . . . to recap the top stories of the day—Local anesthesiologist Michael Carlucci was killed late last night when a tractor trailer collided with his vehicle on Route 283. State police spokesperson, Chip Zimmer, is saying it looks like Carlucci fell asleep at the wheel in the dangerous construction zone, precipitating the accident. Police are recommending extreme caution through the construction area and urging motorists to follow the reduced speed limits. Fines are doubled in the area, and speed-watch patrols have been beefed up."

"Holy batshit!" Rusty shouted as he leapt off the sofa, scattering the remains of the hoagie.

CHAPTER THIRTY

Bryan Marshall checked the digital clock on his desk—1:00 a.m. Things were getting out of control. But he'd deal with it—he always had. Landry was on call tonight and Raskin said he'd take care of everything, but Marshall had his doubts about that. Raskin was acting increasingly bizarre; the stress must be too much. Probably not a good idea to trust him to get this right. In fact, he wondered whether he could trust him at all. Too much at stake.

Marshall sat behind his desk, unlocked the bottom drawer, and opened it. Leaning close, he used the key around his neck to unlock the metal box inside. He reached in and pulled out two gleaming revolvers. He held them lovingly, one in each hand, hefting them and feeling their reassuring weight. He checked to see that both were loaded; they were. He smiled—he had foreseen this eventuality.

Marshall tucked each gun into a different side-pocket of his long white coat. He reached down to close the metal box, but hesitated. He should be taking care of business, but he could never resist the folder with the pictures. God, he needed to get a grip on this. It would only take a couple of minutes, though. He slid several issues of *Hustler* magazine out of the way and pulled out a plain manila folder. He opened it and flipped through the stack of photographs. A close-up of Sharon DeCorso, circa 1974, looking particularly fetching, caught his attention. He leaned back in his chair and let the picture transport him twenty-four years into the past.

Summer is my downfall. Marshall sat at his desk, fingering some enlarged glossies. Do they have to wear such clothes? He was bemoaning the latest fashion trend of the mid-seventies—hot pants and halter-tops. His photographs showed several of the nursing students walking into the hospital in their abbreviated civilian garb. "It's just not my fault," he muttered, beginning to breathe hard. A large proportion of his photos were of one particular student, Sharon DeCorso, who was scheduled to meet with him momentarily. God, she's a peach! What would she be wearing today?

Marshall paused to pat himself on the back; he had handpicked all the anesthesia students. He was a firm believer in the maxim, "knowledge is power" and prided himself on his extensive background checks of prospective students. There was always a long line of applicants eager to enter the lucrative ranks of nurse anesthesia. His selection criteria were simple really—female, young, intelligent, attractive, and most important, an exploitable weakness. Like taking candy from a baby.

Marshall knew he held all the aces today. No more screw-ups, like with Karen McCarthy. He had perfected his technique, honed his craft. Yesterday he had caught Sharon, red-handed, stealing cocaine. Today's meeting had been scheduled to discuss this unfortunate occurrence.

He, of course, had known all about Miss DeCorso's predilection for controlled substances. Her application mentioned several instances of altered narcotics records from her previous nursing job, but he had chosen to overlook these. Everyone deserved a second chance, right? Could he help it if someone had left some cocaine lying about last night? He certainly didn't make her steal it.

There was a knock at the door. Marshall got up and opened it.

"Come in Sharon." He positively beamed when he saw her. "Good of you to stop by early. My, my, don't you look nice this morning!"

Marshall sat back in his chair, staring off into space, his heart pounding. Something was pulling him back to the present, but he resisted; the fun was just beginning. He continued to watch the scene of Sharon's encounter play across his mind. He saw himself slamming his fists down on the desk just as he screamed the word "cocaine." He saw her crumble before him and beg for mercy.

With a start, Marshall opened his eyes. He realized with fresh insight that this part, this euphoria of power, was just as delectable, perhaps more so, than what inevitably followed. This surprised him mildly, and he wondered where this had come from and why now, after all these years? The image of Sharon's pretty face, twisted and littered with tears, triggered an even older memory. He saw a small, helpless boy crying, a large man looming over him with a leather belt clenched in his angry hands.

Marshall felt an unexpected twinge of pity for Sharon and the other women in these pictures. This surprised him even more. What the hell was going on? Was he going soft like Raskin? He quickly packed up the photos and shook his head to clear away these troubling thoughts. He put his hands back in his pockets and caressed the guns, drawing comfort from their cool, smooth, metallic surfaces.

Guilt had never been a big problem with him. Since an early age, Marshall had learned that the much larger, real concern in life was not getting caught. His father had taught him that lesson well. Guilt had too many supernatural or religious overtones—something he really didn't go in for. Who cared if he did something wrong? In fact, if you removed some all-powerful God from the equation, there was no right or wrong—just rules and consequences.

That was Raskin's problem. He suffered from a heavy load of guilt—his damned Catholic upbringing at work. Through the years, Marshall had carefully cultivated Raskin, molding him as necessary, always relying on the twin motivators of greed and guilt to prod him along. He remembered it had not always been an easy process; there had been a turning point. He recalled clearly their conversation after he had had his way, right here on this desk, with Miss DeCorso.

"So Bryan, you, uh, conducted another interview this morning?" Raskin said sarcastically. He was sitting in the same chair Sharon had occupied hours ago and Karen McCarthy had refused to sit in one year before that.

"An interim evaluation really, not an interview," Marshall said matter-of-factly, pretending not to be ruffled by the question. "You know what I always say, Joe—a bird in the bush is worth two in the hand." He slapped his knee and laughed heartily.

Raskin didn't join in. "Oh, I see. Forgive my error—It's just I can't keep them all straight."

He shot Raskin a burning glare. "Listen, Joe. That will be quite enough—"

"Will it?" Raskin was out of his seat now, stabbing the air with his finger. "Don't you think you're carrying this thing a bit too far? Have you no fucking self-control?" If the desk hadn't been in the way, Raskin's finger would have been tattooing his chest.

"Sit down!" Marshall hammered the desk with his fist. "I don't need any lectures on morality from you. I know what I'm doing."

"Look, I just don't want any suspicions aroused, OK? We don't want the police or the feds probing around here asking questions."

Raskin was obviously still hot, but must've realized it was not wise to anger him any further, and sank back into his chair.

"Look Joe, I said I'd handle it. I've got things under control. You worry about—shall we say—how neat and tidy the books are."

Raskin looked hurt. "As long as we don't trigger an audit, there's no problem. If we do, we can shuffle things around quickly. It'll work—Bart said he'd give the whole thing his seal of approval."

"And you trust a freaking CPA?" Marshall said, shaking his head with disgust. "That little weasel."

"Yeah, I do. He's in over his head, too."

"It better work. I don't feel like going to the lockup for your bloody incompetence. What about Hinkson—any problem there?"

"Hinkson?"

"Yes, Hinkson. He's too fucking righteous. Why'd we ever hire him?"

Raskin shrugged his shoulders. "I don't know—seemed OK at the time. You voted to make him a partner."

"Yeah, yeah, don't remind me. He fooled all of us."

"Pickings were slim at the time, as I remember," Raskin offered helpfully. He ran his fingers through his hair and appeared to weigh his words. "Listen, if Hinkson catches wind of any of our creative bookkeeping or your interviewing techniques, we're screwed big time."

"We've got to get rid or him," Marshall said.

"On what grounds? He's too damned honest?" Raskin moaned. He stood up and paced about the small office.

"Look Joe, you helped me write the blasted corporate bylaws. Don't you remember?"

Raskin looked puzzled.

"We don't need a reason," he continued. "All it takes is a majority vote."

"Will the others go along with it? It's pretty nasty."

"Of course they will, after I explain it to them," Marshall said with conviction. "They won't like it, but they'll do it."

"So we vote him out." Raskin stopped pacing and looked at him. "When?"

"Next corporate meeting—I don't think we should wait on this."

"But, we need another guy," Raskin whined. "This place is getting too damned busy."

"No problem, Joe. We'll take a graduating resident—these guys are much easier to control and keep in the dark. We'll pay him peanuts and enroll him in the infamous five-year partnership track," Marshall said with a laugh.

"Think we'll find anyone?" Raskin asked.

"Sure. Peanuts will sound like a king's ransom to these starving residents."

"Yeah, I guess you're right," Raskin said. "Funny how fast you forget."

"After three or four years, we'll regretfully announce that it's just not working out; we're not quite as compatible as we thought—sorry old chap—no renewed contract, no partnership, no hard feelings."

"You've got this all figured out, don't you?" Raskin said. Understanding was dawning across his face.

"We save big on salary—but here's the *pièce de résistance*— they don't collect any retirement money because they're not vested until after five years. Check the fine print."

"You're slime," Raskin said, but his voice carried an unmistakable hint of admiration.

"So, I've been told." Marshall stood up, walked over to Raskin, and put his arm around him. Then he continued in a lower voice, "Joe, the real money is in the bonus money—you know that. Think about it. The fewer partners we have, the bigger our slice of the pie." Raskin's eyes lit up, and an evil smile began to stretch across his face. "We can probably clear over a hundred thousand per man in bonus money this year."

Raskin whistled and said, "You don't say." He was fully on board, now.

"Anyway, the process repeats itself with the next sucker and we dance our way into retirement—filthy rich retirement!"

"Amen, brother!"

"And remember, Joe, it's like I always say—a women's behind is under every successful man."

This time, Raskin joined him in raucous laughter.

Bryan Marshall opened his eyes, stood up, and walked to the door. He was aware of the heavy loads in his pockets. He flicked off the light switch and locked the door behind him. His days of having his way with the nursing students were gone, but he still knew how to amuse himself. He patted his pockets as he headed down to the OR. Time to take care of business.

CHAPTER THIRTY-ONE

Doug entered the surgeon's lounge and thought he was seeing a mirage—a pot of steaming coffee. *My lucky day.* He poured a cup and drank the styrofoam flavored coffee as usual—in three hurried sips the vile tasting fluid was gone leaving a blackish residue inside of the cup.

Hospital coffee was notoriously bad. The coffee in the surgeon's lounge at Mercy Hospital was no exception. It derived its unique aroma and taste from three separate factors. First, the ground coffee was the cheapest variety available. Second, the glass coffeepot used to brew the coffee had a black tarry substance coating the inside—the by-product of years of continuous service. The pot looked more at home in an oil refinery than in a hospital. Finally, the coffee frequently cooked on the burner for hours, especially at this time of night. Nobody seemed to mind that too much. You drank this coffee for its punch, and in this category, it scored very well, thank you. You didn't drink this coffee to celebrate the moments of your life.

Doug barely noticed the funny, bitter, slightly metallic taste of his fourth cup of coffee of the day; he'd tasted worse from the venerable Bunn-o-matic. His first inkling that anything was wrong was a slight blurring of his otherwise sharp vision. He initially dismissed it as a symptom of overwork and fatigue, which wasn't uncommon on a call night. However, the slightly out of focus vision quickly converted to double vision, which he couldn't ignore. He shook his head several times, but the lounge continued to swim in double images. Differential diagnoses from his medical school days flowed unbidden into his mind—brain tumor, cerebral bleed, embolus, myasthenia gravis, multiple sclerosis, etc. Feeling suddenly very tired of standing, Doug sat down and tried to collect his thoughts. He was becoming noticeably weaker by the second.

Gotta keep cool—gotta think. Panic threatened to overwhelm him; all his training and experience under fire seemed useless. With great effort, he thrust the panic aside and forced himself to concentrate. His mind, functioning in overdrive, completed the necessary connections: blurred vision—double vision—weakness—muscle relaxant—coffee poisoned—not much time—wait, one last chance.

Doug attempted to stand and immediately collapsed to all fours, spilling his coffee on the floor. His trunk muscles were already too weak to support his weight. He crawled out of the lounge, his hands slipping on the coffee, into the hallway. His head felt like it weighed a hundred pounds, and he couldn't lift it to see where he was going. It didn't matter because he knew the layout of the OR complex in his sleep. He headed for the anesthesia workroom, which was only about twenty feet from the lounge, and the closest place that had what he was looking for.

Doug knew he had to race down the hall as fast as he could while he still had some strength. He was facing a grisly battle with time. He couldn't get it out of his mind what a horrible way to die this would be—mind alert and unable to breathe. This is what

Stephanie, the obstetrical patient from his residency days, must've felt like.

Focus, he commanded himself.

He ignored the ever-increasing weight of his limbs.

He ignored the work it took to suck in a deep breath.

He ignored his heart hammering wildly in his chest on an adrenaline frenzy.

He had gone fifteen feet down the hall when he collapsed onto his chest. His arms and legs were giving out under the crushing weight of his body. Odd thoughts sparked across his mind: *Luke, his six-month-old nephew—this is what it must feel like to be a baby, to have flailing arms and legs, but not enough strength to propel the body. Very frustrating. Maybe that's why babies cry so much? Focus! Focus! Get to the workroom.*

He crept down the hall snakelike, scraping his face on the cold linoleum floor.

Four feet. Three feet. Two feet.

He grasped the doorjamb and taking advantage of the extra leverage managed to pull himself to the doorway threshold. His legs were now useless pillars of lead. *Get the lead out—gotta get the lead out boys*, his brain gibbered. Pushing against the inside of the doorjamb, he crossed into the interior of the anesthesia workroom.

Here were countless drawers and cabinets containing hundreds of different drugs and assorted airway supplies. Doug could no longer move his body any further on the floor. However, he could still move his arms and hands. Barely able to reach, he quickly opened the drawer marked with the letters M - T. *Thank God for my gorilla arms.* Lying on the floor, he couldn't see inside the drawer. He frantically scooped out the contents. Several ampules shattered on the floor, leaving slivers of glass strewn about. He searched the intact vials and ampules, cutting his fingers in the process. *Where is it? Where is it? Must be here. Not much time.*

Finally he found what he was looking for—a small bottle of Tensilon. He reached into his jacket pocket where he knew he had some used syringes. *Won't worry about a dirty syringe and AIDS today.* He quickly drew up approximately 100 milligrams of Tensilon into one of the syringes. Tensilon was a cholinesterase inhibitor drug, which acts to antagonize a drug-induced neuro-muscular blockade. In short, it was the antidote to his paralysis.

Doug, of course, knew two other important considerations of reversal drugs, like Tensilon. First, they are typically given intra-venously when used in the O.R. Intravenous administration pro-vides quick access to the bloodstream, and from there to the entire body. Doug also knew he had neither the time nor strength to start an IV, even if he had all the equipment right at hand. Still, the medicine would work intramuscularly, although the onset would be slower. There was one other route that he knew would be faster.

Doug rammed the needle through the skin underneath his chin, upward into the fleshy underbelly of his tongue. No alcohol swab today. He injected the contents rapidly into his tongue, ignoring the exquisite pain elicited by this maneuver. The tongue was a highly vascular muscle, allowing for relatively rapid absorption—not as fast as the intravenous route, but far superior to a shot in the arm, leg, or buttock. He knew seconds counted.

Doug was also acutely aware that Tensilon had some potent side effects. These are routinely countered by the administration of a second drug—Atropine. He didn't have the luxury of time to give two injections; besides, he couldn't reach the A-G drawer. Tensilon by itself causes a severe vagal response, which if unop-posed may cause a profound slowing or even cessation of the heartbeat. Doug knew he had run out of options, and would have to chance it.

Doug's breathing became markedly labored. He needed to do one more thing. Just inside the doorway in the corner of the workroom was a green E-cylinder of oxygen fitted with a regu-lator device and Ambu bag attachment. Using all his dwindling strength, Doug managed to topple the Ambu bag off the top of the cylinder. Propping his left arm with his right, he reached the oxygen flowmeter and turned it on. A loud hissing noise of the gas flowing down the plastic tubing and into the Ambu filled his ears. His left arm crashed down uselessly to the floor, crunching some ampules underneath. He felt sharp stabs of pain as several shards of broken glass embedded in his arm. The Ambu bag came to rest about a foot from his face. He felt the stream of oxygen emanating from the mask wash coolly over his face. It would have to be enough.

Doug could not move. He continued to breathe in short rapid gasps, as his diaphragm continued to struggle. Even though the diaphragm is the most resistant muscle in the body to neuromuscular blockers, it too could not stand up long to the paralyzing onslaught. Doug took his last gasp. He could still see and think clearly, if you counted suffocating awake conducive to lucid thought.

His chest began to burn as he ached to breathe. How long could you hold your breath? One minute, maybe two at tops. He knew that I.V. Tensilon took about three minutes to work—intramuscular probably double. The hissing of the oxygen became a roaring in his ears like the surf crashing over his head. Mixed in with the roar, he heard his heartbeat pounding wildly. His surroundings began to dim, and he realized he was slipping into the black oblivion of unconsciousness.

Please God, don't let me die like this. He recalled the panicked look in Stephanie's eyes and realized he must look just like her. His mind wandered, and he saw his three boys playing tag on an impossibly green field. The boys' faces were resplendent with their innocent child-smiles, although Anthony's toothy grin always tended toward the impish. He saw Laura standing off to the side, gazing at him with her beautiful smile and long black hair; her clear laughter surrounded them.

For perhaps the first time, he fully fathomed the enormity of her love, of their love, and it shook him to the core. He saw that his whole life of burying emotions and love was a fool's game. He was hurting the very people he loved. Because of his cowardice, his unwillingness to risk vulnerability, he had cheated himself out of the fullness of love, deprived himself of unknown heights their relationship could've attained. Doug saw all of this as clearly as he saw his death approaching. He ached with intense regret and shame; what he'd give for a second chance. Although he felt he had failed them, Doug immersed himself in the protective womb of his family, trying to attain a measure of peace as he waited for the end. His last flicker of conscious thought noted that his run-away heartbeat was slowing rapidly.

* * *

Raskin removed the sterile cap from the end of the epidural catheter and attached a ten cc syringe filled with 0.25% Marcaine. He injected with the surprising amount of force necessary to overcome the resistance of the two-and-a-half foot, narrow-bore tubing protruding from his patient's lumbar spine.

"There, there, Mrs. Concepcion. That should take care of the pain," he said to the sobbing woman, trying to sound like he gave a shit. Raskin realized he had a problem. Ordinarily after reinjecting an epidural, one waited and observed the patient for at least fifteen minutes for any side effects. Most common was a fall in the blood pressure. It was also possible, although rare, to see grand-mal seizures following an inadvertent intravascular injection of Marcaine into an epidural vein. Raskin didn't have fifteen minutes.

He knew he had a tight schedule to keep if he was going to rid himself once and for all from that meddlesome creep Landry. He also had to get rid of that coffeepot before anyone else drank from it. He checked his watch again for the hundredth time—1:05 a.m. The Atracurium should be taking effect right about now.

His plan was simple, but required his presence. He went over it again. Raskin wanted to be first on the scene to aid the good Doctor Landry. He would pretend to resuscitate him in case anyone was watching. He intended to inject a lethal quantity of cocaine intravenously during the "resuscitation." Then his death would look like an unintentional overdose, not a strange asphyxiation with no apparent cause.

Raskin smiled inwardly at the simplicity of his plan. So, Doctor Landry is revealed as an IV drug abuser. Not much sympathy there, he thought. Another victim of the high-stress OR environment. Regrettable. Not really. People always wanted to believe the worst about fat-cat doctors anyway. Raskin chuckled, then abruptly stopped.

One small problem remained. What if someone had already found Landry? He reasoned this was unlikely, since he had heard no 'Code Blue' announced over the hospital intercom. But even if they had, he would immediately take over the code, being the most appropriate ranking physician in the house. He would then give the cocaine, which he had already labeled as epinephrine, a standard drug given at resuscitations. This would guarantee an unsuccessful outcome of the resuscitation, had it in fact begun before Landry was actually dead from the Atracurium. It would also ensure that the toxicology screen would be positive in spades for cocaine. Nobody would bother to look further for traces of Atracurium, a drug all but unknown to the pathologists. Anyway, even if they thought to look for it, the Atracurium would be long gone, owing to its ongoing molecular disintegration.

But he needed to get downstairs immediately. So he left the wailing Mrs. Concepcion, assured her the epidural would kick in soon, hoped her blood pressure would remain stable, and hightailed it down to the OR. He, of course, couldn't have cared less whether her blood pressure fell, or for that matter whether she seized and died. He was beyond all that. However, he didn't want any suspicions aroused toward him that he was behaving peculiarly and not following standard protocol. Or worse, if

Mrs. Concepcion had a problem, they would be stat paging him just when he planned to be occupied.

Raskin took the steps two at a time down to the OR. He burst through the automatic doors, almost walking into them as they failed to get out of his way quickly enough. The OR complex was darkened and had an eerie quality about it; a place of such usual frenetic activity, crowded with all sorts of scurrying people, seemed unnaturally still as if some large catastrophe had befallen mankind and he was the only survivor. He entered the surgeon's lounge.

Empty. The coffeepot was there, looking guilty as sin. The only light issued tentatively from a small table lamp in the far corner of the room. There was a spilled cup of coffee on the floor. No Landry, though. He can't have gotten far. He dumped the coffeepot and ran down the main corridor into the OR complex. He quickly scanned all six operating rooms. Nothing.

Luckily, the place was devoid of people. No pain-in-the-ass cleaning personnel or night nursing supervisors roaming the halls. Where the hell was Landry, though? Could someone have found him? No, he reminded himself, they would've called a code, and he would have heard it on the overhead page. He's got to be here somewhere. Maybe the recovery room.

Raskin reversed his direction down the corridor and made a left to the hallway, which led to the recovery room. Soon, he heard a hissing sound coming from somewhere up ahead. The workroom—and aha!—here was the good Doctor Landry looking rather dead; at least he didn't see any evidence of respiration. Strange, he didn't look more cyanotic. No matter. If he wasn't entirely dead, he would be in a matter of moments. Chuckling to himself, he whipped out the syringe loaded with enough cocaine to send ten men to their graves.

Raskin turned toward the row of drawers to get a tourniquet to allow him to carry out the lethal venipuncture. He found one and knelt down beside the prone body. He rolled Landry's limp body over onto its back and roughly cinched the tourniquet around his right arm. He tapped briskly at the crook of Landry's elbow, coaxing a large antecubital vein to stand out. He paused for a moment and bent down until his beard was practically touching Landry's right ear. He said in a low voice, "You two smart guys fell for the oldest trick in the book." He took the syringe and deftly inserted the needle into the vein and prepared to push the plunger. "Goodbye Doctor Landry."

CHAPTER THIRTY-TWO

Doug regained consciousness slowly. He imagined he was lying on the beach in Hawaii, the surf pounding in his ears. But the roaring gradually coalesced to a hiss different from the ocean, and his head throbbed miserably. His body seemed to be pinned down by some unseen force, gravity perhaps, as if he had awoken on the surface of Jupiter. The air was very thick, and he had tremendous air hunger.

Doug opened his eyes. The sight of the workroom jolted his memory back into place. *God, I'm alive!* Amazing! The Tensilon and the oxygen must have done the trick. He tried to leap up from the floor, but was horrified to discover that his muscles were still flaccid lumps. Slight twitching rippled down his arms and legs, but nothing actually moved. Fear quickly returned. His breathing was steadily improving, but he knew he was extremely vulnerable. Although he could feel strength seeping back into his frozen limbs second by second, he guessed he probably needed at least ten more minutes to have any respectable power. He wondered who was behind all of this. In answer to his question, he heard the OR automatic door open and loud, determined footsteps echo off the floor. Someone had undoubtedly returned to finish their business. The footsteps receded—probably down the main OR complex hallway. OR doors opened and slammed shut. The menacing footsteps grew louder.

Doug could now move his arms and legs, but still couldn't get up. *Shit, what can I do?* He scanned the room, desperate for ideas. Doug decided his only hope was to play possum as long as he could and hope he would be strong enough to defend himself when the time came.

The footsteps were on top of him now. With his eyes shut, Doug ceased breathing for the second time within fifteen minutes—this time voluntarily. He strained with all his remaining senses to figure out what was going on.

An unmistakable hulking presence, complete with offensive body odor and stale cologne, knelt down beside him. Raskin! That's Raskin!

Drawers behind him opened and slammed shut. When he felt the rubber tourniquet being roughly applied to his arm, panic again threatened. What horrible substance would he be exposed to now? Surely something lethal—potassium, epinephrine, fentanyl, morphine, cocaine? Wasn't one poisoning enough for a day? He squelched further panicky thoughts and concentrated hard.

Gotta wait 'til the last possible second. Surprise and delay are my only hope. Doug knew he had no way to gauge his recovery until he actually moved, and he couldn't risk that yet. He hoped it would be enough. Then he felt the needle pierce his skin.

Doug jerked his arm violently away from the needle. He ignored the sharp, stabbing pain as the needle ripped a gash in his arm. Simultaneously, he screamed as loudly as he could—mostly for the shock effect it would have on Raskin, who no doubt thought he was dealing with a corpse. He also hoped someone might hear.

Raskin, looking like he had seen a ghost, recoiled in horror, his eyes bugging wide. Doug propelled himself backwards a few feet. He noted he was still woefully weak. Raskin recovered quickly and pounced on Doug, all two-hundred-and-sixty pounds pinning him to the floor. His meaty hands rapidly encircled Doug's neck and squeezed with tremendous force. Doug thrashed about with his legs and punched wildly, but the blows carried no real force and Raskin ignored them. Raskin's face turned dark red, his facial muscles locked in strain. Several ragged cut marks running across his left cheek oozed blood; it looked like he had been clawed recently. But his eyes told the real story; sanity was no longer a major player.

Doug became frantic; he realized he would not regain his strength in time. He only had about a minute of consciousness remaining before he sank into the abyss—this time for good; no clever pharmacology would pull him back. *It's over! Beaten.* Doug's feeling of failure was complete. He felt he almost deserved his fate.

"Say hello to Carlucci for me!" Raskin said, as he throttled him harder. "His crash was no accident, by the way." He laughed and added, "I slipped him a mickey. He fell for it, same as you."

Mike! He's talking about Mike! He didn't deserve his fate! The thought of this slimy bastard murdering Mike went through Doug's brain like a lightening bolt, illuminating the deeper recesses of his mind.

Inside every person there is an irreducible core; when the chaff of civilized nature and nicety are burned away, one finds out what one is really made of. Doug discovered his sphere of titanium steel buried down deep. He had never seen it clearly before, only gotten vague hints of its presence once or twice when his back was against the wall. Perhaps the frost, coating his deepest feelings, had obscured his view. But he had never been pushed this far or this hard. Now his extremity demanded more. His being shrank to embrace the sphere and no further. He drew strength from his inner self and from sources beyond.

It was time to take a stand. Doug still couldn't break Raskin's death grip, but even though it was nearly impossible, he arched his back for all he was worth. Every muscle in his body strained prodigiously and his neck cords felt like they would snap any second. He managed to squirm six inches to his left. And again another six inches.

Doug was now just able to reach the cabinet where the Suprane was stored; he opened the door with his outstretched left hand. If he could just reach a bottle or two. Suprane was one of the newest anesthetic agents that had a very rapid induction and emergence time. A small amount of Suprane vapor inhaled would cause rapid loss of consciousness. The only problem was that Suprane existed as a liquid, not a vapor at room temperature. To vaporize the liquid, one needed either a higher temperature or a larger surface area to serve as a wick. Doug knew of both.

With his strength approaching fifty percent and with his air hunger becoming unbearable, Doug frantically waved his hand inside the cabinet, searching. Raskin had a smug smile on his face. If Raskin would just ignore his flailing hand for a little bit longer. Finally, Doug connected with something solid. Two or three Suprane bottles smashed against each other and shattered. A sharp glass edge of one of the broken bottles gouged deeply into the palm of his hand. Suprane spilled out onto his cut hand and burned tremendously. Doug ignored the pain. He quickly withdrew his arm, his hand dripping with blood and Suprane, and smeared the mix all over Raskin's beard.

Raskin shrieked and sucked in a gigantic breath—and then promptly passed out. The air rushing through his beard must've vaporized enough Suprane, because he lost consciousness within seconds. He slumped on top of Doug, his hands releasing their death grip. Doug's head spun from a combination of not enough oxygen and too much Suprane. He pushed the limp but massive body of Raskin off him and wobbled to his feet. He stood hunched over with his hands on his knees and drew in several more deep breaths. Ah, sweet air—it felt so good to breathe normally. He staggered to the doorway, thinking he would call for help.

Raskin rammed him with a flying tackle that knocked the wind out of him and sent them both sprawling out into the hallway. Raskin had regained consciousness almost as fast as he had lost it. The manufacturers of Suprane would have been proud.

Doug's head hit the floor, opening up a gash above his right eye. His anger knew no bounds; it ignited and burned through his brain, like rocket fuel fed by liquid oxygen.

He ignored Raskin's bulk on top of him again.

He ignored his heaving chest, convulsing to retrieve air into his lungs.

The blaze inside his skull permitted only one thought—revenge.

This time, he vowed, the fight would be different. The playing field was level now, even though Raskin outweighed him by seventy pounds. Doug had all his strength back and then some. Energized by his hatred, fueled by his anger, he shrugged Raskin's body off and freed himself from the clutching hands. They both clambered to their feet, faced each other, and began circling.

"Why'd you kill him, you bastard?" Doug shouted, breathing hard. Blood flowed freely into his right eye causing him to blink.

"I didn't—that trucker did." Raskin was wheezing loudly, but drew his fists up in a protective boxer's stance. "I only gave him something to help him sleep."

Doug stopped circling for a moment, stood up straight, and stared at Raskin; all the pieces of the puzzle slammed into place. *Mike and Rusty were right—should've listened to them.* Raskin took advantage of Doug's hesitation and landed several solid jabs to his chest. Doug rocked back on his feet to help absorb the blows. "You killed him because he was onto you—you sabotaged Mike's case and killed his patient, too!" Doug shouted.

Raskin sneered back at him. "I didn't kill that fat, Polish S.O.B. Just because you guys couldn't deal with a little V-tach—it's not my fault."

Doug resumed his crouch and looked for an opening. He yearned to smash Raskin's smirking face. "You put epi in my syringes too, didn't you? And screwed up Ken's vaporizers!"

"Of course I did! I had no choice. I wasn't about to lose my job to the likes of you."

"You sick bastard." So that's what this was all about. Doug shook his head in disgust.

"You're the one who's sick," Raskin fired back. "The whole hospital knows about you and that sleazy SICU bitch—how you get a fucking hard-on every time she walks in the room."

Doug tasted his own blood and then feinted to the left. Raskin appeared confused by Doug's quickness and reacted slowly. Doug delivered several piston-like right crosses and a crushing left hook to his head, knocking Raskin to the floor senseless. "What's wrong, Joe? Not so much fun fighting someone who's not paralyzed?"

Doug straddled him, wrapped his hands around his neck, and squeezed with all his might. Raskin made sputtering sounds as he tried to say something, his eyes wide with panic. Doug wasn't interested in hearing anymore. "Payback is hell, Joe!"

CHAPTER THIRTY-THREE

"Hold it right there, Landry!" boomed the deep baritone of Bryan Marshall, brandishing a jet-black nine millimeter Walther pistol in his gloved hand. "Let him go!" Marshall shouted. Marshall was positioned fifteen feet down the hallway, near the cysto room, gun trained at Doug. Too far to rush him.

Doug released his stranglehold on Raskin's bull neck and stood up slowly. Raskin rolled to his side, sputtered, coughed and took in several ragged breaths. He rubbed his neck vigorously, but could not erase the reddened imprints left by Doug's hands.

"Should've figured you'd be involved in this Marshall," Doug said, trying to conceal his shock. He had thought the puzzle had been complete. Marshall was greedy, no question about it, but Doug didn't see him involved in sabotage and murder to keep his job. Marshall, for all his faults, was a competent anesthesiologist. He was still missing some critical link between these two.

"For Chrissakes, Bryan, shoot him!" croaked Raskin hoarsely from the floor.

"Not so fast, Joe. You had your chance, and you screwed up. I'll take care of things *my* way now." Marshall closed the distance to about ten feet, just across from the door to cysto. "We need to ask Dr. Landry, here, a couple of questions first."

"I say shoot first, ask questions later." Raskin pulled himself to his knees with difficulty, still trying to catch his breath. His green scrub shirt was sweat soaked under the arms and down the front; Doug could smell him. Dried blood—Doug's blood—was still crusted on his beard. "He almost fucking killed me!"

Marshall was the only one of the three who seemed calm; as if he were at a business meeting. "Now, Landry, why don't you tell us what you know," he ordered in schoolmarm manner as he adjusted his glasses.

"Go fuck yourself, Marshall!" Doug shot back and wiped blood from his eye. His left hand ached miserably where the Suprane bottle had cut it.

"Tsk, tsk, that won't do," Marshall said tauntingly. "You can do better than that. A clever man like you." Then without a trace of humor, his eyes suddenly cold, he asked, "How did you figure it out? Who else knows?" He raised his arm, cocked the gun and aimed it at Doug's chest.

Doug was rattled by the gun, his thoughts scrambled, but he was determined to keep Marshall talking—buy any time he could to come up with a plan. But what should he say?

"So, you knew about the sabotaged cases, Marshall?" Doug practically shouted, hoping the increased volume would mask the fear in his voice. Marshall didn't answer, but stared back, poker-faced.

"Of course he knew," Raskin said. "It was his idea!"

Marshall eyed Raskin with surprise, eyebrows raised. Doug glanced over at Raskin.

"It doesn't matter if he knows now," Raskin said as he climbed to his feet. "He'll be joining his friend, Carlucci, soon enough."

Doug turned to face the gun again. "Why in God's name, Marshall? Those were innocent people."

"You fool! We weren't trying to kill anyone. Raskin may have been a little overzealous with the adrenaline dose."

Raskin scowled briefly at Marshall.

"But why, Marshall?" Doug asked, although he was pretty sure he already knew the answer. "You still haven't given me a reason."

"Pinnacle's coming in here, Landry. I got the official word last week—I only told you guys the half of it. They're cleaning house and only a few of us are going to stay."

Marshall paused for a moment, cocking his head as if he'd heard something. "We just wanted to stack the deck in our favor."

"So you murdered innocent people." Doug realized that he had badly underestimated Marshall's callousness. These two would stop at nothing—Marshall would certainly not let him leave here alive.

Marshall ignored him. "Now tell us who else knows!"

"You can still go fuck yourself!" Doug's fists bunched; all his muscles were taut. His body demanded action, but he was still pinned down by the gun.

"Listen, Landry," Marshall said, and a cruel smile slid across his face. "If you're trying to protect Melissa Draybeck, well let's just say you'd be wasting your time."

"Why!? What have you done to her?" A sickening dread descended on Doug like a heavy curtain, making it hard to breathe.

"Me, nothing," Marshall responded, "but Joe did seem to have a disagreement with her about her cat."

A strange look crossed Raskin's face, and he absently fingered the cuts on his cheek.

"Her body was just discovered tonight," Marshall said with a feral grin.

Doug gasped. He felt as if he'd been sucker punched and might be sick at any moment. He wheeled to face Raskin. "You butcher! How many more, Raskin?" Doug's fingers coiled and uncoiled, aching to return to Raskin's neck and complete their job. Unable to control his seething, Doug took a step toward Raskin, arms outstretched, until he was almost within reach.

Marshall fired. The bullet whistled right by Doug's head; the report was deafening in the confined hallway.

Shit! That was close. Doug froze in his tracks, his eyes darting back and forth between the Walther and Raskin. The smell of spent gunpowder was already noticeable.

"The next one won't miss, Landry," Marshall said and continued to point the smoking gun at Landry. "Don't try it again!" The veins on Marshall's head bulged dangerously. Doug's ears were still ringing, and he had trouble hearing Marshall even though he was shouting.

Raskin stared hard at Doug, his eyes daring him to make a move. "There's one more thing you should know, Landry," Raskin said.

"What's that?" It was all Doug could do not to jump him; anything was better than this hellish immobility.

"Remember that nurse anesthesia school that used to be here?" Raskin continued.

"Yeah, it was shut down right after I came," Doug said.

"Well, Bryan here used to have a thing for the nursing students. Right, Bryan?" Raskin shot a glance toward Marshall, who was eyeing him curiously.

"Shut up, Joe," Marshall said evenly, but his eyes betrayed a touch of alarm.

Finally, things were beginning to make sense. "So that's why you put up with him for all these years," Doug said to Marshall. Marshall shrugged noncommittally.

"I'd heard rumors," Landry said and turned back to Raskin. "What happened Raskin?" This was the critical connection!

"I said shut up, Joe!" Marshall said louder. His tone brooked no refusal.

"Look," Raskin said, pleading slightly. "I just don't want Landry going to his grave thinking I'm the only slimeball around here. Besides, it feels good to get it off my chest."

"You're not in the bloody confessional!" Marshall screamed, his accent thickening. Marshall and Raskin traded glares.

"What happened, Raskin?" Doug prodded softly, sensing a wedge was being driven between the two and that this might be his only hope. If only Raskin would keep talking.

Raskin ran his fingers through his hair and coughed. "Well, let's just say one of the girls got into a family way and had an unfortunate accident," Raskin said, a touch of defiance evident in his voice.

"Who was it?" Doug pushed. Out of the corner of his eye, he saw Marshall sighting down the barrel of the gun.

CHAPTER THIRTY-FOUR

Rusty pressed the gas pedal hard to the floor. The engine of his beat-up Jeep Wrangler coughed first and then sputtered up to full roar; it was an unhealthy roar though, a whine really, that sounded like a piston or connecting rod might go at any moment.

"I need more power, Scottie," Rusty said, imitating James T. Kirk of the Starship Enterprise.

"Aye, Cap'n—warp nine," Rusty replied to himself as Mr. Scott with his best Scottish accent. "But Jim, I cannot guarantee this bucket of bolts will hold together." He smiled and glanced at his dashboard clock. It was vibrating badly as the Jeep topped out at seventy-five mph, but he could make out the time—1:05 a.m.

Twenty minutes later, Rusty screeched to a halt in front of Mercy Hospital's Emergency Room entrance. He jumped out and bolted for the door. Once inside, he bounded up the stairs two-at-a-time to the second floor operating room complex.

Gotta warn Doctor Landry.

The hallway leading up to the automatic OR doors was deserted. Rusty ran forward. Just before he came within range of the optical door sensor, he heard a gunshot ring out from within the OR complex. He stopped dead in his tracks, his sneakers squeaking on the floor.

"Shit," he mumbled to himself. "My spider sense is tingling." Security would quickly mobilize, he thought, but then remembered he wasn't at the Med Center. Mercy, the sleepy little community hospital, had no armed security. But surely someone would call the police, having heard the gunshot. Except this would take time—precious time he didn't have.

Rusty quickly abandoned the idea of a frontal assault through the noisy OR doors; a stealth approach made more sense. There was a side door into the cysto room that the X-ray technicians used to enter the OR. But he had to hurry.

Rusty opened the side door and crept noiselessly into the cysto room. As the door closed behind him, he was immersed in utter darkness. He paused to let his eyes adjust. Soon he could make out a sliver of light beneath the far door which led into the main OR hallway. He tiptoed carefully across the room toward the faint light, his hands stretched out in front of him like a blind man. In this fashion, he soon located the OR table in the center of the room and saved himself from banging into it. He maneuvered around the table, and just when he thought he was home free, his right foot connected with something solid. A metal bucket mounted on wheels went flying across the room and crashed into the wall, making a tremendous clanging.

Rusty froze, held his breath, and listened. He waited for the door to fly open and a hail of bullets to greet him. His heart was hammering so loudly in his ears, he could barely hear.

A minute passed. Nothing happened.

Rusty started to breathe again and closed the distance to the door. Angry voices were coming from the hallway, but he still couldn't make out what was being said. He searched the smooth metal door's surface; no window was evident. The door was one of those thick, lead-lined jobs, and this had probably saved him moments earlier.

He decided to risk cracking the door ever so slightly so he could hear. A glimpse would also be nice. He prayed the door wouldn't creak as he inched it open.

The door opened silently. The unmistakable smell of spent gunpowder leaked in. Rusty shivered and focused on the conversation.

"—thinking I'm the only slimeball around here."

That's Raskin! Rusty swiftly put his eye up to the crack. He got a good look at Marshall, not five feet away in the hallway, wielding a large gun, looking like he meant business. Rusty shuddered. He couldn't see Raskin, but figured he must be further down the hall toward the recovery room. Was Doctor Landry still alive?

"I'd heard rumors. What happened Raskin?"

That's Doctor Landry! Thank God he's alive. Rusty remained crouched by the door; he was paralyzed by fear. What should he do? He couldn't take his eye off Marshall's menacing gun. This really wasn't his fight; he'd only known these people a couple of weeks. Plastic-man wouldn't bother to stay. Maybe he should hurry away and get help? Shouldn't the police be here soon? He turned to inspect his line of retreat, but something held him; he realized the extent of his attachment to Dr. Landry and Dr. Carlucci. He was also mesmerized by the conversation, and his legs remained frozen.

Raskin answered. "Well, let's just say one of the girls got into a family way and had an unfortunate accident."

Accident! What the hell was he talking about?

CHAPTER THIRTY-FIVE

"I said shut up! Both of you!" Marshall screamed, spittle flying from his mouth, as he waved the gun around wildly. Doug felt intense panic as he realized he may have pushed the unstable Marshall too far. He watched in horror as Marshall suddenly took aim. His trigger finger flexed smoothly, and the Walther spouted flame followed by smoke. Another deafening explosion.

The bullet emerged from the muzzle at supersonic speed, ripping a path through the thick air before piercing the front of Raskin's cranial vault. In a time measured in microseconds, the bullet's energy was transferred to the contents of the vault as concussion waves reverberated all through the bony confines. Raskin's head exploded as the exiting bullet tore a five-inch, ragged hole in the back of his skull. Pureed brain matter and blood showered the wall.

Raskin's lifeless body, minus half a brain, crashed to the floor.

Doug blinked. He had thought the bullet was meant for him and was surprised to be still alive, although he quickly realized it was probably only a temporary reprieve.

"Don't look so baffled, Landry," Marshall said, chuckling. "It's unbecoming—yours is coming soon enough." He leveled the Walther at him.

"Why Raskin?" Doug was desperate to keep him talking, although he was losing faith in this strategy; he still had no plan. He couldn't help glancing at Raskin's sprawled body and the grisly sight of his shattered skull now resting in a growing pool of blood. Raskin's eyes were wide open, and a look of surprise could still be made out on his face.

"Oh, he had quite outlived his usefulness," Marshall said. "A real liability, if you know what I mean." Doug turned back in time to see him reach into his lab coat pocket and produce a second gun, a .38 caliber revolver. He pocketed the Walther.

Doug stared down the gaping barrel of the .38 and realized this one was meant for him. "You planned to kill him all along, didn't you?"

"Very good, Landry. You are quick. You see, the two of you will have had a bitter fight, presumably over these sabotaged cases, and ended it with a shoot out, both parties regrettably killed. Enough talk, Landry." Marshall took careful aim. "You've heard way too—"

"Answer me one question, Marshall," Doug said quickly, his tongue having difficulty navigating the dry terrain of his mouth.

"What?" he asked impatiently.

"The girl—what was her name?" Anything to keep him talking—he must be proud of the death in some twisted way.

"I suppose it will do no harm to tell you. Her name was Karen McCarthy." Marshall paused as if some inner memory stirred him. The .38 grew heavy, and his arm sagged a bit. "Such a sweet girl. Hated to lose her." But his daydream was short-lived; his arm snapped back up, the .38 seeking the center of Doug's chest. "Say your prayers, Landry." Marshall squeezed the trigger.

CHAPTER THIRTY-SIX

"—Her name was Karen McCarthy."

Rusty didn't hear the rest. Pain detonated inside his head; he felt like he had been hit with a sledgehammer. Breathing ceased as his throat closed off. His blood ran cold, so cold that the icy fluid threatened to clog his heart. Stuttering and misfiring, his heart labored on lamely; Rusty's whole body sagged as he wavered on the edge of blackness. Only leaning heavily on the doorjamb kept him from collapsing to the floor.

Karen McCarthy!

That was the name he'd retrieved from the microfilmed newspapers.

That was the name on the death certificate—"Camp Hill, June 1971. Cause of death—cerebral hemorrhage."

That was the name of the girl who had died in a traffic accident on Peter's Mountain.

His mother!

Except now, Rusty knew her death was no accident.

His adrenaline flow became a torrent, reviving him. His shock quickly turned into anger, the flames of which were fanned by the adrenaline wind into white-hot rage and fury.

His paralysis broke. Muscling the lead door out of his way as if it were made of bamboo, he took two running steps, oblivious to the gun, and launched himself at Marshall.

CHAPTER THIRTY-SEVEN

As Doug said his prayers and Marshall's trigger finger began to work for the third time, both men turned abruptly toward the sound of the cysto door being flung open. In freeze-frame fashion, Doug caught Rusty suspended in mid-air hurtling directly toward Marshall, screaming something that sounded like, "Flame on!"

The gun discharged, but the bullet missed Doug by at least a foot. Marshall tried to duck, move his arm, and fire at his new assailant, but his efforts were cut short by the slamming force of the two-hundred-pound human projectile. He got off one more shot at Rusty, but it wasn't even close. Rusty caught him square in the shoulder; the sickening sounds of popping ligaments and rupturing capsule were clearly audible as Marshall's shoulder forcibly dislocated. The .38 flew out of Marshall's hand and clattered across the floor, coming to rest ten feet from Doug.

Marshall crumpled to the floor, howling in pain as Rusty bore down on him, grinding the newly dislocated shoulder further and further out of joint. Rusty swiftly righted himself and pummeled

Marshall's face, drawing blood almost immediately from his squashed nose. Marshall made no effort to ward off the blows, but instead fished around in his pocket with his good arm.

Doug saw the Walther emerge, but also saw that Rusty didn't notice it; he was too intent on pulverizing Marshall's face. Doug knew he couldn't cover the distance fast enough to stop Marshall, so he dove for the .38 and shouted to Rusty, "He's got another gun!"

Rusty quickly twisted and grabbed Marshall's left arm, but he was too late. Crack! The bullet lanced through Rusty's right shoulder. Rusty shrieked in pain, but held his grip on Marshall's gun hand. As Rusty slammed the gun to the floor repeatedly, Marshall kept firing, rapidly emptying the clip. All of the shots were wildly erratic, most hitting the ceiling. Finally, the useless gun squirted free, skidding several feet away.

Meanwhile, Doug hit the floor hard but managed to scoop up the .38, his right hand finding proper purchase on the knurled handle. Coming out of a roll, he leveled the gun at Marshall, but didn't have a clean shot because Rusty was on top of him.

Something was wrong with Rusty, though; he looked much less vigorous. Marshall was now busy slamming his fist at Rusty's wounded shoulder. Rusty screamed again and again and then sagged completely; he looked like he must've passed out. Marshall pushed him off and scrambled to his feet, still crouched, keeping Rusty's body between him and Doug.

"Don't move, Marshall!" Doug shouted. "I'll shoot." Doug knew he had no real shot because Rusty was still in the line of fire. He fired one round high though, hoping to scare Marshall.

"The boy's hit bad, Landry!" Marshall shouted back, sounding unfazed. "He needs help." With that, Marshall turned and sprinted down the hall, keeping low.

Doug fired again. The shot missed and drilled into the wall, sending pieces of plaster raining down. Marshall disappeared into one of the far ORs. Doug got up and ran over to Rusty, who lay

groaning on the floor. He was coming around, his eyes beginning to focus. Doug assessed the situation quickly—it was worse
than he had thought. The bullet had entered Rusty's right upper
chest near the shoulder joint. He was probably dealing with a collapsed lung. Marshall had not been lying either; Rusty was bleeding badly. There was no question about it. If he left him to chase
Marshall, Rusty would likely bleed to death before Doug could
return. Marshall had probably had enough anyway—that shoulder
had to hurt. He was most likely high-tailing it out of the hospital
right now.

Doug pocketed the gun and ran to the workroom to get wound
dressing material. He came back and knelt beside Rusty, his hands
filled with supplies. Rusty looked up at him, pale and in obvious
pain, but lucid.

"Go get him," Rusty got out between gritted teeth. He reached
out and grabbed Doug's arm. He stared up at Doug with a look of pure
anguish. "Don't let him get away—he killed my mother. I'll be okay."
Rusty grimaced harder for a moment as a spasm of pain rocked him.

"I'll go in a bit." Doug noticed Rusty's shirt was saturated
with blood and becoming redder by the second. "You're bleeding
pretty bad, Rusty—gotta stop the bleeding first."

"Hurry, Doug."

"Look, Rusty. You saved me with that flying tackle back
there—I'm not gonna let you bleed to death." Doug opened some
thick, sterile gauzes. "Hang in there—this is gonna hurt some."
He applied the gauzes to Rusty's wound and pressed hard.

"Ow!" Rusty screamed in pain. He looked like he might lose
consciousness again.

"Sorry, Rusty. Gotta stop the bleeding." And hope you can
breathe okay. "I'll put an elastic pressure dressing on it. That
should hold the bleeding until we can get you some real help—
you're gonna need surgery. Doug looked on in alarm as the dressing soaked through with fresh blood. Shit, Doug thought, he needs
surgery soon or he's not gonna make it.

"Thanks," Rusty said weakly. "Where's Marshall?" Rusty turned his head feebly to look around.

"He probably left town by now." Doug stood up and started toward the cysto room and the nearest phone. "I'm going to call for help." Suddenly the hallway lights went out.

The darkness was so complete that Doug could feel the blackness pressing in on his eyes. A strange squeaking sound came from further down the hallway. It was coming closer.

"It's Marshall," Rusty said, his voice thick with fear.

Doug whipped the .38 out of his pocket. His hands were instantly sweaty, and his mouth went dry. He tightened his grip on the .38. A horrifying thought crossed his mind. How many bullets did he have left? Two? Three? Raspy breathing came from down the hallway.

"I know you're out there, Marshall," Doug said. "Don't come any closer. I've got a gun, and by God I'll use it." Doug strained to hear something, anything. All he could hear was Rusty's labored breathing. "It's over Marshall. I've already called the police. Time to give it up." Doug hoped his eyes would adjust to the dark soon. Where was he?

Suddenly the hallway filled with noise, and he heard Marshall running toward him, screaming, "I'm coming to get you, Landry!"

Doug aimed at the sound of his voice, both hands on the gun to steady it. He fired twice in near panic.

The room exploded with sound, and the bright muzzle flashes illuminated Marshall's body, not five feet away. He couldn't have missed this time.

The first thing he heard after the roar of the gunfire faded was Marshall cackling. Marshall flicked on the lights, and Doug saw him step out from behind the portable x-ray shield, a large transparent, vertical sheet of leaded Plexiglas mounted on wheels. Two bullets were embedded dead center with spider web fracture lines radiating from each. Marshall had something in his hands.

Doug pulled the trigger three more times; each followed by dreadful clicking sounds. He threw the .38 with disgust at

Marshall's head. Marshall ducked and the gun sailed past him. He howled with laughter. "All out of bullets are we, Landry? Such a pity." Marshall grinned fiercely.

Doug's heart sank when he saw what Marshall was holding. It was the Midas Rex—the high-speed bone saw used to cut through the skull like butter. On cue, Marshall revved the Midas Rex; it made its horrendous, characteristic whine as the blade spun up to better than 10,000 rpm.

Marshall advanced slowly at Doug.

What could he do? He could easily still run; there were many avenues of escape. Doug shot a glance at Rusty. It looked like he had passed out again and his breathing had become uneven. If he ran, Rusty was a goner.

"C'mon, Landry," Marshall interrupted his thoughts. "Just you and me—no guns."

"Yeah, a real fair fight," Doug replied. Marshall's face looked bad; his right eye was puffed up hideously and swollen shut. Dried blood was smeared over most of his face. His nose was bent unnaturally, obviously broken in several places, with fresh blood still dribbling out of it.

"If you leave, the boy dies." Marshall nodded toward Rusty. He was clearly goading him into a fight.

"I know."

"You always wanted to be chief." Marshall's voice had a new nasal quality to it, undoubtedly related to the beating. "Now's your chance."

"You're a fool, Marshall. I never wanted it."

"We'll see who's the real fool," Marshall said and laughed.

Doug backed up into the darkened cysto room; perhaps the dimness would favor him. His eyes were glued to the infernal saw. He groped for anything he could use as a shield. He grabbed an IV pole and held it in front of him to block the hungry blade.

Marshall pushed forward relentlessly, carefully blocking any escape now. His right shoulder was visibly disfigured, but it didn't seem to bother him. He lunged at Doug leading with the blade. Doug held the pole in front of him to parry the saw. He watched in horror as the blade sliced through the pole easily, sparking terribly, but barely slowing down. Doug fell over backward, and Marshall pressed the attack standing over Doug. He thrust the saw down, trying to pin Doug between the blade and the concrete floor. Doug rolled hard to his right; the blade just missed him, grinding into the floor with a horrible racket and more sparks.

Doug scrambled to his feet but now was backed against the sidewall. Marshall walked forward, a determined half-smile on his mangled face. Doug grabbed frantically for anything to put between himself and the whirring blade. His right hand snagged the tangle of gas lines feeding the anesthesia machine. The hoses were thick and stiff, made from heavy-grade industrial rubber.

Marshall sliced through them like limp spaghetti. A tremendous hissing filled the room as the oxygen and nitrous oxide spewed out of the cut gas lines at fifty psi. Doug still had the live ends in his hand. The hoses writhed around like snakes while Doug fought to tame them. Once under control, he aimed the blue and green hoses at Marshall, who was now five feet away and closing.

Marshall belly-laughed again. "What are you gonna do, Landry? Blow me away?"

A flash of insight blazed across Doug's mind. He knew that nitrous oxide was very flammable, even explosive, in an oxygen-rich atmosphere. All he needed was a flame to ignite it. Marshall advanced with the saw, again revving it. In the dim light, Doug caught a glimpse of something wonderful—little sparks of blue lightning in the motor housing of the Midas Rex.

As Marshall neared to within two feet, Doug pointed both the oxygen and nitrous hoses directly at the saw in Marshall's hands. The nitrous caught in explosive fashion; a loud roaring could be heard as the makeshift flame-thrower erupted into life.

Doug was temporarily blinded by the flashing fire but managed to aim the torch at Marshall's body. Above the roar of the burning flames, he could hear Marshall's screams. Marshall danced about frantically, but Doug kept the fire on him. Soon, Marshall crumpled to the floor in a heap, and the smell of burning flesh became overpowering.

CHAPTER THIRTY-EIGHT

Doug walked slowly out of the hospital toward the parking lot and his pickup truck. He glanced over his shoulder at the building. In the glow of dawn, the hospital looked much less malevolent; in fact, it appeared almost serene, as if it had been relieved of some inner burden.

Rusty had done well with his surgery and now was resting comfortably in the SICU. Doug noticed the cold snap had finally broken, and the wind had died down. He gazed at the horizon as he walked. The sun was in no hurry to show itself, but judging from the clear skies, it looked like it would turn out to be a nice day.

An approaching vehicle crunched on the loose gravel and broke the morning silence. Doug stopped walking and waited for the familiar Explorer to be parked. Ken Danowski climbed out, grabbed his duffel bag and ambled over to Doug.

"Morning, Doug," he said. Doug saw Ken do a double take when he took a closer look at him. "Wow, you look like shit. Bad night?"

"I've had better," Doug replied with a tired smile.

"What the hell's going on? Does this have anything to do with all the police cars I saw out front?"

Doug gave Ken the complete story of what had happened last night. Ken let out a big whoop when he learned the truth about the sabotaged cases. He'd obviously been wallowing in guilt and self-doubt ever since his awareness case with Mrs. Lubriani. Ken skipped into the hospital, now apparently ready to tackle his day on call.

Doug continued to make his way to his truck. He was physically exhausted but was strangely more at peace with himself than he had been in years. He was still broken up over Mike's death, but he realized he had not been responsible. Mike's drug abuse had nothing to do with his death; he had been murdered. Turning him in wouldn't have changed a thing. Doug felt certain of this and was greatly relieved.

He stopped by the trashcan. He had two things to dispose of. He unzipped his bag and retrieved the letter to Dr. Nichols. Doug stared at it, unwilling to part with the letter just yet. It was a link to several days ago when Mike was alive. He would miss Mike badly; as a friend, he was irreplaceable. Several tears surfaced, and one managed to drip onto the letter. "Goodbye, friend," he whispered as he ripped up the letter and tossed it in, watching the shreds flutter down. No point in telling anyone now.

But there was something else, something more important, contributing to Doug's peace. When he had been close to death, with Raskin's hands coiled tightly around his neck, he had been forced deep inside himself. He had discovered that his inner core was really a fusion of his own being with that of Laura and the kids. The very emotions he had sought to keep frozen for so long had actually saved him. This was where his strength really flowed from.

A wellspring of love and commitment for Laura bubbled forth. Its headwaters traced their origin almost twenty years ago to their young romance when they had first met, passionate and vigorous. Several years later, marriage vows added force to the gathering waters. Downstream further, with the addition of each child like a feeding tributary, the stream was transformed to a river, complete with areas of turbulence and calm but always joined by a current of conviction. The river grew in width, depth, and strength as they shared the trials of parenthood and suffered through the heartache of losing their grandparents and two of their parents.

It had all become clear to him.

His attraction to Jenny was revealed for what it was—a life-less, ghostlike imitation that was swept away like debris before the raging floodwaters of his true love. He reached into his bag a second time and pulled out his hotel reservation for the Hyatt on the Inner Harbor. He tore it up and hurled it into the trashcan. Who's in charge, anyway?

He hopped up into his truck and gunned the engine. He couldn't wait to see Laura and make up for lost time.

Dr. John Benedict, husband and father of three sons, graduated cum laude from Rensselaer Polytechnic Institute and entered post-graduate training at Penn State University College of Medicine. There, he completed medical school, internship, anesthesia residency and a cardiac anesthesia fellowship. He currently works as an anesthesiologist in a busy private practice in Harrisburg, Pennsylvania.

Author website: johnbenedictmd.com
Author email: johnbenedictmd@yahoo.com
(The author welcomes all feedback and correspondence.)

Don't miss *The Edge of Death*, John Benedict's mind-bending sequel to *Adrenaline*. Available Now!

From the Back Cover:

Powerful creatures have long been rumored to roam the Earth—demons, wraiths, the undead, vampires. What if they are not just the stuff of legend? What if there is a scientific basis for their existence?

There's a secret lab in the basement of the prestigious Buchanan Medical Center, where the newly declared dead become subjects in pathologist Gunter Mueller's research in cutting-edge resuscitation medicine. None of his subjects have survived—*until now*.

Not only is he alive, Nick Chandler has undergone a chilling metamorphosis into a man of supernatural prescience, superhuman strength, and absolutely no remorse—as Chip Allison and his friend Kristin Duffy quickly discover. Chip is on duty as monitor watcher in the ICU when Chandler is wheeled in; mere minutes later, Chandler has fled into the night, leaving behind a violently murdered nurse, the first of many victims.

Besides being an avid dog lover, Kristin has an interesting hobby: she takes Kirlian photographs—images of the auras all living creatures give off. When she applies the technique to a photo of Chandler inadvertently captured on the night of his escape, *Chandler has no aura*. And somehow, Chandler knows she has that damning photograph...

Still suffering flashbacks after being attacked by his former boss wielding a bone saw three years ago, anesthesiologist Doug Landry is teaching residents at the Buchanan Med Center during a six-month sabbatical when his wife Laura is seriously injured in a biking accident. When things go terribly wrong on the operating table, Laura is delivered to Dr. Mueller for resuscitation...

EXCERPT FROM *THE EDGE OF DEATH:*

CHAPTER ONE

Tuesday, 5:00 p.m.

Consciousness crept slowly into Nick Chandler's brain, fingers of awareness snaking into his mind like shafts of sunlight penetrating the morning haze. Here, in the meadow where he lay, there was no time—or pain. He was content to bask in the warm sun and drink in the mingled scent of freshly mown grass and the heady nectar of honeysuckle. Such peacefulness was beyond his experience.

Voices that seemed miles away hummed lightly about his ears. Or was it just the sound of insects flitting about in the hedgerow? The only other sensation he felt was the rhythmic whoosh of air being forced into his mangled chest.

Thoughts began to coalesce, disturbing ones. Questions queued up for attention, threatening to perforate the fuzzy cocoon of his mind. *Where am I? What happened to me?* Then a stranger thought, more insistent, jumped the line. *Am I dead?*

Chandler shooed these thoughts away—he didn't want to deal with any questions right now. Answers usually brought pain and he preferred the tranquil limbo of his nonexistence. But one question buzzed back, like a pesky horsefly, refusing to be ignored: Was this what it felt like to be dead? He couldn't be sure—and, he realized, he didn't care. Deep down, though, he remembered that people were *supposed* to care about such things.

He sensed that something was different about him, changed somehow, though he couldn't put his finger on it; the feeling was way too vague. But he knew he was right.

Chandler sighed. Too much work for now—he was bone-tired. Besides, the sunlit meadow beckoned. He let his mind submerge again, bobbing just beneath the surface of consciousness.

An unknowable amount of time passed as Chandler drifted in and out, until the buzzing returned and grew louder, finally nudging him awake. He sensed other people around him, picked up bits of conversation.

" . . . congestive heart failure secondary to viral myocarditis . . ."

" . . . overwhelming sepsis with full-blown ARDS . . ."

" . . . multi-system organ failure with progressive renal and hepatic shutdown . . ."

Later an older male voice, deep and resonant with a professorial tone, commanded his attention. "Lauren, bring us up to speed on what happened yesterday."

Chandler struggled to focus and stay awake to hear this part; the meadow would have to wait.

A young female voice, crisp and assertive, answered. "He coded around noontime and we consider it a miracle that we brought him back in the first place. An hour later, though, he arrested again and this time we couldn't get him back. He was pronounced dead. He was then rushed to PML."

"You mean Dr. Mueller's lab?"

"Yes. The postmortem lab."

"I assume you are all familiar with Dr. Mueller's groundbreaking research into resuscitation science?" the professor said, garnering quiet murmurs of assent. "Go on, Lauren."

"The patient was immediately placed on full cardiopulmonary bypass. His heart was stopped with a hyper-cool cardioplegic solution, ultra-low oxygen therapy was instituted, and a slew of cerebral protective drugs and antithrombin agents were administered. After twenty-four hours of this treatment, combined with sufficient resting of the myocardium, they attempted to restart his heart. Amazingly, after several countershocks, his heart resumed beating and he was soon transferred here to the ICU. The patient hasn't regained consciousness, though."

That certainly answers a lot of questions, thought Chandler. *Carol Sue was right about the virus—should've listened to her.* And now that they mentioned it, he *did* remember signing some weird form dealing with resuscitation. It was from the Buchanan Med Center Bioethics Committee and was so chock-full of legalese, he hadn't been able to make heads nor tails of it at the time. But the gist of it was, if any of it came into play, you were basically fucked. And by signing it, you had just helped the hospital install an ironclad covering for their collective butts.

He had been so sick when he was admitted that this particular form and all the others he signed had been a complete blur to him. Except now, he could call to mind clearly the five-page experimental resuscitation protocol that dealt with the Mueller lab. He could page through the sheets in his mind, backward, forward, and zoom into any paragraph for a closer look. He had no idea how this was possible.

The professor spoke again. "So, what is his prognosis at this point?"

Prognosis? The word was delivered with such grave overtones. Again, Chandler fought off a wave of drowsiness.

"The patient is basically terminal and will be lucky to survive the night," Lauren answered, delivering her clinical assessment with a tasteful touch of sorrow.

Talk about your good news-bad news. He wasn't dead, but it didn't sound like he had long to live. Except again, Chandler *knew* they were wrong, as they'd been about the consciousness part. He couldn't say how he knew, or why, just that he felt certain. *But what was it the perky med student, Lauren, said? She considers it a miracle that I'm still alive.* A tiny smile curved his swollen, cracked lips and pulled painfully at the tape holding his endotracheal tube in place. *Miracle might not be quite the right word for it,* he thought, drifting back down into the narcotic haze of the soft meadow.